BY PHILIPPE LABRO

The Foreign Student
One Summer Out West

Le Petit Garçon

PHILIPPE LABRO

Le Petit Garçon

TRANSLATED BY LINDA COVERDALE

Farrar Straus Giroux

NEW YORK

Translation copyright © 1992 by Farrar, Straus and Giroux, Inc.
Originally published in French as Le Petit Garçon,
copyright © 1990 by Éditions Gallimard
All rights reserved
Printed in the United States of America
Published simultaneously in Canada by HarperCollinsCanadaLtd
Designed by Victoria Wong
First printing, 1992

Library of Congress Cataloging-in-Publication Data
Labro, Philippe.
[Petit garçon. English]
Le petit garçon / Philippe Labro ; translated by Linda Coverdale.
p.   cm.
1.   World War, 1939-1945—France—Fiction.   I. Title.
PQ2672.A22P4713 1992   843'.914—dc20   92-790   CIP

CONTENTS

Of course, there have already been many deaths in my life. But the most irretrievable death is that of the little boy I once was. And yet, when the time comes, he is the one who will return to his place at the head of my life, marshaling my poor years, down to the very last, and like a young leader rallying veteran troops in disarray, he'll be the first to enter my Father's house.

GEORGES BERNANOS

Le Petit
Garçon

PROLOGUE

As far back as I can remember, those days evoke for me the compact and mysterious silhouette of someone we called the Dark Man. He would arrive on foot, along the gravel path that led from the green-painted metal gate to my parents' villa—the house of my childhood.

We easily recognized his step in the silence of the night, for his brisk footfall made a distinctive sound on the white pebbles and gray cinders. My family would be just finishing our evening meal; that was the ritual hour he had chosen to visit my father, whom he engaged in incomprehensible conversations that would sometimes frighten us, when the two men raised their voices. One evening, as we listened to the crunch of approaching steps, one of the children announced with exaggerated solemnity: "The Dark Man is on the march."

And the nickname stuck. We'd given him others, though, calling him the Man with the Lumber Jacket, because in cold weather he wore a gray one with red leather edging on the sleeves; also Pauloto, since his first name was Paul and he owned an automobile, something very rare in those times of scarcity and hardship. It was a Juvaquatre, a black one, of course, equipped with two gazogene pipes attached to the trunk in the back. We'd christened it the Phaeton. He hardly ever drove it, but it played an important role in the fabrication of his legend.

I don't know whether it was Mother's sensitive nature or Father's literary bent that fostered our mania for assigning a nickname to every grownup in our parents' orbit. It was one of the thousand complicities that unite brothers and sisters, forming that invisible bond among the members of a "large family," so that even today there are certain names I can say, certain onomatopoeias that are unintelligible to all other adults—save for one, two, or three men and women who can't keep a straight face at the merest hint of these sounds, as their careworn masks crack up with the laughter of childhood. Muddle, foolish mistakes, failures, and compromises, all suddenly vanish; small sacrifices and great distress, all swept away! Then I perceive only the intimate whispering of our past, as though an unknown force, through the grace of a few silly words, had cleansed the scars from our faces and revived the emotion of innocent times.

In what shameful business was Merlussy the Cyclops involved? From which foreign country came Monsieur Germain, who seemed never to speak? Why did the mention of the beautiful Madame Blèze bring smiles to men's lips? Who was Sam, who sailed into our life one day, a strange bird with a pointed nose, enormous glasses, and the fluting tones of a castrato? What was little Murielle looking for in the darkness of Lovers' Lane? Now I feel a lump rising in my throat. German officers, booted and holstered, have taken over the upstairs, and my father sleeps fully clothed on the settee in the hall, near the corridor leading to our bedrooms on the ground floor. I'm no longer even sure if he gets any sleep at all at night. The wind blows in the valley of the Tescou River, which is veiled in a bluish haze; in the morning, there's hoarfrost behind the house, and the cones of the seven leafless poplars reach higher than usual into the sky. I listen to the shouts of my brothers and sisters playing on the chalky soil of our favorite field. Enticing and forbidden things are going on behind the merry-go-round on the Allées Malacan, in town, where the gypsies have parked their caravan for a while. A smell of figs, corn, sheep, Chasselas grapes, and moist, heavy clay mingles with the scent of cork oaks, while a thick black 78 record bearing the label "His Master's Voice" plays on the phonograph, whispering a melancholy tune:

> *I'll wait forever . . .*
> *Forever and a day*
> *Till you come back to me.*

The door I've come so far to knock on seems reluctant to open, creaking, refusing to give. Is it still too early to begin this long journey? I must focus my thoughts on the Dark Man, because he was the first vision that came so compellingly to me. He is the one, I sense it, who can guide me toward the place my whole imagination longs to rediscover.

He had a thick head of silver-white hair, a broad, prominent brow, a square jaw, a large, straight nose, and eyes that gleamed with a kind of irony. Small, and short in the leg, he had a body that didn't seem at all suited to his remarkable head and his cocky attitude, which gave him a bellicose air, the stature of a rebel. He always wore a black double-breasted suit. It seemed that nothing could change the cunning look he turned upon the world; he considered other men mere nonentities, and he had the gift of making women feel ill at ease.

And now his step grows a little firmer on the gravel; the simple rhythm of his footfall threshes out new scraps of memory, and gradually things fall back into place. My father rises, tall, solemn, as slender as his friend is stocky, and crosses the dining room to meet him. The two men exchange their first words. Their movements bespeak a constant complicity. The hall, with its tiled floor, echoes my father's dry monotone, the Dark Man's harsh and mocking voice. What can they be saying to each other, night after night? What secret do they share? This is one of the questions that will haunt the little boy's childhood.

Everything is a secret for the little boy. Everything is an enigma, a marvel. In this tranquil, ageless province, gardens that now seem ordinary were once the enchanted forests of Brocéliande, while roads, today banal, promised the thrill of danger, and the most modest dwellings harbored a wealth of outlandish situations, bizarre characters, dramas, and hidden treasures.

As a little boy, I didn't understand that there could be a pattern to life and that people's actions were driven by what we conveniently call the force of circumstances. Around the time I've chosen for the beginning of this story, however, an apparition will leave its mark on my virgin soul.

I am awakened one night by metallic sounds coming from a neighboring house on the other side of the hedge. Some instinct leads me to slip out of bed in the large, dark room and tiptoe past the slumbering figures of two of my brothers. The oldest is by himself in another bedroom, while the three girls sleep upstairs.

I push open the green shutters of the French windows giving onto the back terrace. Outside, all is calm, save for a steady hum rising from the valley. In the distance, at the bottom of the slope leading to the stream where bleak and roach are sleeping, I think I can see a long, dense shape. I know this landscape—it's our familiar horizon, bounded by the fields of sunflowers and the thickets of wild reeds that line the farthest shore of the river, the side we don't explore. But never before have I seen it in the middle of the night, and I'm troubled by its appearance because I've never noticed that opaque mass, which doesn't exist in daylight. Standing on the terrace, unable to let go of the wooden railing beneath my hands, I stare out at the oblong darkness giving off that unreal throbbing noise. How long do I remain transfixed by the vision? Gradually, I become convinced that it's a machine that rises up every night from the riverbed in order to manufacture the passing hours. The noise it makes is coming from that thing adults are always talking about but that I don't yet understand: time. I'd hear them say, "I haven't the time," or, "We've got the time," "We'll need time to do such and such," and "Give me time for this and that."

The Time Factory! I'll describe it the next day, to the closest of my brothers; he'll accept it, just as I know how to take his own fabrications. As I tell him about it, I feel able to draw a picture of it. Emerging from the waters of the Tescou, glistening and streaming wet, it looks like a huge construction made of stones the color of night, without a single door or window. Inside, faceless men dressed like millers watch over a complicated structure of wheels, belts, and pistons, turning endlessly upon itself.

"What're they making?" asks my brother.

I reply with complete assurance. "They're making time. If you don't have any, you can go buy some. Grownups never have enough, so they go there."

"How much does it cost?"

I tell him I don't know the price.

Soon we'll speak of it simply as the Factory. I won't forget that I discovered this astonishing thing when I was awakened by a noise from our neighbor's house. And so, in our secret meetings, we'll establish a connection between the fantastic Factory and the neighbor's house, which is quite real, but equally mysterious.

I

Innocence

1

Only a laurel hedge separated our property from that of Dr. Sucre. It was easy to sneak through the greenery and try to spy on our neighbor. We didn't often dare set foot over there, however, and although we loved to make fun of him, we did it from afar, because we feared certain reprisals that only a member of his curious profession might take.

He was a "sikiatrist," a word without meaning for us until a classmate offered us this definition: "A sikiatrist, he's someone who treats crazy people, and so he's a bit crazy himself."

You have to imagine all this spoken with the strong accent characteristic of the Tarn plain, an accent that rolls and sings differently from the accent of those who live in the Garonne or the Dordogne regions, and which has nothing in common with the sharper intonations of "those-eu" in the big city, in fascinating and inaccessible Toulouse, and has no relation at all to the tonalities of tough, faraway cities: Carcassonne, and beyond, places never visited, Béziers, Perpignan, the ends of the earth! Our accent—or rather, the accent of our classmates at the Lycée de Garçons—favored a syrupy tone that saturated the end of every word or phrase with the inflections "eh" or "eu," so that the definition of Dr. Sucre should be written, phonetically, "Eh sikiaatrist-eu, he's someone-eh who treats crazy people-eu, and so he's a bit crazy himself-eu."

If you really want to capture the accent and speech of this area, you have to replace commas and periods with the four-letter word "fuck." The respectable strata of society in our little town were not affected by this verbal tic, and we had noticed early on that there were two kinds of boys: the ones who indulged in this custom, and those who observed, as we did, a certain decorum in the exercise of the rather brutal language spoken in the red-brick-walled universe of our school playground. Those who said "fuck" at every turn, as a way to punctuate a sentence, were neither the best dressed, nor the best behaved, nor the most promising pupils. Although we were disgusted by their idiosyncrasies, they enchanted us at the same time, for they initiated us into a more vulgar world that rarely touched the edges of our family life up in the Villa, set apart from the street and its language.

So, to be thorough, I'll say that the identity of Dr. Sucre had been revealed in the following manner: "Eh sikiaatrist-eu—fuck—he's someone-eh—fuck—who treats crazy people-eu—fuck—and so—fuck—he's a bit crazy himself-eu. [Wait a beat.] Fuck!"

And I think, now that my memory is lining these sounds up properly, that it was little Pécontal who provided this information. He was the smallest student in our class, with a chubby baby-face, blond hair like the wig plopped on a celluloid doll's pate, and an accent as thick as the sticky molasses of Agen. He would confidently pontificate about all sorts of things in an effort to disguise his physical inferiority. Pécontal had won my admiration on the first day of school when we were put to the test by Monsieur Furbaire. This teacher rolled his *r*'s very strongly. He had a mustache, a coarse complexion, and a large nose he would plunge into a vast handkerchief to produce a noise like the blat of a stopped-up trumpet. Furbaire had directed us to stand up, one after the other, and say our last names out loud.

Petrified by stage fright, we'd stammered our identities, mumbling the words, heads down, eyes glued to the floor. Only one, a little guy with stunted gestures, had spoken with rare self-assurance, boldly announcing, "My name is Pécontal. My buddies call me Short-Ass."

Monsieur le professeur Furbaire had remained frozen on his chair, as incredulous as the rest of the pupils.

"Rrrepeat that if you please, sirrrah," he'd growled.

The dwarf-child with golden hair had calmly repeated, to the utter delight of the entire class, "Pécontal. My name is Pécontal. And my buddies, they call me Short-Ass."

Upon which, instanter, Furbaire had pointed toward the hall and snapped, "Out that doorrr, Pécontal. OUTTHAT-DOORRRPÉCONTAL!"

Little Pécontal had crossed the classroom under the flabbergasted eyes of the twenty-two pupils of the fifth grade and had gone "out the door," a trip we watched him take about once a day throughout the school year, since from that moment on, in response to every sound, every piece of mischief performed behind his back, Furbaire would scream, continuing to write on the blackboard without turning around toward his scapegoat, "OUTTHATDOORRRPÉCONTAL!" to make him pay forever for the insolence of their first confrontation. Without protesting, Pécontal would get up and walk to the door, rolling his eyes at me along the way. I'd watch him slow down when he reached me, with his thick knitted socks of white wool down around his abnormally short ankles, his round eyes buried at the top of his fat cheeks, his ears sticking out, the dainty wisp of blond hair artistically curled on his bulging brow, his fat little butt straining the navy-blue cloth of his trousers. He had a penetrating gaze that made him look as if he were plotting some joke, concocting some amazing piece of news that would dumbfound his audience, as though he'd placed the whole of his tiny stock of energy at the service of an impertinence intended to impress his friends and defy adult authority.

13

Then a wave of tenderness would flow through me, and I would have liked to catch up with him, to fetch my cape from the row of coat hooks just as he was getting his, to accompany him in the courtyard where he wandered in disgrace, but I didn't do any of this. I loved and admired him, while at the same time feeling a kind of compassion for him, because I sensed, without being able to explain this, that he belonged to the race of those whom life condemns even before they live it. Whatever happened to him?

Ever since learning what Dr. Sucre's profession was, we'd badgered our parents to invite him over for an aperitif. Father was less than enthusiastic.

"The man's an Ostrogoth," he told us.

"What's an Ostrogoth?" I asked.

Father loved words. It pleased him to dole them out with a certain parsimony, so that they would strike our imaginations. He played with literary references. He quoted Louis Blanc, Flaubert, Bergson, Paul-Louis Courier, Rivarol, Pascal and Montaigne, Vigny and Michelet, Rostand and Victor Hugo, Anatole France, and a hundred other French writers, whole pages of whose works he seemed to know by heart. During a conversation, out of the blue he would suddenly use a rare word that would astonish us. These words usually had a peculiar, even comical tone. We'd repeat them lustily, making a game of it, until Father supplied us with the definitions. We'd soon incorporate them into our language, the language of brothers and sisters, and that gave us a feeling of superiority with regard to our classmates on the playgrounds of the lycée. Not that we'd ever considered using those words in front of them—the "harridans," "cubicles," "ignoramuses," or "resipiscences" whose meaning had been divulged to us by Father—for they belonged to us, and formed the keys to our closed universe, up there in the Villa on the Chemin du Haut-Soleil, a universe we left only to go to school.

Perhaps Father had thought to put an end to all discussion of the matter with that "Ostrogoth," which sounded like a mixture of "escargot" and "Australian," but the word had filled us with joy, and in a unanimous surge of revolt, we children began to bang our hands on the table while chanting our new acquisition.

"Let's in-vite the Ostro-goth! Ostrogoth! Ostrogoth! Ostro-goth! Ostrogoth!"

Our mother, who was eighteen years younger than her husband and lived attuned to her boys and girls, considering herself our older sister, now joined the concert. Father broke into one of those fond smiles that infrequently brightened the regular features beneath his receding hairline. He gave in to our demand.

And so it was that one Saturday afternoon we watched Dr. Sucre, dressed in white, arrive perched on a rusty bicycle. Everything about him fascinated us. He'd decided to use his bike to come over when it would have been simpler to walk three yards, cutting through the laurel hedge separating our two worlds. He was dressed like a Pierrot, a loony clown: white jacket, white shirt and tie, white shoes. He wore tinted glasses that concealed the glint in his eyes. And, finally, he didn't take off the two enormous bicycle clips he wore to protect the cuffs of his white trousers. He had small, tobacco-stained teeth, clumsy hands, and a sly look about him. "Weasel-faced," Father would have said. Dr. Sucre considered the children lined up to observe him (and their efforts to stifle their laughter), then remarked to our parents, in a not particularly indulgent tone, "So these are the children whose shouting I so often hear."

"I trust they don't disturb you?" said Father.

His guest didn't bother to answer. Father escorted him to the back terrace overlooking the valley, the poplars, and the river. Mother brought out some crackers and quinquina, an aperitif wine. Father tried to make light conversation, and all seven of us children, four fatheads and three idiots, remained on the alert, straining our ears to detect some intonation in the "sikiatrist's" words that would confirm his own dollop of madness. But nothing happened. The girls tired of this game and went to their rooms, as did our oldest brother. Three boys stayed hunched down on the carpet in the large dining room, continuing their surveillance of Dr. Sucre's legs. It seemed more and more strange to us that he hadn't taken off the two clips of yellowed wood that made his legs look so silly. All our passionate attention was now focused on these objects, whose size and ugliness we criticized, exchanging our impressions in low voices interspersed with hiccups of glee.

"That's enough, children!" barked Father.

We kept quiet until the moment when Dr. Sucre hinted that he was ready to leave. No one pressed him to stay.

"I'll see you to the door," said Father.

We follow, a few yards behind them. At the door, where Dr. Sucre bows to my mother, I screw up my courage and ask him a question. "Tell me, monsieur, is it true that you treat crazy people?"

He leans down to me and nods wordlessly.

"How can you tell if a person's crazy?" I inquire, following the plan decided upon a few minutes earlier with my brothers.

He deigns to reply, in a pompous tone, weighing each word. "Lunatics are recognizable by many details," he tells me, "but there is one characteristic that is unfailingly reliable. They habitually wear bicycle clips on their trousers, even and above all when they're not on a bicycle." Then he lets out a hoarse laugh, which ends on a note left hanging in the air, and takes his leave. We're stupefied.

There's a touch of amused irony in Father's eyes and Mother's smile, but we haven't time to put up with their sarcasm because I must carry out the rest of our prearranged plan. The idea is to take advantage of the detour Dr. Sucre will make on his way home by having someone slip through the laurels to explore his property and, if possible, the inside of our unusual neighbor's house. I'm the one who has been chosen for this mission, since

I'm the youngest, the thinnest, and able to sneak easily through the hedge. It's also true that my brothers have formed the habit of assigning all reconnaissance missions to me. I'm insatiably curious, and although I'm also constantly afraid, my pride compels me to hide my fears to show my elders that I'm able to do anything, quite worthy of belonging to their gang and of cutting a heroic figure in the notebook that contains part of the collective family memory.

I don't know who started this tradition, Mother or my oldest sister, Juliette, but ever since they've been old enough to write, Juliette and her two sisters, Jacqueline and Violette, have set themselves to filling the pages of the Album. It's a notebook of a larger format than the ones used in the lycée, and Mother bought several of them at the Papeterie Centrale, the stationer's store on Rue de la République, better known by its nickname, Rue Delarep. The Album is the register of our exploits, follies, fables, and legends. It's a precious object, which we are not required to show to our parents. Every so often, in the evening, we read them short excerpts out loud, but most of the time it stays in the drawer of Juliette's worktable. Every child is permitted to consult it.

It's the repository of our myths, the nicknames we give to adults, phrases gleaned on the lycée playgrounds, slogans encountered during our forays into the outside world. Far from constituting a diary of several voices, the Album resembles a repertory, a catalogue without time or date, the jumbled nomenclature of our inventions. Feelings are expressed within it only by exclamations ("Yikes!" or "Oh, la la!"), and the style is rather telegraphic. The Time Factory made its appearance there, of course, quite a while ago, along with Pauloto, alias the Dark Man. The Album reinforces the tribal feeling that unites us and that we carry along with us whenever we leave the Villa, its gardens and property.

When we set out for the lycée in the limpid morning air, the fourteen wheels of our seven bikes, with their spokes and chains, make a music that belongs only to us. Going down Chemin du Haut-Soleil, with its poorly tarred surface, is the pretext for a proud display: the girls in front, followed by the boys, and myself last, taking in the calls and glances of the neighbors or passersby. I hold my head high, on my little bike, and when we arrive at Carrefour La Capelle, the intersection where the girls turn in a single, graceful sweep to the left, toward their school, while we continue straight on to ours, I feel a pang as our battalion breaks up, but I know we'll all meet again at the end of the afternoon to climb back up the long slope toward Haut-Soleil, leaning on our handlebars, and there'll be new absurdities to consign to that Album, the true meaning and value of which are known only to us.

What secrets will I find for the Album at Dr. Sucre's house? Panting, I break through the laurel hedge; crawling across the grass, I hide behind a gardening shed to await the owner's return. I study his house, which is smaller than ours, ugly, made of gray stone, and completely dark. The building seems empty, but my imagination leads me to believe there's someone inside. Have I been spotted? Am I being watched through the dirty window-panes by I don't know what inmate of the insane asylum where Dr. Sucre works, someone he might have brought here to perform various household chores? This is where the strange metallic noise that awakened me came from, the night I discovered the Time Factory. While I wait, huddled in the grass, as the shadows steal in and make everything look different, I regret having been chosen to carry out this raid.

My imagination plays tricks on me. The others often say of me, "He sees things that aren't there," and I'm the most frequent contributor to the pages of the Album. Even though I'm the youngest, I sometimes send my brothers off to sleep by telling them stories I make up as I go along. This propensity can back-fire on me. At first, people find it hard to believe what I tell them. For example, the "Short-Ass" business with Pécontal: "That's not true, you've invented the whole thing!" Which leads to my protests and a fight I invariably lose. I end up pinned to the ground by the fists and knees of an older brother who keeps repeating, "Swear that it's true! Promise me you're not lying!"

Sometimes I get carried away and trip myself up. The most bewildering situations and solutions swirl around inside me; then fear takes the upper hand and so overwhelms me that I call for help from the only authority able to stem my panic: my parents. And so I'm a very sensitive little boy, tormented by several demons. There's the need to win over my audience, to gain acceptance and admiration. There's the desire to explore and discover everything that can feed my compulsion to show off. And, finally, there's the demon of imagination that changes into fear, driving me to seek refuge in my mother's arms or in my father's protective shadow—with a demand for kisses, a need to be physically reassured. All this sweeps over me in conflicting waves, so that I have no idea where these demons come from and am helpless to control them.

The sound of Dr. Sucre's bicycle is coming closer. I scrunch down behind the gardening shed. He arrives, gets off the bike, and leans it against the wall of the house. I can't distinguish his features in the darkness, but I can make out his movements. Dr. Sucre bends down to take off the bicycle clips, one after the other. He seems to study them before shoving them into his pocket. He bursts into laughter quite different from his hilarity of a short while ago, shouting, "HAH! HAH! HAH!" like a tenor exercising his voice. He remains standing before the front door and I'm afraid he has discovered my presence, but I'm mistaken. I witness an even more baffling scene: Dr. Sucre talking out loud.

"I put one over on those little cretins," he announces to the surrounding gloom.

And he laughs once more before going into his house. An electric light comes on. Through the windows, I see the long-limbed silhouette of the doctor, and I can hear him exclaim again and again, until he's had his fill, "They're little cretins!"

Then silence. I get to my feet and leave, convinced I'll never be able to describe the scene without incurring the usual accusations that I'm making it all up, certain that I've just witnessed an obscene spectacle: a man—a grownup!—laughing all alone and talking to himself, unaware of being watched.

Later, I told my story to Juliette so that she might record it, like a registrar, in the Album. I thought her summary faithfully reflected the seriousness of my testimony. "It is not clear," she wrote, "that our neighbor Dr. Sucre is mad. But one thing is obvious: he *hates* children!!!"

2

To evoke the time I'm talking about, I take pleasure in rediscovering—and this recovery must be effortless—the vocabulary of that French poet and troubadour who throughout his life knew how to use simple, old-fashioned words, once filled with magic. Words that today are drained of their life and meaning, set aside on the shelf, once used to be strong and straight to the point, as clear as the sky over rooftops, as pure as young love, as direct as a mailman streaking across fields on his bicycle.

How words have changed, along with their use, and how fashions have tarnished the adjectives that formed a part of the language passed on by our parents! When they described a girl as "pretty," this term was enough to express that harmony and feeling of delight provided by her maidenly form—more words that would later give rise to smiles. Today, when I read no matter what sentence and come across such hyperbolic adjectives as "superb," "sumptuous," "magnificent," I don't recall ever having heard them during my childhood, and the poet I revered above all others would never have chosen them to describe the girl in question. "Pretty" took care of everything quite nicely. Words had a different weight, a different ring to them; their music translated the reality of their time, but it's useless to bemoan the passing of this music, because the times that have followed have needed other words, since new sciences and techniques, new trades, new images, have created new customs, and thus a new language, one almost irrelevant to the language I inherited.

When my father first handed me his copy of *Les Misérables*, published by Julien Rouff and Company (14, Cloître Saint-Honoré, Paris), he pronounced the words "a masterpiece" in a tone that filled me with respect. It took me six months to read the enormous volume bound in gold-tooled red leather and studded with engravings by Brion, Vogel, Morin, Valnay, with a drawing by Victor Hugo himself on page 325, a portrait of the sinister Thénardier! From then on, I began to judge "masterpieces" by the standard of the one that had been offered to me: a masterpiece was something that had to be as powerful, teeming, captivating, as the story of Jean Valjean, Cosette, Javert, and Monsieur Madeleine—something that would touch my soul as deeply, stimulate my dreams as grandly, fire my imagination as strongly. These days, the term is on everyone's lips, this goes without saying. At that time, for me, the word had taken on a grave, almost religious resonance.

In the same way, I'd been marked by two other words my father used one day when he was speaking "to the children."

When he addressed us all with a single reprimand, it was to correct our collective madness, an explosion of noise, of shouting, of racket and rumpus, a tide of bodies racing down the stairs and corridors and which could be stopped only by the intervention of authority. We called this "cavalcading."

At the end of the day, when the older children—the "big kids"—had finished their homework, they seemed possessed by the need to rejoin the other three—the "little ones"—who were off playing by themselves, one in the back rooms, another in the attic, still another beneath the seven poplars planted by our father, one tree per child. The oldest boy, Antoine, would open his window and shout to whoever was within earshot, "Cavalcade! Cavalcade!"

The first reaction would come from the wing occupied by the girls, with Juliette's voice echoing, "Cavalcââââde! Cavalcââââde!" because she prolonged the ends of her words by adding a few circumflex accents in the hope of sounding like Edwige Feuillère, an actress she admired, whose diction and air of distinction she wished to emulate, while the rest of us found her accent affected. (We hadn't yet learned to use the word "snob," which would arrive when Sam came into our lives, but I'll speak of this later, when he makes his appearance in this story with his pop eyes, his heron's neck, and his feminine hands.)

The rest of us would answer from all corners of the property, and we'd set out at a run toward one another, heading for a rallying point in the central field below the terrace, around a large pile of logs that served, depending on the game of choice, as a fortress, a packet boat, a locomotive, or a Roman chariot. When we were all together, our band began its "cavalcade," the principle of which lay in not stopping for anything and in trying to remain at all costs at the crest of the onrushing wave. That meant grabbing one another—but not too roughly—by the shirt, the pants, the skirt, the arm, the shoulder, each one ousting another from the favored position. Occasionally someone stumbled but would scramble up to rejoin the swarm that invaded the front hall, clattered down the stairs to the cellar, barreled through the laundry rooms to climb upstairs four steps at a time, dashing through sitting, dining, and living rooms, knocking over chairs on the way, slamming doors, squealing and squalling, as the trampling noise resounded over the floors and reverberated beneath the ceilings.

A kind of mini-hysteria would run through our horde. A distant observer might have thought that the one leading the cavalcade was carrying in his or her hands an invisible flame that each of the others wanted to claim, like the first human beings in the quest for fire. I suspect Antoine, who had already developed a limitless passion for rugby (the most popular local sport), of having wanted to impress upon our agitation the same frenzy that drives a line of forwards covering the last few yards to the goal line, when each man who falls passes the ball on to the player behind him. Our ceremony was more abstract, however, and thus more beautiful, since there was no object of conquest, no points to win, and we were galvanized solely by the dynamics of complicity, the need to free ourselves of an excess of energy, the unconscious desire to touch one another, to bump into each other without hurting ourselves, all this transcended by the presence of the three girls, who brought to our cavalcade the higher pitch of their laughter, their more fragile bodies, their wildly disheveled hair, and that constant rustling of their blouses and dresses that aroused in me an emotion I did not understand.

We didn't gauge the effect of our uproar on the adults. Our mother, all tenderness and indulgence, would willingly have joined us in our race, but our father took a different attitude when the excesses of the cavalcade disturbed him in his office, in the center of the ground floor between the large parlor-dining room and some of the children's bedrooms. Despite the madness that possessed us, we carefully avoided this forbidden place. The door was always closed. He spent hours alone in there, reading or reflecting, when he wasn't receiving his visitors, whom he never spoke of as "clients." When the cavalcade drew near the office, it slowed down, as shouts became whispers. One day, though, we went too far, and heard a violent and angry "That's enough!"

He emerged from his office and summoned us children to a lecture, the essence of which was that we had what he referred to as rights, but we also had duties, and the one should never, under any circumstances, take precedence over the other. Rights and duties. Duties and rights.

"These words should begin to mean something to the oldest among you," he said to Antoine and Juliette, "and if they don't, then I despair of you. And as for you others, the younger ones, even if you don't understand what I said, try to remember it this way: you have two lungs in your chest that allow you to

24

breathe. It's a law of nature. You'll have trouble breathing if you use only one lung. Well, you must give equal weight to your rights and duties. You have the right to amuse yourselves, but you have the duty to respect the silence and labor of others."

He was standing surrounded by his seven children, whom he had invited to sit down on the tile floor of the entrance hall. The thick lenses of his tortoiseshell glasses concealed the unusually gentle expression in his blue-gray eyes, which the children felt were fixed sternly upon them. He was an athletic and graceful man, white-haired, and almost six feet tall. The children gazed up at this statue of severity, trying to understand the lesson. To illustrate his argument, Father placed his right hand over his right lung, his left hand over the left lung. Then he lifted up his right hand, saying, "Your rights," replaced it on his chest, and made the same gesture with his left hand, on the side of his heart, saying, "Your duties." Then he dropped his arms alongside his body and took a deep breath, followed by an equally impressive exhalation, to show that his two lungs were working splendidly, now that he'd given the same chance to both duties and rights, to the left lung as well as the right one.

Feeling vaguely guilty, our buttocks chilled by the tile floor of the hall, we looked on, intrigued by the demonstration and aware of the seriousness which our father had attached to it, as he did with so many things. Antoine had leaned close to Juliette; they looked like a very young couple who had suddenly become fearful of the future. I felt a twinge of jealousy toward them, because I loved them more than I did my other brothers and sisters. I admired Antoine, whom I wanted to emulate, but he seemed distant with me, indifferent to my stories of bravery, which I multiplied in an effort to win his confidence. As for Juliette, I would have liked her to give me lots of hugs, so that I could smell the scent of her hair with the same freedom I enjoyed in my mother's arms, but she didn't oblige me in this, to my sorrow.

I don't know what effect Father's explanation of those two words had on my brothers and sisters. In my case, when Monsieur Furbaire alluded later on to the concept of duty during our weekly civics class, I couldn't help jumping up and striking my chest, shouting, "The left lung, the left lung!" This earned me a burst of laughter from the whole class and an equally spontaneous "OUTTHATDOORRR!" from the teacher.

And finally, after the cold weather arrived, when it came time to ride off on our bikes, my mother would remind us, "Bundle up, keep your chests warm." She'd come out to wrap me in a long woolen scarf beneath my cape, carefully crossing the ends of the scarf over my chest. I'd savor the tenderness of her gesture, enjoying being all muffled up while the others waited, ringing the bells on their handlebars and shouting, "We're going to be late!"

I thought to myself, as I watched her crossing the ends of the scarf, that my mother was warming the lung of my rights as well as the one of my duties, and that I could set out to brave those unknown elements that would surely arise in the classroom, on the playground, or along the streets of our departure and return, for now I felt safely provided with a certainty that I had not possessed before.

3

Among the other words that impressed me deeply was this one: "hero." It seemed to me that there were several kinds.

First of all, the ones I found in my books: Jack London, Fenimore Cooper, James Oliver Curwood, the swashbuckling novels of Paul Féval, the exploits of Captain Corcoran—a name that simply thrilled me. I dreamed of the lands he'd seen, the perils he'd surmounted.

Daily life offered other, more prosaic examples. The heroes of our lycée playground were those who displayed some exceptional physical accomplishment—an attitude that reflected the mentality of our small town, whose inhabitants had always worshipped strong men, those who were good at sports, men with speed and endurance at their command, local champions who drew admiring glances from flirtatious women on the main street or beneath the plane trees of the Allées Malacan. Prowess at a sport meant a guarantee of social or scholastic immunity. One teacher, newly arrived "from up north" (an undefined region that designated all territory situated above the foothills of the Limousin area), had dared to punish the lycée's best rugby player, a certain Labartête. Besides giving him a zero for not turning in his homework, the teacher had thrown in a few hours of detention. In an indignant chorus of consternation, the students had revealed the unwritten law to this ignoramus: "But, monsieur! No one punishes Labartête!"

And no one punished Julien Darbezy, either, for he held the French junior division high-jumping record, a leap of 1.77 meters. He was tall, slender, and pale, as most of those who specialize in this event seem to be. We'd watch him cross the schoolyard, indifferent to the murmurs that preceded or followed him: "It's Darbezy—fuck—the record-eh holder-eu!"

The only people worthy of catching his attention were other athletes like Labartête or Marquez, another rugby player, powerful and ferocious. The three heroes spoke only to one another, a small group apart from the rest of the pack of students.

We wondered what they could be talking about; none of us, and certainly not we younger ones, who sometimes ventured into the older students' courtyard, would have imagined they were merely chatting about the food to be served later in the dining hall, or the weather predicted for the coming match on Sunday. Labartête had curly black hair worn in a pompadour wave off the forehead; Marquez was also dark, with a more olive complexion, a nose already flattened during a brawl after a particularly brutal tackle, and lips that were puffy, as though swollen with an excess of blood. Both were boarders at the school. The "boardies" all wore gray smocks, but Marquez and Labartête had quickly dispensed with that formality, and the principal, one Monsieur Poussière, was not up to making an issue of it. Monsieur Poussière resembled his name: "Monsieur Dust." He was puny, stoop-shouldered, wore a mustache, and avoided people's eyes as he slunk through hallways, hugging the walls. He often wore a cape so long it dragged slightly on the ground, hampering his flight from the tedious realities of his job.

Darbezy wasn't a "boardy." His blondness, pallor, and height contrasted with the more Latin, bovine appearance of the other two. Rumor had it that a few minutes before setting his historic record, he'd eaten several pieces of sugar moistened with a few drops of ether. Two of my classmates and I had decided to check out this recipe, to see if, "like that, you can jump higher."

Little Desquinesse, whose father was a pharmacist, had supplied the ether in a flask wrapped in cotton and secured by a rubber band. As his contribution, Bonhomme, a redhead with jug-handle ears and a jolly face, had swiped a few sugar cubes from home, just as I had. It hadn't been easy. We didn't know why, but sugar was becoming an increasingly precious commodity that our mothers used sparingly and hoarded on the highest shelves in the cupboard. The whole point of the experiment was that we should eat the sugar just before doing the high jump at the sand pit during recess. That way, we'd discover the truth about Darbezy's glorious reputation.

There we are at last, one freezing winter morning, with our supplies stuffed in the pockets of our smocks, beneath which we're wearing our gym outfits: undershirts, shorts, ankle socks, and espadrilles. At recreation time, we crouch behind a pile of sand over by the playground shelter. Desquinesse is in charge of the operation.

"Have your sugar ready! I'm getting out the bottle."

Each of us holds out his sugar cube to Desquinesse, who uncorks the flask and dispenses a few drops of the liquid; the harsh, unfamiliar odor stings my nose. We all hold our little ether-soaked cubes in the hollows of our hands, but Desquinesse has misjudged the dosage. The ether quickly dissolves the sugar cubes, so we have to decide either to swallow the sludge or to throw it away. Bonhomme gets rid of his.

"Chicken!" hisses Desquinesse.

But when his turn arrives, he isn't any more courageous, and he ditches both sugar and flask, burying them in the sand pile. I hesitate. That's when I see Monsieur Machigot, the upper-class mathematics teacher, heading our way. He's a frightening man. He's tall, deathly pale, and wears a wig that has made him a figure of fun and speculation in our conversations as well as in the pages of our Album. He's never without a rag he uses to wipe the blackboard; he calls it an "eraser," and Antoine, who's unfortunate enough to be one of his students, has already recorded in the Album that the eraser is used to swat the faces of those who make mistakes in their math problems. Machigot is one of the few teachers in the lycée who speak without the local accent, in a sharp and stentorian voice. That's the tone I hear echoing under the roof of the shelter. "What's going on over there, hmm?"

I'm flanked by Desquinesse and Bonhomme, who draw near as though to protect me. I bring my hand to my mouth and swallow the sugar. The immediate sensation is not pleasant: my tongue feels coated, my ears plug up. Machigot waves his eraser in front of my eyes and questions me. "Tell me, my boy, what did you just swallow?"

"Nothing, monsieur."

I keep my eyes riveted on his yellowed wig, a ridiculous rug whose fringes flutter above his forehead and along his ears in the gusty winter wind. The twisted eraser, chalky and grayish-white, swings at his fingertips.

He turns to the others. "What are you three getting up to over here?"

"Nothing, monsieur," reply my friends.

To my surprise and relief, Machigot seems to lose interest in us. He pockets the eraser and straightens up, his eye fixed on other horizons, the courtyard of the older students, at the other end of the playground, where he knows he'll be better able to exercise his authority and vent his perpetually nasty temper.

"I leave them to you," he remarks to the gym teacher, who has just joined us.

Machigot trudges off. Less curious than his colleague, the gym teacher has us line up with the other students. The ether has had an effect and I feel weaker, but light and airy, as well as slightly sick. Desquinesse and Bonhomme whisper to me: "Well?"

"Nothing," I tell them. My stomach flip-flops; I'm about to faint.

We take off our smocks for the high jump. The cold pounces on our bare arms and legs. When it's my turn to jump, I back off to get a good running start at the red string held taut over the sand pile by two wooden stakes, an arrangement grandly christened "the high-jump ground" by our gym teacher, a friendly young man who shouts encouragement at the appropriate moment with a phrase that seems to amuse him no end, and which he repeats several times a day: "*Sursum corda!* In other words: let's get over that cord!"

His name is Pouget. His face might have been quite ordinary, but he was blessed with singularly round, apple cheeks, scarlet mounds with a tiny pale spot right in the center. It seemed as though a makeup artist had drawn two circles of rouge around a dot of white powder. With our passion for nicknames, we'd invented one for Pouget: Red-Cheeks-except-in-the-Middle. Juliette considered it too childish, unworthy of inclusion in the Album, but that's what tickled us younger ones: the nickname's stupidity as well as its realism.

I start my run, hopeful of both flying way over the string, like the Archangel Darbezy, and flushing out the unbearable taste of the ether. As I arrive at the jump, my legs go out from under me and I sprawl full length, nose in the sand pile, bringing down stakes and string in my fall. Amid the hoots of laughter, I recognize the voices of my accomplices, Desquinesse and Bonhomme, and I can tell they're feeling a kind of satisfaction, because despite my brave action (unlike them, I was plucky enough to swallow the sugar), nothing extraordinary happened. I didn't become a hero.

Furbaire who rolled his *r*'s; Machigot with his wig, his stare, and his military bearing; Red-Cheeks-except-in-the-Middle with his pathetic "Let's get over that cord!"; Dr. Sucre and his bicycle clips; the principal, Monsieur Poussière, swathed in his cape and trotting his little legs around the establishment he was supposedly in charge of; how many other adults had we pinned like bugs with our stabbing sarcasm? Why did they all—or

31

almost all—seem like ridiculous characters, the buffoons in a comedy whose rules and roundabout plot we were too young to understand? What drove us to make fun of everything outside the sacred precincts of the Villa, to mock every grownup except our parents and our father's friend, the Dark Man?

We heard only snatches of their conversations, but these turned on the vulgar triteness of society, the ups and downs of which the Dark Man would relay to my father, who would in turn describe to his friend the faults and weaknesses of the visitors he received, closeted in the office of his house over-looking the town below. Then both of them would indulge in their favorite pastime, the skeptical and disenchanted contem-plation of human nature and the state of a world that was fast disappearing.

My father would use certain words: absurdity, idealism, suf-fering; the Dark Man would reply with derisive laughter and say: profit, vanity, lust. They'd tackle the relationship between men and women, and soon move on to the evocation of a past they seemed to have in common. At that point, the verbs would switch to the imperfect tense, their voices would grow more confidential, and in those moments, we sensed that they shared a secret and that this secret was still a living bond between them. My mother would leave the two of them to themselves, and it was only thanks to my small size that I could lie around under the furniture or behind the big sofa, where I'd hear them talk about what "he" and "she" had said and done.

They were our most tangible heroes. The ones in my books lived only in my dreams; those of the lycée playground quickly revealed their limitations; but these two white-haired men, older than most of our classmates' fathers, were figures of authority, wisdom, and real-life virtue. To us their features seemed noble, their bearing unblemished by any comical flaws, their gestures free, in our eyes, from the slightest hint of caricature. Above all, at the heart of this family and the Villa, the presence of a mother whose every thought and action sprang from love reinforced the feeling of security that belongs to childhood: one is afraid of everything but not afraid of anything, because "they" are there. These adults represented reassuring stability, and we clung to them when buffeted by our fears and anxieties, our ignorance of the realities of life.

Heroes don't cry, however, and one evening Antoine had seen them cry. He'd tried to hide this discovery, but it had weighed too heavily on him, so finally he'd told Juliette, and they'd sworn not to tell another soul. No one was ever to know!

4

Yes, he'd seen them cry. These two middle-aged, devoted friends, these pitiless judges of their fellow men—he'd seen them weeping brief and silent tears, sitting in their armchairs set in a half circle before a squat piece of furniture made of wood, steel, and mica, which at the time we still called a wireless.

It was a huge, brown, clumsy thing placed at the end of the big parlor-dining room, against the wall, parallel to the clock that chimed the hours, a marvelous instrument that poured out words and music, with round dials that only our parents were allowed to touch.

That afternoon the weather was pleasantly mild; the days had begun to lengthen, casting a golden light on the eastern bank of the Tescou, a late-afternoon light in June, scented by the hay strewn beneath the poplars where Mother and we children had decided to linger over a snack laid out like a picnic, with pears, peaches, plums, cherries, and cookies galore—delicious short-bread fingers, crumbly and sprinkled with sugar, made at the Biscuiterie Loupe on the far side of town. The owner was a regular visitor at the Villa, and as my father had refused to accept money for his consultations after he'd reopened his office, he was paid in kind, so in exchange for his fiscal expertise, he had received a giant delivery of the very finest products from the firm of Monsieur Loupe, who drove fast cars, Delages or Delahayes, and had a statuesque blond wife. The cartons of biscuit tins had been stacked in the attic over the girls' wing; every week we treated ourselves to a cookie orgy. When the tins were empty, we took them down to the laundry room; in those days, an empty tin was always handy to have around.

Since it was still hot, out under the poplars, and we picnickers had run out of cold water, Antoine had been sent to refill our two thermoses. He'd returned to the Villa and to his surprise had found the French windows closed, locked from the inside, so he'd used the side entrance, a small flight of stone steps leading directly to the kitchen. There he'd refilled the thermoses, and while the tap was running, he'd noticed a strange sound. It was like a faint crackling of words, a drawn-out, monotonous, unfamiliar voice droning on about things that Antoine couldn't quite decipher, down in the kitchen. So he'd tiptoed closer, along the hall that led to the dining room. The door to the parlor was shut, but when he'd pushed aside the voile curtain covering the panes of glass in the door, Antoine had seen his father sitting on one side of the wireless, and the Dark Man on the other, both in the same posture, leaning toward the speaker, gripping the armrests of their chairs as though they were two paralytics clinging to their wheelchairs, and he'd been struck by that sight: they'd seemed old, sick, unhappy, and above all, if you looked closely—and the late-afternoon sun shining through the French windows was strong enough for him to be sure he'd seen clearly—above all, the two men were weeping. As Antoine remembered it, the Dark Man would wipe a white handkerchief along the edge of his lower eyelids for a few moments, then replace the hankie in the pocket of his black jacket, only to take it out and dab at his eyes again.

Painfully astonished by his discovery and not yet knowing what to make of it, Antoine had considered retreating, but curiosity and distress had made him kneel to place his ear at the keyhole. Then he'd understood that the strange hissing noise, that senile voice unknown to the familiar universe of the Villa, was coming from the wireless, and he'd thought he'd heard a phrase he wouldn't have remembered if the two men, after twisting the dial to turn off the broadcast, hadn't repeated it several times, as though to convince themselves that they'd both heard the same thing: "I will devote myself body and soul to France to alleviate her suffering."

They stood up from their seats the way people with bad backs gingerly straighten out their stiff bones and muscles. They seemed stunned. Their eyes were now dry. Father began his habitual pacing from one end of the huge room to the other, while the Dark Man remained frozen, leaning against a wall. Antoine was afraid of being caught eavesdropping, but he felt he had to know more, so that he might be able to live with the devastating memory of grown men crying. Father and the Dark Man didn't have anything like a discussion, however; instead, each of them seemed to want to unburden himself, to free himself from thoughts accumulated during the broadcast, and neither of them waited for the other to finish talking, so that their sentences bumped into and overlapped each other all up and down the room, which made them difficult for Antoine to understand. He could distinguish some words, however: Pétain, lies, armistice, disaster, resignation, and France, a name that recurred frequently in these two intersecting monologues, this France about which they spoke as though it were a human being, a woman who'd just been the victim of a terrible accident, and whose serious condition left them grief-stricken. Resentment and fury overwhelming his sorrow, the Dark Man repeated over and over in his harsh voice, cursing lavishly, "The Boches, sonovabitch, can you believe it, the Boches!"

"Yes," Father would answer, more soberly, "I know."

"You were right," his friend would continue, "sonovabitch, you saw it coming!"

Finally, Father repeated after his friend, and in the same incredulous tone, "The Boches! France!"

Then they fell silent and looked at each other, suffering, their arms hanging helplessly, their shoulders sagging, defeated.

Antoine had run off to rejoin the picnickers with his thermoses of fresh water. Later, during the night, he'd gotten out of bed, left his room on the ground floor, and gone upstairs to where the girls slept, where he'd awakened Juliette and told her what he'd seen. In the great silent house, the two adolescents had agreed not to reveal a thing to the rest of us children. Juliette spent most of her time with Jacqueline and Violette—the three girls living at their mother's side in what Father called, somewhat condescendingly, "a woman's world"—but the sharing of this cruel information had strengthened a secret bond between the two oldest children, bringing them closer together. Sometimes they'd meet at night, in her room or his, and under the pretext of going over the Album, they'd talk about what they feared (as did our parents, but unbeknown to us) would one day come knocking, like misfortune, on the door of the Villa.

5

We didn't speak of our home as a house, we called it the Villa—probably because it was nothing like the few other residences of Haut-Soleil, which wasn't a neighborhood, but rather a large wooded area on the principal hillside overlooking the town, which was what's called a lowland town. I suppose that today Haut-Soleil has become a real neighborhood, with streets, intersections, traffic lights, zoning regulations, and doubtless neon streetlights, concrete, and a few other urban horrors.

At the time, the only access to it was via a single badly surfaced road that wound its way through trees, natural parks, untended gardens, wild grapevines, and bramble bushes that were so many stashes of succulent blackberries—picked right from the thorny canes, they'd leave black-and-purple stains on the fingertips and an exquisite taste in the mouth. There were a few rather ugly buildings here and there, in the style of Dr. Sucre's house, made of fired bricks molded from the gravelly red clay of the terraces overhanging the town.

On Sunday, people liked to come wander through the woods. They'd leave their bikes by the side of the road and sit surrounded by greenery, resting from the steep climb in the shade of the water tower, a giant mushroom whose ungainly bulk marked the official town limit. Beyond lay "the countryside."

Certain couples used to take a long dirt path snaking down to the river in the valley, a path that was practically hewed out of the brambles that arched over it like a bower. They were young couples who walked with their arms about each other's waists, sometimes stopping to kiss, and so the path was called Shadow Street, as well as Lovers' Lane. Children didn't go there, because we felt uneasy and embarrassed around these couples, and because they'd often shoo us away with a brusque gesture, or a few sharp or vulgar words. And anyway, if it was "shadowy," that meant the path might be dangerous. Whenever I passed by its entrance, an opening in the brush that seemed to lead only into darkness, I hoped I'd never have to go there alone, or all the way to the end. We preferred to run and play in the rank weeds around the cedars, redwoods, larches, chestnuts, acacias, oaks, the cherry, wild plum, and walnut trees, or beneath the seven poplars planted in the large open area surrounded by an endless laurel hedge, an area we called the garden, and at whose center stood the Villa. Our house was so incongruous, set right in the middle of Haut-Soleil, that some people made it their destination on Sunday afternoon walks. They'd come to peer through the bars of the front gate at the house built by that tall, aloof man, who rarely deigned to come into town but on whom the local leading citizens, merchants, and farmers would soon come calling.

The Villa was spacious and new: three floors, an attic, a cellar. It had white walls, a large peaked roof of red tiles, wooden shutters painted a vivid green, a fresh, cheery air, and it made a bright spot in the mass of trees that flourished on the humid, fertile soil. Father had insisted that it be designed after the fashion of houses in the Basque country, where he'd spent many a pleasant vacation, and he'd christened the house Haut-Soleil, after the hillside, but we still called it the Villa.

It was a refuge, a haven, a cocoon, a paradise; the mountains and the jungle; the Far West and the Red Sea; the here-and-now and infinity.

•

At some point after Antoine saw Father and the Dark Man weeping in the parlor, we learned that German soldiers had invaded and occupied part of the country; we'd assimilated that bizarre term, Boches, which began to be used as an insult or point of comparison—pejorative, of course—during recess or in the classrooms ("lying like a Boche," Machigot had said about a student caught out). But we knew we were safe from their army, their cannons and uniforms. We lived in an "unoccupied zone." We didn't feel involved at all. The only echoes of this global turmoil reached us from my father's conversations with his friend, but the adults didn't tell the children what was going on in the world, and we didn't speak of such things among ourselves—at least not in the beginning. And yet, if we were living in that house with its extraordinary garden, it was truly because of the Second World War (although that's not what we called it at the time).

Father had divined it, foretold it. His deep pessimism, bolstered by an analysis of what he'd seen and experienced throughout the thirties, had pressed him early on to make a radical decision. While many of his contemporaries were still blind to the danger, he had realized how things would turn out, and he knew that if there was one place where it would be difficult to raise so many children, it was Paris, "*la Capitale*," the city where he had himself begun his career, fresh from the provinces, and where he'd succeeded beyond the fondest dreams of his mother, the humble widow of an accountant. And then, at the age of fifty, my father had completely disrupted his orderly life by abandoning his prosperous financial and legal consulting business on Avenue Niel, in the seventeenth arrondissement, by moving wife, daughters, sons, books, papers, and furniture to the southwest of France, well before the Exodus, to install them in the villa he'd had built for just this purpose.

"You were right, sonovabitch, you saw it coming," the Dark Man had told him.

40

Paul was his oldest friend and, unlike my father, had remained faithful to his native region. They'd met when Paul was nineteen and my father eighteen. At that age, one year's difference can seem like ten. Paul was an assistant teacher at the local lycée, and even then, people had found him strangely attractive. Short, handsome, "well put together," as the expression went, passionately interested in literature, he'd captivated the tall, timid young man with glasses whose studies he supervised. Paul had understood how fragile my father was and had looked after him. He knew about his friend's secret trauma: in class one day, my father had been notified that his own father had just died of a heart attack, while sipping an aperitif on the sidewalk terrace of a café.

The young man, an excellent pupil, had faltered in his studies and behavior. Through willpower and sacrifice, and thanks, as well, to the fraternal friendship of the young teacher who'd taken him under his wing, my father had pulled himself together, although he'd never shaken off his obsession with death, a fear as well as a sense of impending catastrophes, and a sporadic tendency toward neurasthenia. Those demons would haunt him throughout his life. Paul had cherished and helped him. Sublime friendship! My father had worked fiercely, made rapid progress, and passed the civil-service tax examination that Paul had failed. Soon fortune turned her smile from one man to the other. My father succeeded, as though driven by the adversity that had befallen him at such an early age, and he felt himself growing stronger. He toughened his body at French boxing, transforming himself into an imposing man, distant, capable, and efficient. After the First World War, he left the civil service to start his own business in Paris, becoming a consultant to several companies he would help to make quite wealthy—and himself as well. The other man, Paul, tries his hand at several professions, drifting from job to job, returning regularly to his land, his inheritance from his father: a small farm of grapevines, cornfields, and sunflowers.

"What's mine is yours," my father writes him. "Come. I don't know what to do with my money."

Paul goes to live with my father in Paris; together they weather the madness of the twenties. Recommendations from my father win Paul positions in several firms, but something calls him back to the land, to his farm, saddled with debts, poor soil, stunted vines, and scrawny livestock—but which he can't bring himself to abandon. For more than ten years, between reunions in Paris or in their native province, the two men send each other letter after letter, while a one-way correspondence carries a steady stream of money orders, until the day when my father, who has married in the meantime and begun raising a family, confides to Paul, in a letter of some twenty pages, his conviction that the whole world is on the brink of disaster.

"I've no need to earn a living anymore. I intend to retire to the country, where I can bring up my children far from the suffering and privation that must surely come. The children are not ready for the bombs, or the blood, or the tears. It's true that no one is ever ready for that."

He senses the grim fate awaiting Europe's democracies.

"I'm fed up with all these complacent bourgeois, and I don't care about leaving Paris, where I had to smile and put a good face on things for twenty years."

He's sure of his prophecy: world chaos, the fall of France. Finally, his plan: to return to the country. The letter ends: "Find me some property and do it quickly. I have full confidence in you."

That's why Paul will acquire a few hectares of land for him in Haut-Soleil.

And that's why, on the evening of June 25, 1940, a "day of national mourning," he'll tell him: "Sonovabitch, you were right."

Was there any bitterness in the Dark Man's last remark?

Even at the early age of nineteen, something had set him apart from the other assistant teachers and brought him closer to the young lycée student shattered by the death of his father: a sense of irony, a cold eye cast upon human pettiness and weakness. As for my father, his long acquaintance with the world of finance had accentuated his natural penchant for skepticism, his disdain for pretense, his need to philosophize. Paul had vague Communist leanings, while his friend had voted Socialist at first while calling himself a Liberal. On that point, as on others, they confronted each other daily in verbal jousts during which Paul, who had found his niche at the head of a small agricultural cooperative, took a malicious pleasure in poking fun at my father's comfortable and "bourgeois" life. My father liked to be scolded, seemed unconsciously to encourage this criticism and denigration from his friend, welcomed his sometimes derisive laughter. Thus, each man maintained a complex bond with their past: the youth they'd spent together, their numerous separations, sustained by a correspondence in which they'd told each other "everything" (including their love affairs), their bachelor days in Paris.

When they began to speak of those years, at that precise moment the irony and bluster would fade from their voices, which dropped to a whisper, steeped in that complicity whose hidden source so tantalized the little boy and his siblings.

A child knows nothing. A child feels everything.

I had no way of coping with the many puzzling questions that arose within the complicated world of the Villa. I could clearly see that Antoine and Juliette told each other secrets from which I was excluded, and I could sense as well the burden of mystery that weighed on the lives and words of the grownups. But my imagination, thriving on books, made up for my ignorance of how things really stood, and just as I'd been convinced, when younger, that I'd discovered how and where Time and the Hours were made, I was confident that a gust of fresh air would soon disperse all taboos and enigmas.

6

Three women filled my heart. A fourth attracted me like a flame.

I was in love with Juliette, my oldest sister, and with little
Murielle, a neighbor. Juliette was my permanent love, and if I
was fooled and perplexed by Murielle's schemes, I knew I could
return to Juliette, her light, her fragrance.

Everything came easily to her, and she wanted to do everything: dancing, fencing, horseback riding, tennis, watercolor
painting, pottery, the flute—and her grades in school reflected
the same aptitude. But in our small town, with its undistin-
guished girls' school, the odds were against her continuing the
activities that had been so freely available to her in Paris. Mother
had spent days ferreting out a tutor, looking for a studio, private
lessons, a club, whatever!—anything that would correspond to
her gifted daughter's aspirations, and this had meant trips into
town, appointments across the river, advertisements posted in
the bakery, constant comings and goings in an effort to make
up for the pathetic lack of cultural life in the region.

"She's talented, that girl," Mother would say. "It's a shame
to let such talents go to waste!"

Juliette was stifled by this provincial environment. She loved
the Villa, as we all did, and she was happy there, but as soon
as she set foot outside Haut-Soleil, she felt she was entering a

world of cramped streets and shabby lives. She'd dreamed of spreading her wings, not having them clipped! She'd taken over three-quarters of the upstairs where my sisters lived, and had set up one area for painting, another for pottery. It was there, after climbing the steps of the main staircase, that I'd go looking for a hug or a kiss, which she dispensed, in my opinion, in uncommonly meager doses. I'd gaze at her, as she bent over her potter's wheel, or studied her canvas, and be captivated by her beauty. She had a broad forehead, blond hair with reddish highlights, like Mother's, and unusually long, straight brows that gave her eyes something special that the other girls didn't have, with their squarer faces and closer resemblance to Father. Juliette's gestures were deft and precise, performed by hands with fingers that seemed drawn by the most delicate pencil. She possessed a kind of serenity, an ability to smooth over all irritations, to brush aside any vulgar or mean behavior and thus advance, limpid, fearless, transparent, guided and protected by who knows what angel.

"Why don't we try the Russians?" Father had suggested.

Surely the Russians were artistic. Surely the Russians would not pass up a chance at a bit of money. Surely the Russians knew how to fence, perhaps how to teach dancing, how to play the flute.

In the neighborhood of Les Moustiers, near the barracks, where the river had flooded ten years before and reached highwater marks, lived the people called the Russians. They were the only Russians in town, and even though they'd tried not to draw attention to themselves, they were "Russian," which was food for comment whenever they turned up at the grocery store or bought chestnuts from a vendor.

"Here come the Russians-eu, fuck, they're not the same-eh as us, fuck."

Their name was a prestigious one: Tolstoy! Father, Mother, and the Dark Man, all three for different reasons, would have liked them to be descendants of the great writer. Hardly had they appeared in town when my father had asked his friend Paul to investigate this possibility, but the results had been disappointing. They were perhaps distantly related cousins, but it was impossible to know for certain. All the same, they were Russians, White Russians. The men wore their hair too long, the women wore theirs in braids or chignons, and their faces betrayed the pride and humility of refugees, which they so obviously were: thin, pale, with a haunted look in their eyes. The oldest son, Igor, had agreed to give fencing and music lessons to Juliette. Father had guessed correctly: those people had the souls of artists! Since there wasn't much space in the garret where more than twelve of them lived piled on top of one another, Igor walked all the way from Les Moustiers to the Villa.

"Bonjour," he'd announce, "I've come to teach matters martial and musical."

Father had gone himself to open the entrance gate at the end of the gravel path. Our usual visitors, as well as the Dark Man, knew that they didn't need to wait at the gate and had only to walk on up to the Villa, but Igor Tolstoy had no way of knowing this. Besides which, he seemed to have an innate sense of good manners. The unexpected and unusual sound of the bell had sent us scurrying to the windows.

"Who is that scarecrow?" Father had murmured, peering out at the gate. "Well, of course, it's a Russian!"

He'd gone to let him in. Our guest had waited for Father to open the gate and had bowed to him with those curious words: "matters martial and musical."

"Why 'martial'?" Father had asked.

"Arms, monsieur, arms," Igor Tolstoy had replied with a charming accent.

And taking a step to one side, he'd opened the front of the wretched coat draped over his gaunt body to produce, one in each hand, two swords with engraved pommels.

"My daughter fences only with a foil," Father had said, without hiding his surprise.

"It is of no importance, monsieur," the Russian had answered. "Cold steel is cold steel, whatever the size, weight, and name of the weapon."

Father had smiled and said, "Follow me," for he was already amused and touched by the Russian's vocabulary and turns of phrase.

We watched them coming toward the house, side by side; the young Tolstoy was as tall as our father, which impressed us no end, as we hadn't yet met anyone that tall—except, perhaps, Monsieur Loupe, the wealthy cookie manufacturer.

"He really is a scarecrow," exclaimed one of us children, for the expression, like all those chosen by our father, had proved perfectly apt.

"Yes," replied Mother, "but he's a handsome scarecrow."

The girls had murmured their agreement. He was just twenty years old, with a long, lean face, perfectly romantic.

"You walked through the entire town with those swords under your coat?" asked Father.

"Yes," replied young Tolstoy. "We haven't the means to travel about via bicycle."

"It must have been difficult for you . . ."

"An interesting experience," allowed the young man. "Walking in a town that is a priori hostile while concealing on one's person a brace of ancestral weapons, heirlooms of history, cannot fail to engender a certain internal gaiety as well as a heightened sense of altruity."

"You mean alterity," suggested Father. "A feeling of otherness."

"Quite so, monsieur," agreed Igor Tolstoy.

"Naturally," remarked Father, "although your idea is indeed to the point, you realize that these two words are barbarisms."

"Monsieur," said the young man, nodding, "so you have just informed me."

Then Father, all smiles, stopped his guest just a few yards from the front door behind which we all stood in the entrance hall, awaiting the arrival of Juliette's music and fencing master.

"Young man," said Father, taking his arm, "I'm beginning to like you."

"My feelings are not dissimilar," replied young Igor, thus earning himself a fresh wreath of smiles.

The door opened, and my father, stepping aside to introduce the Russian, announced to us all, "He didn't bring a piano—it would have been a little hard to manage."

Mother took the young man's hand with a solicitude we'd seen her show only to us, and led him to where our green-lacquered grand piano stood proudly in the parlor. Hesitating between jealousy and attraction to this new character who seemed to put his parents in such good humor, Antoine took the swords from Igor and placed them across the arms of a chair. The swords weren't used; they were too heavy, and Juliette couldn't have lifted one; but the piano lesson was a success. Juliette would have preferred a private lesson, but her brothers and sisters didn't see things her way. At the end of the lesson, the older children decided to take Igor back to Les Moustiers by bicycle, seating him on the baggage rack of Antoine's bike, since it was the sturdiest. That's how they got their first look at the refugees' quarter.

Because the Russians weren't the only ones. It seemed that, almost every day now, the town swelled with the arrival of a family or a group of men or women from the north, from the occupied zone. A few years earlier, there'd been a great influx of Spaniards, Republicans escaping the repression that followed the Civil War. They'd settled in the town, most of them working in the brewery, the cookie factory, or hiring out to the farms in the area. It was said that some of them weren't all that honest. There'd been thefts, some brawls, and a few refugees had wound up in jail. Sometimes we heard their voices when we rode our bikes to school. The route we took down from Haut-Soleil to the lycée ran by the municipal jail.

It was a crude building, and it frightened me. Its high walls were dark gray, dirty, polished smooth by rain and time, cliffs that I refused to look at. When we approached that part of our itinerary—which happened twice a day, since we stayed to have lunch in the school dining hall—I would speed up, pumping the pedals, looking straight in front of me, with my head down, trying to ignore my brothers' jeers: "He's scared of the prison! He's scared of the walls!"

I hated those walls. I couldn't bring myself to accept that behind their thickness, which I had no way of measuring, men were busy eating or sleeping. The huge stone mass blocked out the sun, so we felt a chill as soon as we came alongside those walls; a shadow would fall across my bicycle, and sometimes I just burst into tears, hearing the voices of Spanish prisoners calling from a few barred cell windows I was too small to see: "*Niños! Niños!*"

Should I answer? I was convinced they were calling to me rather than to the others, and when I'd learned from Juliette that the word meant "children," I was even more upset. Why were they calling to us? Perhaps, as charming as the song of a swiftly flowing river, the sound of our fourteen bicycle wheels speeding toward the promise of education, friendship, joy, had become for them a bitter reminder of the freedom they no longer possessed. Be that as it may, I suffered; yes, that's the word: in my own way I suffered every time I bicycled past that damned wall, and the suffering lasted the entire time we lived in the Villa of Haut-Soleil. Even though I would be growing up, learning to ignore cruel words or malice, becoming accustomed to the hardships of war, experiencing real dangers, discovering my own sensuality, and finally understanding some of the mysteries I had found so baffling, the dark, heavy mass of the old prison would still oppress me, instilling in me a feeling of guilt, the foreknowledge of impending menace, an awareness of unjust sorrow and pain.

7

"Niños! Niños!" cried the voices of invisible men from behind the high walls of dirty stone, and the voices pursued the little boy pedaling so feverishly away on his silly bike. The voices echoed inside him. Sad or salacious, hoarse and angry, they grabbed hold of him, insinuating themselves even into his wooden-soled clogs, his blue cloth cape, his round black beret, his beige wool mittens; he felt as though the only way he could be free of them would be to jump into the river that sometimes erupted from its banks and stained the refugees' quarter with indelible traces of blackish-brown silt, of red and greenish mud. Thus, in the same waking dream, without rhyme or reason, he jumbled together these unhappy places and unfortunate people: the prison with its Spaniards, Les Moustiers marked by the great floods, the Russians and all the other fugitives arriving every day from that half of the country in the grip of a foreign army, refugees climbing down from trains smelling of tangerines and cardboard to seek lodging along the lanes and alleys of the community, imperceptibly changing the atmosphere of that sleepy little town whose indolence was the despair of his older brothers and sisters, but which seemed to him a rich lode of sounds, colors, shapes, and masks that transformed life into a theater, flamboyant and awesome, where danger lurked at every step.

8

Igor Tolstoy gave no more than three piano lessons to Juliette. He disappeared one day with his two swords as swiftly as he had arrived. The "Russians-eu" had left town.

All Father told us was: "They went farther south."

He had the look of someone who knew more than he was saying. We'd noticed Igor's father, old Dimitri Tolstoy, entering Father's office, and then we'd watched him take his leave with a lengthy handshake that seemed as much the sign of some agreement as an expression of thanks. The Dark Man had been there, too. Later, that kind of scene was often repeated, and we soon came to distinguish two categories of "visitors" to the Villa. On the one hand, there were those who came in search of legal advice, the town's merchants or bigwigs. They'd come and go through the front door, often bringing packages, a present, cases of wine, poultry, fruit for us children. Father wanted no more to do with "clients" or a "profession," vulgar words. His sole desire was to read, to think, perhaps to write—a joy and a dream that had been denied him by life's twists and turns—and he wanted to devote himself to raising his children with his beloved wife at his side. But he couldn't bring himself to say no to the slightest courteous request, so that little by little, given the soundness of his opinions and the accuracy of his advice, the town and the surrounding area had contrived to reestablish his practice almost against his will.

After a few years, he gave in and accepted the customary fees, although he disliked intensely any sort of financial transactions. He hated money, which "drives people mad." He'd known what it was to be without it, however, and eventually he bowed to the inevitable. In a letter to Paul he wrote, "I've always refused to indulge in excess, while at the same time desiring and enjoying material comfort, and it's a weakness."

The other "visitors" had no names, or only first names: our parents would refer to them as Monsieur Marcel, Monsieur Jean, Monsieur Maurice, Monsieur Germain. They'd appear out of nowhere, turning up at one corner or another of the garden, arriving by the back terrace and leaving just as furtively. We hardly ever heard the sound of their voices. They didn't seem to fit in with the landscape, and their outfits were very strange: a hunting jacket with ski pants, or a raincoat on a beautiful sunny day. They wore warm clothing, scarves, mufflers, woolen caps, as though they'd traveled through cold lands and sleepless nights, or, rather, as though they were getting ready for such a journey. They didn't all suddenly turn up at once; with hindsight, their intrusion into our world at the Villa seemed to us to have begun around the time of the Russians' departure.

We asked all sorts of questions—and there was the Album to think of, naturally! But the answers we received were vague. "They're old friends of your father and mother."

Because there were women, too, of all ages. They didn't look like our classmates' mamas, like any women in the town, or like our neighbors in Haut-Soleil. Their complexions were less robust, and a few of them had almost olive skin; others had thick black hair, cut short, which was unusual at the time. Some of them had beautiful mouths, and occasionally I'd notice mauve shadows under their eyes or along the rims of their eyelids, shadows that came not from makeup but from another skin, another flesh, another blood—an impalpable difference that made them even more fascinating.

We accepted the idea of "old friends," particularly for our mother, because we knew she herself had come from far away. Although Father hadn't told us anything about his background (we lived in complete ignorance of his past, for everything began and ended with us at the Villa, everything revolved around our family group), we did have a better idea of our mother's earlier life. That's why we hadn't been surprised when she'd shown such immediate and tender solicitude for young Igor Tolstoy.

9

She had Slavic blood in her veins.

She had told her story to Juliette, for the two of them were very close. Juliette had given us the gist of it, without too many details, with the same sense of discretion that led Mother to say, "I don't want to talk about all that."

Her eyes were slate-blue, flecked with green; she had delicate features, and although she was thirty years old, she still seemed quite youthful. It was hard to believe she'd carried seven children in that slender, girlish body. She had that alien quality, that element of the unexpected which Baudelaire calls the indispensable seasoning for all beauty.

When she braided her sandy hair and wound the plaits around her head like a crown, she inadvertently showed off a soft, downy nape I loved to touch and kiss. Her mouth was lively, her lips curved in a constant smile, even at moments of great irritation. It seemed she always found a reason to keep her dimples, those two little convex commas, in place right up by her cheekbones, which were high and rounded, giving her face an Oriental cast. It was as though she were thereby defending herself against the attacks of a world that had been none too kind to her before she met my father. Fortunately, she'd passed on this smiling disposition to her oldest daughter, and it pleased her when people took them for sisters, but of the two, Juliette seemed the stronger, the more determined, while my mother's pure and beautiful face betrayed, ever so faintly, a kind of fear of her own vulnerability.

During the first years of her life, she'd been carted all around Europe like a suitcase, tossed about like some cheap piece of goods. She had only a dim recollection of the mother who'd abandoned her when she was two years old, in an orphanage in Austria. She was the illegitimate daughter of a Polish noble-man and the family governess, who'd come from Paris only to get herself dismissed. The child had been sent from Salzburg to Zurich, where another governess, a distant relative of her moth-er's, took pity on the child and cared for her. Later she'd been sent to a religious institution in Reims. She herself was unable to remember anything about how she'd gone from Austria to Switzerland and on to France.

Her childhood had been a succession of adult faces and voices that would vanish, without excuses or explanations, just as she'd barely begun to grow used to them; of beds and rooms devoid of warmth, character, or gaiety; of trains and stations that would always fill her with stubborn anguish; of parks, gardens, dor-mitories, or playrooms too fleeting for her to feel at home in them, for she never returned anywhere. She hadn't gone without hugs or kisses, because children who are passed from hand to hand often receive a great deal of attention, but she hadn't been able to become familiar with the touch of the same hand, the scent of the same skin, the texture of the same face powder, or the fragrance of the same perfume. She'd been "in withdrawal," as people would later say about drug addicts, but this depri-vation hadn't destroyed her. It was the cause of her frailty, but also of her resilience. She had survived.

In Reims, she'd been fortunate enough to be adopted by the headmistress, Madame Mygan. She became her daughter, her pride and joy, because she was an excellent student: industrious, vivacious, with a natural gift for poetry, which she liked to write, or, even better, to recite up on stage during awards ceremonies. She'd stayed with Madame Mygan (whom she'd always called Marraine, "Godmother") when her benefactress had established her own boarding school in Versailles.

My mother was sixteen when she accompanied Marraine to an evening of bridge at the house of some bourgeois friends, near the Parc Monceau in the eighth arrondissement in Paris, where she saw my father for the first time. He was eighteen years older than she was. He was struck by the singular beauty and waiflike appeal of "the little Polish girl," and had accompanied the two women back home that evening. He'd been living on a grand scale at the time, with a car and a chauffeur—and he'd returned to Versailles the next day to invite Marraine and Juliette to tea at the Grand Hôtel. He'd married the girl six months later, to the amazement of his relatives and the delight of Paul, who'd crowed, "So, you're just a dirty old man corrupting a pretty young thing!"

But he'd secretly envied my father, who'd asked his friend to shield him from all the women they'd known, women who'd been complicating his bachelor life ever since the early twenties. Reluctantly, Paul had done so. Nine months later, the couple's first child was born: Juliette, followed eleven months later by my brother Antoine.

I've said that I was in love with my mother and my oldest sister, but it was little Murielle who filled my thoughts. I was baffled by her attitude, attracted and repelled by her affectations, clumsy and unspeakably ill at ease in her presence.

Murielle was the daughter of a couple who owned a store and had a house down the road on Haut-Soleil. She had freckles on her button nose and a naughty gleam in her eye, along with a figure already filling out, at the age of eleven, around the hips and bosom. She wore dresses in a simple checked material, with sashes that tied in the back. She would come into the Villa's garden from the west side, where several openings in the hedge allowed her parents' dog, a rather unruly mixed breed, to come snooping around looking for food to steal. We'd try to chase him away from the area where we usually played, but he'd keep coming back, and only Murielle seemed able to make him behave. That was her pretext for coming over to our place and challenging me with her sly looks.

"Filou, come here, Filou," she'd call softly, in a singsong voice.

The mongrel would run around in circles, yapping and drooling; after a while the familiar voice of his little mistress would calm him down and bring him to heel. Then Pierre and Michel, my twin brothers, would announce to Murielle, "You can go now."

They didn't like her. In their opinion, she'd broken the most sacred rules by boldly invading the territory of the Villa without permission. They'd decreed, via the pages of the Album, that Murielle was "depraved."

"You don't even know what the word means," Juliette had said.

"Oh yes we do! We asked, and we know," they'd replied.

Me, I didn't know. I shared their desire to protect our playground, but I wasn't as intransigent as they were regarding Murielle. She had "Why not?" written all over her, and a disarming way of looking at me that I found very attractive. I was younger than she was.

"I'm perfectly willing to leave," she said, "but you come with me."

My brothers turned their backs on her disdainfully. Facing little Murielle on my own, I gave in. We walked over to the gaps in the hedge, with the dog trotting alongside.

"Filou is a *filou*, a rascal," she said laughingly. "You know what a rascal is?"

"Sure," I replied.

"Hold my hand."

I turn around to see if my brothers are watching, but they've gone off to another part of the property. I take Murielle's hand.

"You're a rascal, too," she says.

"No," I protest. "A rascal's someone who cheats, and I'm not a cheater!"

She laughs, and pulling her hand from mine, she waves away my words. I miss the touch of her skin already.

"Have you been down Lovers' Lane?" she asks me.

"No, I don't like that place."

"Me, I go there every day, but I've never been all the way to the end. You want to go all the way down it with me?"

"I don't like that path," I insist. "It's too dark."

Murielle doesn't answer. I see a hungry, greedy expression on her face. When we bend down to go through the hedge, we draw closer to each other. Suddenly the little girl kisses me on the cheek and runs off, with Filou scampering after her. I can hear her laughter and singing.

"Filou! You're a cheater, like our rascal Filou!"

I want to shout that she's wrong, that she hasn't the right to shout over the treetops of Haut-Soleil that I'm something I know I'm not. And when she repeats her provoking claim, I can't contain myself any longer.

"It's not true! Not true!" I shriek fiercely in my despair.

She's gone, and I turn back toward the Villa, excited and humiliated.

Shouting has made me feel better, but I'm all discombobulated, to use a silly word Father has recently taught us. Tearing across the big field that lies between the hedge and the Villa, I go looking for Mother, or Juliette, looking for a warm, ripe body, a "grownup" body, so that I can hide my upset feelings in its embrace. I promise myself I won't give in anymore to Murielle's invitations, but the next time her dog shows up, when she reappears in her plain checked dress, I'll be overcome by the same sensation of weakness and paralysis, and I'll submit, in the same way, to her saucy and imperious will.

•

One day around that same time, at the end of the afternoon, I discovered a woman who was to tantalize my curiosity and stimulate my fantasies. Her name was Madame Blèze.

We'd heard people mention her name a few times, and whenever it came up in adult conversation, men lowered their voices, while a knowing smile would play about certain lips. The Dark Man would fairly quiver with glee, shooting off snide remarks and allusions in all directions, warbling a little refrain he seemed to have composed just for the occasion, the words of which I had difficulty understanding between snatches of whistling. Father would make him be quiet, while Mother would put on an offended expression, but like Juliette at her side, she showed an indiscreet interest in this Madame Blèze who had the whole town talking.

She lived alone in an apartment downtown on Rue La Capelle, where she made hats. She was from Paris, where she was said to have been a modiste in a famous milliner's establishment. She'd created outfits for the prettiest women in the capital, but war and the Exodus had driven her south with her husband. No sooner had they taken the apartment in town than the husband had gone back where they'd come from, back "up" to Paris, as the phrase went, to take care of some business there.

People went *down* to the country, and *up* to Paris: this was how we pictured such things throughout our childhood, so that I imagined France as a country shaped like a single giant hill, the only summit of which, the epicenter, was in Paris. From there, on all surrounding sides, the terrain descended in a steady slope to the rivers of the north and south, then on to the seas and oceans. I figured that trains, cars, roads, and travelers who went "up" to Paris were obliged to make a mighty effort, and that there were certainly rest stops all along the way where people could take a breather and get refreshments before returning to the endless climb toward that fabled metropolis, way up there at the end of the map—toward which converged all energies, efforts, and desires.

I supposed that when travelers reached Paris, they needed a few days to rest up from the journey, and I wondered if the air they breathed, on the top of that hill, changed people's habits and constitutions. I reasoned that the same vehicles or people had to keep an eye on their speed when they set out again, going down home or elsewhere, because now they were coasting, the way I did on my bike sailing down the road in Haut-Soleil. It seemed to me that going downhill was easy; it mussed up your hair, which was why everyone arriving from Paris had more or less the same lively air, and why there was something different about them and the clothes they wore. It explained why people would say about them, "They're from Paris! They're *fast*."

Madame Blèze didn't seem "fast," strictly speaking, but her figure and bearing were certainly eye-catching—if you were lucky enough to get a glimpse of her in the streets of the town, because she didn't go out much. You went to her place to try on the hats she made, but she didn't have many customers, since few women could treat themselves to these subtly extravagant hats, fragile creations intended to perch delicately atop chignons, but too showy for this provincial town. In all truthfulness, I must say that no unaccompanied man ever knocked on her door, and that no one could have accused her of the slightest impropriety. Rumor had it, however, that she led a riotous life, and her supposedly dissolute past fueled slander and envy.

"She's been around, all right, when she was making her hats up in Paris," they said. "She must have mixed with all sorts of people."

Or again, "But what can she possibly do by herself, shut up all day long in that apartment?"

That was enough to foment a climate of gossip and cruel speculation around her and her vanished husband; he'd hardly set foot on the train station platform before he'd gone off again, leaving her with her suitcases, hatboxes, and yards of fabric on rolls that stuck out at each end of large flowered canvas carryalls. Her rare appearances in public, her pert figure, her long legs and dark eyes—all grist for the mill. It didn't seem possible that such a beautiful woman, practicing such a frivolous profession, could be completely respectable. The first time I saw her, Madame Blèze struck me as an extraordinary creature. Perhaps the state of my health played a role in the emotion that so overwhelmed me that day.

10

I'd been ill, terrifying my parents, who'd thought I wasn't going to make it. A serious bout of diphtheria had almost strangled me in my bed. Struggling to suck in as much air as possible, my mind benumbed by fever, my eyes sunken with exhaustion, I'd temporarily lost the ability to speak, and it would be thirty hours before the serum would have an effect. I'd seen the faces of my mother and father bending over me; their voices seemed to be filtered through a thick layer of cotton.

"Can you speak? You can't speak? Give us a sign if you can hear us."

I tried to answer but could produce no sound, so I nodded my head to let them know I could hear their questions, but from very far away. My chest burned, my lungs were shriveled up, my ribs constricted, my eyes stung with such heat I couldn't keep them open; I felt myself drift away, then back, then away again, and so I learned to recognize the sound of death's voice at a very tender age.

Death came along quite early, slapping me gently with a despotic hand, sowing the seeds of anarchy in what had been until then the reassuring order of my young existence. Dying didn't frighten me. What I knew about death I'd learned from books, and they'd taught me nothing; in general, it was all over in just a few words or sentences, after which the novelists ended the chapter or book and started talking about something else. What I did know was that there'd be a lot of crying. There'd be heaps of sad people gathered around me, and that was more important to me than death itself. In the midst of my pain and fever, the idea gave me a certain pleasure. Oh, how they'd miss me! And how they'd sob over my lifeless body!

The anxiety displayed on these faces looming close to mine added to my certainty that I'd never make it back up to the surface; the more they questioned me, the more I sensed that insidious forces were pulling me down toward a sleep I hadn't desired, a night whose rhythm I'd never known before, black water without end.

I'd so often wanted to have my parents' affection all to myself; I'd so often pretended to moan or cry, just to draw them to me and away from the Villa's full crew of brothers and sisters, who in my opinion received more parental attention than they deserved—and here were Mother and Father, devoting themselves entirely to me. They'd quarantined my room, sent the rest of the family away upstairs to avoid all contagion, and were taking turns sitting by my bed, changing my compresses. Both of them were all mine, gigantic statues leaning over the hot sheets, over their "littlest," who'd been such a handful and had pestered them so often for displays of affection that he'd frequently driven them to distraction. Now the little boy was suffering too much to savor these moments of communion, and he was in no condition to demand his place in the spotlight of this drama. He saw his parents with different eyes.

If he'd been able to move his tongue and lips at all, he would have liked to ask them just one question: "Why does it hurt?"

He understood that he was being punished; he would have liked to know why. And when the serum had finally begun to act, when he recovered his voice and could speak again, he was able to say, "It doesn't hurt as much."

This first encounter with death would leave him a lasting

legacy: an instinctive withdrawal into himself at the merest breath of wind, the first hint of a chill. This slight lag between him and the other boys his age marked him as what adults call a "weakling," but in reality it meant he was by nature acutely conscious of how dangerous and precarious life can be. He'd known how it felt to see his parents and the world as if through a window. The experience had given him a sense of detachment that made him "interesting" to grownups. He was aware of this, and would learn how to take advantage of it later on, for he believed he was different from his brothers and playmates.

He settled into a long convalescence. Slowly he regained his strength, realizing that his frail condition gave him the right to all sorts of privileges. One afternoon when he was lying under a fluffy coverlet of orange wool on the sofa in the parlor-dining room, waiting for his brothers and sisters to get home from school, he heard his mother announce a visitor to his father.

"Someone's here to see you. It's Madame Blèze."

The sofa on which I was slowly recuperating had been positioned in such a way that my father, sitting at his desk, could turn around and check on my condition by glancing over his shoulder through the open folding doors, which were usually kept closed.

As for me, when I wasn't dozing I would watch his broad, reassuring back, clothed in a comfortable beige jacket, and I could follow even the tiniest movements of his head and neck, the gestures of his arms, which I'd soon studied enough to allow me to guess what he was doing with his hands even though I couldn't see them: writing with his fountain pen, leafing through a book, or drumming with his fingers on the desktop. I spent long moments as well studying the hazel-colored earpieces of his glasses where they curved around behind his ears, nestling between his skin and his fine white hair. It got so that I was almost more used to seeing his back than his face, and could gauge his moods according to the set of his shoulders under the cloth, the stiffness of his spine, and the way he passed his hand over the back of his head. And of course I was at leisure to observe his visitors, a privileged position that enabled me to enrich the anthology of our Album.

I'd watch Father escort them into the room and ask them to be seated, after explaining the presence of this silent little boy lying down in another part of the parlor, observing them from under his orange blanket. Father would go sit behind his desk in his usual chair, sometimes blocking my view of the visitor, but I'd learned to shift my position discreetly to retrieve those lost faces and note their changing expressions. Most of the visitors spoke in lowered voices, as though unsettled by the presence of a third person, even that of a convalescent child. Then I would pretend to go to sleep, closing my eyes, and the conversation would soon become louder. I was more interested in their faces than in what they were saying.

That's how I witnessed the appearance of Merlussy, nick-named the Cyclops, whose right eye was held shut by what looked like scar tissue from a burn. We didn't know why he came to see Father, but his disfigurement—plus the hat with the overly large brim covering the hair long past due for a trim—led us to suspect there was something irregular about him, a man up to his ears in business worries.

"So, Monsieur Merlussy," Father asked, "how are things going?"

"It's always the same," Merlussy replied, "always the same old crap."

He had a hollow voice, and sounded overwhelmed by his problems. The conversation became incomprehensible, full of numbers, with the word "debts" recurring frequently, so I lost interest. When Merlussy rose to leave, he settled his felt hat firmly atop that alarming visage and shook my father's hand with a few words of thanks.

"I'll have one or two turkey hens sent up to you," he said.

"Oh no, Monsieur Merlussy, please don't bother."

"I insist, they're quite plump, you'll see—nice plump birds."
And off he went, trailing a cloud of questions.

I also observed a certain Monsieur Floqueboque, a short, ungainly man, fat but pale, with thick features and a flabby chin, who wore a jacket too short for him, with lapels sporting all sorts of sewn-on bits of red, blue, and green ribbon. He was glib and conceited, constantly shaking his finger at my father as though lecturing him, holding forth on the state of the world. From time to time, he would fish from his pocket a tiny comb, like something from a doll's set, and run it rapidly through his abundant head of long, dirty hair, as though he'd just arrived after a lengthy voyage and hadn't yet had time to go to the barber. His mannered delivery and his tone, which reeked of the efforts he must have made to erase all trace of an accent and acquire a polished and affected style, reminded me of the way one of our most despised teachers at the lycée talked. I detected the same vanity, the same certainty of never being wrong. He punctuated his monologue with both references to himself and a kind of verbal tic, "I might add."

"As for me—in my opinion—and I might add—having personally experienced—and I might add—I can guarantee—I insist on this—let me emphasize—in my eyes—when I was there—and I might add—may I remark that," and so on.

I thought I could read impatience and resentment in the stiffening of my father's back.

"But, Monsieur Floqueboque," he finally managed to interrupt, "I don't quite understand the purpose of your visit. What can I do for you?"

"Nothing, actually," replied the self-satisfied little man. "I simply wanted to meet you, and I might add, to mark an occasion, in a way."

He was another one who had crossed the Demarcation Line. He belonged to what he called the "Administration." He waved his hands around in the air as though to embrace it, and harangued away, puffed up by the importance and omnipotence of this Administration whose acolyte he was so proud to be. He launched into a speech on the nation's future. I heard a few words, a few names: the national awakening, Vichy, the Maréchal. That's when I saw Father spring from his chair and indicate with a particularly curt gesture that the conversation was at an end. Monsieur Floqueboque did not return to the Villa, but thanks to him we learned a new expression. After showing his visitor to the door, Father made a detour over to the sofa on his way back to his desk. He took my wrist in his hand to check my pulse, which he'd been doing ten times a day ever since my close call with death. I felt his fingertip feel for my vein, and was comforted.

"You'll be able to tell your brothers and sisters," he observed, "that you were treated to a fine specimen of a stuffed shirt."

Finally, one afternoon, Madame Blèze appeared. She'd moved her chair closer to the desk than the other visitors had, and was seated in such a way that I saw her in profile. She was wearing a hat of blue-black material: short, flat, and round, without raised edges, a little pancake decorated with a veil she had raised to disclose a pale, delicate face. She wore her wavy brunette hair in loose, springy curls. Her lipstick was dark red, almost garnet-colored. I found her fascinating in every way, and she stirred up an emotion in me that none of the other "women in my life" had been able to arouse.

You see, she wasn't the least little bit like them. An aura of elegance floated around her; her manners were ever so refined. Juliette, little Murielle, my own mother dressed and moved with natural simplicity, whereas Madame Blèze gave the impression of having considered and arranged every accessory she wore, every gesture she made, even her very immobility: legs crossed, bust held high, chin up pertly as she faced my father, lips slightly parted, garnet-red lipstick gleaming after a dainty moistening with the tip of her small tongue. She wore a suit that matched her hat, with a narrow skirt that showed off her legs in their clinging stockings of transparent black silk. I wanted to run my hands over those beautiful long limbs, and this sudden and completely new desire was so strong that I told myself, at that very moment, that it had to be illicit, and that this was the explanation for the sneering laughter and whispers of the Dark Man: Madame Blèze made you want to touch her, but you were doubtless not allowed to do so. Now I remembered the little verse composed by Pauloto:

Madame Blèze went a-wooing!
Tell me, whom is she screwing?

I was so captivated by the sight of that woman, so absorbed in my discovery of the temptations she'd unleashed that I couldn't pay attention to her conversation with my father. I had the impression she expected something from him, that she was afraid of financial difficulties. Her voice was plaintive, as though she was seeking to move her listener to pity, and the girlish tone used by this mature and expertly made-up woman added to her charm and its disturbing effect. A few days earlier, deathly ill from diphtheria, I'd believed myself detached from the world of other people. My desire for Madame Blèze, the vision of her legs, her figure, the curving shape of her backside on the chair, the confused longing to touch that transparent material covering the skin of her slender ankles—all these things set me apart once more from the rest of the world.

I was oblivious to my surroundings; only my hands, resting on my abdomen, connected me to my body, but there wasn't any pain this time. I discovered a tiny flickering of pleasure, and somehow linked the memory of my fever and illness to these delicious moments of sensual awakening. Once again I was being carried away, far from other people, but I wasn't frightened, and I owed this discovery to that woman, a woman as dark and strange as my mother and sisters were blond and familiar. This was a discovery I would keep to myself. I decided not to write anything about it in the Album. And then I changed my mind. Madame Blèze's visit was definitely an event, and I realized that my brothers and sisters wouldn't understand how I could pass over it in silence, when not a day had gone by until then without my contributing a few remarks about the visitors I'd seen parade by. Why had Madame Blèze aroused such emotion? I didn't know, but I had a small, intimate secret that I sensed could not be shared by Antoine, Pierre, or Michel, still less by the girls! So, to give them the slip, I wrote: "Madame Blèze arrived and left in a vélo-taxi."

Because she'd turned up at the Villa in one of those curious vehicles that were starting to replace automobiles in the town streets: pedicabs pedaled by sweating men wearing caps, their shirt sleeves rolled up, their faces straining with effort. I'd gotten off my sofa to go watch her departure from the kitchen window. She'd lowered the little veil of her hat and seemed even more disturbing to me, as I gazed at her through the window, both because she apparently expected someone to come assist her, poor helpless creature that she was, and because of her sophisticated and provocative allure, which clashed with the peaceful setting of Haut-Soleil.

Completely absorbed in the contemplation of this vanishing mystery, I didn't hear the door open, and my father raised his gentle voice in astonishment. "What do you think you're doing, standing there on the cold floor with bare feet?"

11

Madame Blèze got out of the vélo-taxi on the corner of Rue Delarep and Place des Acacias to walk a hundred yards or so to her apartment. On her way, she passed the Café Delarep, which did not go unnoticed by habitués of this establishment, who commented thereon for quite some time. Where had she gone, all dressed up like that, hiding behind her black lace veil?

There were several watering holes in our little city's various neighborhoods, but the Café Delarep outshone all its rivals, thanks to its convenient location, the diversity of its clientele, and its role in the daily life of the town. Its terrace and windows gave onto the main square, which was officially named Place de la Préfecture, but which everyone called Place des Acacias, because of the four clumps of giant acacias growing in the center, with thick, straight trunks and gnarled branches.

All rumors, information, and news converged on the Café Delarep. We considered it a magical and dangerous place, and when our parents took us there as a special treat to have ice cream or a glass of grape juice, we felt prickles of excitement, because we were at the heart of things, at the hub of a universe entirely different from our Villa's. I observed those unfamiliar faces, watched waiters bustling about with their trays, and in the back, where the café regulars sat on banquettes of worn brown leather, I saw some strange characters, wreathed in clouds of cigarette smoke, who all seemed to be in on the same secret, so that I wanted to climb up on the marble top of our little table and shout, "What do you know that we don't?"

The Café Delarep was a clearinghouse for the reception and dissemination of news (actual events, personal experiences, eyewitness reports, or complete fabrications), and this clearinghouse was operated by the combined energies of several shifts of clientele. There were the regulars, who never missed their noon or afternoon aperitif; there were the idlers, who settled comfortably into the empty, off-peak hours; there were those who just dropped in for a quick one. The Dark Man was not above stopping by briefly after work, on his way to his evening visit to my father, to pick up the latest local gossip. He knew all the customers. His position at the cooperative, his long residence in the area, his natural air of authority had won him access to the inner workings of this information center. He liked to sip a Raphaël or a "green parrot" (a *pastis* with mint) with all and sundry, the riffraff as well as the gentry, and he didn't consider it demeaning to listen to their smutty stories or off-color remarks. My father disdained such activities and waited, up in the Villa, for his friend to distill the essence of what he'd learned. The townspeople said my father was a haughty man, and claimed he'd spent too much time in Parisian financial circles, but what they took for disdain was actually indifference, skepticism, misanthropy.

At the Café Delarep, rugby (pronounced "rruby") was a favorite topic of conversation, and the local club managers, businessmen in heavy topcoats with loud, confident voices, would sometimes invite players to the café, especially the Barqua-Rondo brothers, a couple of massive quarterbacks in top condition, stars of the team. There was also the town's "artistic fringe," a collection of weirdos who flocked around a man called the Stork, a giant well over six feet tall with a beaky nose, who was never seen without his beret; he'd arrived from Paris with a collection of records and magazines and established himself as an authority on American jazz. Some of the young people of the town would gather at his place to listen to him pontificate about this music, which was becoming harder to hear in the capital but was growing more and more popular in the south, in the unoccupied zone. The Stork held court among his followers, and boasted of having personally known Louis Armstrong and Bix Beiderbecke. A few local dandies, members of an amateur theater group who dreamed of going up to Paris one day to "break into movies," had joined forces with the jazz aficionados, and they all smoked, chattered, and laughed at the witticisms of the Stork, who had a gift for barbed commentary on the ups and downs of daily life, making his points with a cast of caricatures.

The Café Delarep's cachet was thus divided among several social groups whose members, through their professions, reputations, business backgrounds, or personal prestige, assured the constant ebb and flow of news. Slander and lies circulated freely, of course, but its central location and the diversity of its information had made the Café Delarep the dominant voice in the town, one whose monopoly on truth was rarely questioned. And so, over the years, the Café Delarep had become something real in itself: people spoke of it as though it were a person, someone who enjoyed the full trust of the community, a being whose pronouncements and judgments answered a universal need, the desire to fall back upon an unchallenged authority: "If that's what he said, then that's what happened." And if the Café Delarep said so, then it was true.

That's why, even though all sorts of honest and respectable people had already announced *their* arrival, even though the newspaper or the radio or the latest rumors from other areas had proclaimed that it was now just a question of days and that the same thing that was going on in all the towns of France would soon happen here, as long as the Café Delarep hadn't confirmed *their* presence, no one would believe it.

And so *they* had to be discovered right there on Place des Acacias, and it had to be the Café Delarep that saw *them* take over the town, noting the curious color of *their* uniforms, *their* bizarre goose-stepping march, and the impressive deployment of *their* military hardware, before the whole thing could become a reality: the Germans had arrived.

II

The Visitors

12

They were preceded by a prolonged rumble, like a roll on a set of big bass drums, coming from down below, from the banks of the river that flowed by the town.

It was November; the air was brisk, not cold, and the winds whirling down from Les Causses had finished scattering the dead leaves of the plane trees along the reddish, clayey soil of the Allées Malacan. The two ice-cream vendors, moved by some vague foreboding—was it going to rain?—had parked their respective carts and taken hasty shelter beneath the corrugated iron roof of the Bazar Montaut variety store. The two women hated each other. They'd staked out their territories about twenty yards apart on one side of the Allées, and each freely insulted the other's wares, warning the children not to patronize her rival.

"Her ice cream is poisoned," Madame Donzelli would say.

"Donzelli's stuff isn't ice cream," Madame Tasty Treats would huff, "it's peepee."

But the disturbing noise had united the two sharp-tongued competitors in the same anxiety, and it was they, standing in their aprons, their fat bodies wedged between their gaudy carts and the store's front windows, who spotted the first helmets and the first uniforms. Madame Donzelli, the more daring of the two, shouted toward the Place des Acacias, "They're here!"

Her cry plunged down the narrow, tree-lined avenue to the square and the Café Delarep, where some of the customers stepped out to stand stock-still on the sidewalk despite the foul weather, while others held back, remaining inside. All of them, however, had risen spontaneously, and a brutal silence had invaded the big, smoke-filled room usually alive with the sound of voices and laughter, the clinking of glasses and china. They understood, just as the two ice-cream vendors had realized only moments before, that what had sounded like the booming of many drums was only the song of motors humming along in vehicles painted the color of verdigris, rolling smoothly in impeccable formation, driven or escorted by soldiers whose shirts, jackets, pants, caps, and helmets all flaunted the same new color. Only their boots—and weapons—were black, and shining.

The new color was an unfamiliar one. In that town (which was in turn gray, white, calcareous, chalky, red, clayey, pink, or shaded in pastels, depending on the district and the season) with all its inhabitants (those swarthy, dusky, vain, and chatty people, lively and close to the ground, all this humanity that had tripled in less than two years through the incorporation of paler, citified Parisians, as well as refugees with even more sharply contrasting complexions and accents), everyone was struck and dismayed by this new color, for there was something about it that did not harmonize with the character of the town: it wasn't so much the novelty of the color that disturbed and offended us, but rather its ugliness, its artificiality. And it was obvious that this new color meant business, that it didn't care what anyone else thought, and that it would have to be obeyed, or resisted.

The new color came equipped with new faces and new bodies, with freckles, light eyes, different pigmentation, milkier skin, arms and legs that didn't move in the usual way, noses and ears cast from different molds, in shapes that were less round, more angular. They marched to the sound of a different drum, and their superior officers, at the head of the column, had a different air about them: satisfaction, gravity, certainty. And even though people in the town and the surrounding region knew perfectly well how to recognize the conceited attitude of a landed proprietor, the overweening manner of the local cookie king, or the haughty bearing of a wealthy livestock dealer, these soldiers and their leaders bore the signs of a different, preconceived superiority. An arrogance out of all proportion to that conferred by wealth or birth.

When most of this troop had filed by in the direction of the Caserne Doumercq, down Cours Foucault, they were immediately followed by a second group of soldiers, before anyone had had the chance to make the slightest comment, and these new arrivals were not wearing that verdigris color the café patrons, still rooted to the spot, had already decided to compare to the mold one finds in storerooms or the moss on certain oaks. These men were clad in black, with silver buttons, braid, and insignia, and their masklike faces, with their fixed stares, made the soldiers who had preceded them seem almost debonair. Their eyes appeared narrower, their cheekbones higher, and their impassive features betrayed a trace of the Orient. Such coolness, such harshness, such iciness increased the distress that had seized the habitués of the Café Delarep. All of them felt a sudden chill, those inside the café as well as the spectators out on the sidewalk.

And the sight of a little white death's-head framed by two bleached bones, embroidered on the black background of a fluttering pennant attached to the front windshield of the lead vehicle, confirmed the vague impression that in this land of wine and rugby, of plums and grapes, peaches and corn, veal and poultry, chestnuts and mushrooms, one of those decisive moments had just occurred, in all its overbearing insolence, when life—as it has been understood until then—changes meaning, cast in a new light by the sudden flickering of flames.

Up in the Villa, on top of our hill, we hadn't realized this yet.

13

Up on the hill, the twins had invented a new game. Although it didn't last long, it made us understand that life in the Villa had changed. We'd had no idea what was coming, but now our eyes were abruptly opened.

Pierre and Michel had gone on an expedition down to the banks of the Tescou, the river flowing at the foot of the hills on which perched the Villa, and they'd brought home some long, sturdy reeds they'd whittled into peashooters. At first they concealed the existence of these choice items, which they stashed in one of their many hiding places. The twins—mischievous, industrious, imaginative—knew how to exploit the varied resources of the entire giant garden surrounding the Villa. They constructed huts among the cherry trees; they set snares on the chalky, bushy slopes where wild rabbits sometimes played; they shut themselves up in the attic above the girls' wing to emerge disguised as Sioux Indians, daubed in all the colors of the rainbow, and disappeared into the underbrush near the water tower to track down an enemy tribe.

I envied their complicity. That powerful bond underlying each action, each peal of laughter, each adventure, seemed blatantly unfair to me. I would have liked to become one with them, to experience their astonishing mimicry. I was as yet unable to understand that what I saw as a gift of nature might already constitute something of a handicap, and perhaps develop later on into a crippling infirmity.

"We'll be, we'll have, we'll do" was their litany.

Once they'd announced their intentions with these incantatory words ("We'll be Redskins, we'll have scalp-hunting raids, we'll do bloodcurdling tortures"), they became inaccessible. It was as though they'd entered some sort of hypnotic trance. Their eyes glazed over, their smiles twisted strangely, their gestures became exaggerated, melodramatic, and even though I'd beg them to let me come along with them and join their game, I had the feeling they didn't see or hear me anymore. I was locked out of their theater. I could barely keep track of what they were doing. Their own decision to return to normal ("We'll stop being, we'll stop having, we'll stop doing") was the only thing that would allow me to get near them again. I'd watch them dash off, their two silhouettes becoming indistinguishable in the distance, and it wouldn't be long before I'd go whining to my mother or sisters, who'd tell me, "Leave them alone, they're fine together." And Mother would add, pointedly, "You can see it's impossible to keep them apart."

Whenever Antoine would propose, as a change from our "cavalcades," a pretend game of rugby among "just us guys," the twins would automatically team up. They liked to hit and be hit. The ball was only a short-lived pretext: after the first tackle, the game became a free-for-all, with us piled in a wobbling, seething heap, the trick being not to stay on the bottom, because that's where you got pummeled the worst. Antoine would dominate the brawl, managing, on the one hand, to protect me and, on the other, to dispense enough wallops to check somewhat the onrushing fury of Pierre and Michel, who always pounced on me, and to whom I often screamed in fright and frustration, "You're supposed to fight each other too, you know!"

At times blood flowed, hands got scratched, knees skinned, noses bashed. My heart would pound and I didn't like that, but

I'd do my best to give blow for blow, feeling in the end a kind of bitter satisfaction. This roughhousing would take place on the level part of the lawn, in front of the Villa's façade. Sometimes the fight would stop at the first real ugly blow. When we knew we were being watched by the girls or by our parents, we'd wait for the cease-fire to come from Juliette or the grownups. But I could see that my father would take his time before speaking up, despite the urging of the female side of the family. I didn't understand his attitude. What was he waiting for, while I was suffering so much?

"They'll wind up hurting themselves," I'd hear Mother say.

His arms crossed, undismayed, Father would observe without intervening, and one time I caught him answering that maternal "They're getting hurt" with a "Not enough yet, not really."

In the end, order was reestablished. We'd calm down, lying stretched out, panting, cheeks and hands smarting, me trying not to cry, the twins gleeful, Antoine acting superior. Then, nothing could have robbed us of that moment. Lying there, bathed in the scent of that earth, a scent so hard to define, a mixture of rich, cool, clayey soil and trampled grass, we'd have liked to gobble great mouthfuls of that ground so drenched in the perfume of subterranean fruits or flowers, a sugary sweetness, like wine, leather, chestnuts, mingling with the fragrance drifting down from the cedars, larches, and black mulberry trees in the big garden, the odor of menthol, of resin, sappy wood, bark, pinecones, acorns, foliage, with a strong undertone of wild sorrel, and from even farther away, enveloping the whole, a dominant note of sage and sweet hay. We'd snuggle closer to one another. After fighting, our bodies felt the need to embrace, a desire for reconciliation. Pierre and Michel would welcome me into their alliance, Antoine would enclose our motionless group within his already strong arms, and I would be happy.

During one of these interludes, the twins whispered to Antoine and me, "We've made peashooters. Come on!"

We followed them to the hedge that formed a barrier between

our property and the road through Haut-Soleil. There, under the dense laurels and thickets of euonymus, down by the very roots of the vegetation, Pierre and Michel had dug from the gritty earth what looked like two little steps, on which they now sat while removing their peashooters from a hiding place fashioned of dried leaves. From nearby branches, they picked bunches of little green seeds, hard and round, and filled their mouths with them. Placing the peashooters to their lips, they proceeded to strafe the road through a gap in the foliage. The tiny projectiles made a short, dry sound as they popped from the shooters, and when the first cyclist went by, we understood why our two brothers had seemed so gleeful when they decided to share the secret of their game with us. Because the peashooters blew hard, straight, and true, and the legs of the cyclists, as well as their bicycle wheels, were peppered with these stinging volleys that came out of nowhere.

That was the cream of the jest, its supreme thrill: you could snipe with complete impunity at the calves of men and women riding by, who would brake, and sometimes stop, slapping at their pant legs or skirts, looking for the swarm of invisible insects that had stung them. You could hear them exclaim in astonishment, swearing freely, and then watch them go on their way up or down the road without any idea that behind the dark mass of the hedge a few rascals were amusing themselves shamelessly at their expense without the slightest risk of being found out. We were close to the victims, but under cover, thanks to the density of the vegetation and the twins' clever construction of their hideout. The only danger lay in the irresistible desire to laugh or shout in triumph when you'd bombarded a target really well. You had to try to keep calm, and carry out the operation in absolute silence.

The peashooter game could be played only during the day on weekends, when we weren't in school and when people came to stroll or bike through Haut-Soleil. Antoine tired of this sport almost immediately. He was growing up; this silliness didn't interest him anymore, and when he wasn't busy with his books or studies, he was more attracted by the cheering from the rugby stadium, the intriguing charisma of the Stork and his clique at the Café Delarep, or the glances of the girls he'd pass on the street on the way to and from the café. He'd quickly left us to our ambushes, without remembering to remind us of our father's lesson: we had neither the right nor the duty to amuse ourselves that way at the expense of others. We were so conscious of doing "something bad," however, that two words spoken in an unfamiliar voice behind our backs were enough to make us freeze.

"Not correct."

Or, rather, the words were pronounced this way: "Nott korreckt."

We turned around, trembling. It was Monsieur Germain. He'd spoken softly, almost apologetically. We were flabbergasted, not only because an adult had surprised us *in flagrante delicto*, but also because until that moment we'd never heard the sound of Monsieur Germain's voice. For all we'd known, Monsieur Germain, the somewhat peculiar gardener at the Villa, was mute, and quite possibly deaf as well.

14

For some time already, all cultivable ground around the Villa had been entrusted to a veritable little army of gardeners. In the same way, the cooking and cleaning in our household were taken care of by a raft of female helpers. Some days, it seemed as though the population of Haut-Soleil had tripled. The strangest thing of all was that none of these people was from the local area.

That's how it was with Monsieur Germain. He'd been one of Father's first "visitors," the ones who came more and more frequently to the Villa in the years between 1940 and 1942, and when they'd finished talking to Father, instead of leaving through the front door they'd slip out across the terrace and vanish into the greenery. Monsieur Germain turned up again a few weeks after his first visit.

"He's the new gardener," we were told.

Without saying a word, he nodded his head in greeting every morning when he got off his bike, dignified and discreet, single-minded in the pursuit of his sole objective: to pass unnoticed. He had curly red hair, a mustache, a steel-rimmed pince-nez, a velvet vest under a dark cloth jacket with wooden buttons, and he looked like anything but a caretaker of kitchen gardens and orchards, which awaited his attentions up on the hill crowned by our seven poplars. He wore a perpetual smile on his thick lips, one of those humble smiles that appeal for compassion and seem to say, "Don't make fun of me, I just want to be left in peace." We didn't find him ridiculous at all, and although he may have feared harassment from our band of hooting, name-calling mischiefmakers, in his case we respected the distance appropriate to mystery and prolonged silence. Because he never said one word, soberly shaking Father's hand every day, and bowing to Mother, to whom he would hand over two baskets laden with fruits and vegetables before leaving on his bike, with his own harvest secured on the baggage rack, since that was the arrangement agreed to by my father and the little man: he took his wages in produce from the garden. He was allowed to cultivate his own plot of land, and this permission was extended to the other men who followed him up to the Villa to put in their hours on the property.

Monsieur Germain was in charge of everyone. The rest of the temporary gardeners were all as unlikely as he was, dressed like city folk who'd fled in the middle of the night from a raging fire, some of them having had only enough time to throw a jacket over their pajamas. They would gather around Monsieur Germain out by the broad, gentle, fertile slope that led down into the valley of the Tescou. Chores were assigned. Then they would all go off in different directions, depending on the time of day, on foot or by bike on the road that ran along the river below, returning to the refugees' quarter or going out to the neighboring farms where these men donated their labor in exchange for a meal and a night's lodging. We didn't see much of these activities because they went on while we were off at school. Monsieur Germain sometimes came by of a Sunday to pick up extra food, however, and there were a few other regulars like him, which should have tipped us off to the connection between the situation throughout the country and these "visitors," these silent "gardeners," some of whom were so inept that one of them was seen taking a pickax to cement in an effort to grow potatoes.

"This is Dora, and she'll be helping out in the kitchen."

That's how Mother informed us there was a new inhabitant in the world of the Villa. When we asked, "Who is she, where'd she come from?" they told us, "She's someone we used to know."

That stock reply didn't satisfy our curiosity anymore. We'd recorded in the Album that although Dora did speak, unlike Monsieur Germain, she had a funny, guttural accent, clumsy and harsh; that she was nearsighted; that she didn't know how to make anything except a particularly cloying pumpkin cake; and that she broke lots of dishes without ever being scolded even once. Dora would hide behind my mother, following her around, studying every move she made, and then try to do things the way she did. There was something good and kind in her countenance, and we thought she resembled our mother in some ways: the same tenderness toward the youngest children, the same patience with my perpetual whining, the same indulgence for the caprices of Jacqueline and Violette. The Dark Man, who liked to pop into the kitchen and pantry without knocking, just to throw this "women's world" into a tizzy, had gotten into the habit of bullying Dora, with that pretending-to-be-grumpy voice he used when talking to someone younger than he was, *a fortiori* a woman.

"Well, Dora, are you going to get yourself that pair of glasses?"

Dora refused to venture downtown, where the slightest hint of a different accent would always set people off: "You, you're not from around here."

She was afraid she'd have to reveal her race, background, and illegal status to some shopkeeper, a stranger who might be inclined to gossip.

The Dark Man kept at her, though. "You'd look good in glasses, they'd make you even more attractive."

Dora would blush, shake her blond hair, and busy herself opening cupboards, which just increased her embarrassment and the general untidiness of the kitchen. She wore a blouse my mother had lent her, and the thin material did little to disguise her curves. The Dark Man would cackle and head back to the office, where Father would request in a loud voice that he restrain his penchant for mockery and snide remarks and keep his mind instead on the business at hand.

Both of them were even more secretive than before. Given his many contacts in the local community, the Dark Man had taken on the job of obtaining false identity papers for the men and women my father was sheltering. The two quinquagenarians had had no idea what their initial gestures of hospitality would lead to, and now here they were at the head of some kind of assistance network.

Everything had happened gradually. Because of its location in the unoccupied zone and on the main route to the Spanish border, for two years the town had seen a steady stream of refugees, a mixed bag of Polish Jews, Germans hostile to the Nazi regime, stateless people known as the *heimatlos*. On the whole, the townspeople had helped these poor souls. Some of the refugees had moved on within a short time; others, reassured by the moderate climate, the abundance of food, and the soothing beauty of the hills and valleys, had succeeded in acquiring identity papers and documents to make them seem "in order." They'd become somewhat assimilated into that little town which had thought itself closed to outsiders, but which had proved capable of generosity. Nevertheless, all the newcomers remained temporary citizens, operating under false names, living from day to day, keeping a nervous watch to the north and east, where they feared to see misfortune and persecution raise their ugly heads once more.

When the new verdigris color spread throughout the town, it sent a fresh tremor through the scattered community of refugees. Those who thought they were in serious danger decamped and headed farther south. Others, although secure in their new identities, still felt uneasy, and sought additional protection. There was that Villa, up in Haut-Soleil, that employed an unusual number of gardeners, and that tall, white-haired man who was rarely seen in town and who opened his door, people said, to outcasts in need.

Father had known Norbert Awiczi in Paris, before the war. He was a diamond merchant, a shrewd, intelligent man, fond of the theater, of pretty girls, music, and nights on the town. He'd had the same premonition as my father, and had decided, well before the Exodus, to head for safer ground. One night he showed up at the Villa. He was short, dark, charming, with hands that fluttered through the air like birds to illustrate whatever point he was making. He rolled his *r*'s, not the way they do in the southwest of France, but in a more exotic register, after the fashion of some Romanian actress or other.

"Biarrritz, dearr frriend, Biarrritz! They'll neverr come looking forr us therre!"

"But why Biarritz?" Father had asked.

"Dearr frriend, think of the casinos, and the sea, so therre will be rrich people, and women! That means prrosperrity, wild amourrs, incrredibly juicy deals!"

Then this sophisticated Parisian man-about-town had stopped playing the fool and suddenly become serious, whispering, "And Spain would be right next door, just in case . . ."

Since he'd slurred these last three words together, repeating them several times, Juliette and Antoine—who were old enough to remember him, as he made his appearance only a few days after our move to the Midi—had nicknamed him Justin Case in the opening pages of the Album we were inaugurating. He was originally from Austria, and before setting out again for Biarritz, he'd asked Father a single question: "May I send a few friends along to you?"

"Of course," Father had replied.

It wasn't hard for him to say yes. He was fond of Awiczi, fond of his sharp wit and subtle conversation, and he'd appreciated the fact that the diamond merchant had shared his sense of foreboding about catastrophes to come.

But perhaps, as he watched his wife come and go about the

parlor, my father was also unconsciously associating the fate of that orphaned girl with the universal fate of all those communities threatened by Nazism.

He'd fallen in love with the girl the first time he'd set eyes on her; it had been what's commonly called love at first sight. It's anything but common, however. What had he seen in her that secretly corresponded to his own tragedy, the loss of his father so early in life? The pessimism that had threaded its way triumphantly through much of his thinking had been momentarily banished by so clear and strong a love. He had considered himself—a man pushing forty—to be without any illusions regarding amorous intrigues, experiences, sensations: a man disillusioned with all women. The mere sight of the girl, with her hair in braids, in that bourgeois home where he'd chanced to be a fourth in a boring game of bridge, had awakened what he'd thought to be a blasé heart, a weary body, and an agnostic soul. She had moved, captivated, attracted him beyond reason, and even when he knew nothing of her past, he'd sensed that she needed him just as fiercely as he'd always searched for her. Their union was decided and established then, in the first moment, at the first contact, with the first gesture. Later, they would speak of this only rarely, and only to a few intimate friends, because they knew instinctively that such an experience is difficult to put into words, that by speaking of it to others, one risks encountering incomprehension at best, and at worst (and more often), envy.

When he saw her for the first time, and spoke of his admiration, she lowered her eyes. She'd felt a surge of emotion; she'd received a sign of recognition. He stood straight, tall, and aloof in this room filled with stuffy nonentities and dithering puppets. His already graying hair and tortoiseshell glasses gave him a severe and professorial air, an aura of authority, of success. But she'd sensed something else in his face, heard a different note in his voice. Where my father's business relations and casual friends had perceived only coldness and arrogance, this girl had seen through the icy armor of pride, the disguises of reticence one dons to avoid causing and feeling pain—which amount to the same thing, and lead sooner or later to the chilly wasteland of loneliness.

A few years before, in a letter written aboard the *Île-de-France* as he was returning home after breaking with his American mistress, my father had confided in Paul. "In a corner of my room, awaiting its hour to strike—sometimes choosing midnight, sometimes dawn—I'll see it reappear: familiar, sarcastic, supremely confident, with its twisted mouth and glassy stare—the poisoned face of Anxiety."

"It's a pretty phrase," Paul had said when they'd seen each other again, "but a mite too pretty, too bookish. Didn't you have a tiny bit of fun, all the same, hmm?"

"You're right," admitted his friend.

Better than anyone else, Paul understood the source of that anxiety my father crowned with such a black capital. He knew that his soul brother waged a constant battle against angst, and suspected that this oppressive state of mind wasn't due entirely to the havoc death had brought so early to his life. Sometimes he wondered if it might spring from some mysterious mechanism, some unfathomable laws of heredity.

But the young woman, knowing nothing about the mature man who stood before her, had swept all this away with one look from her innocent eyes. With the strength of her sixteen years bereft of any motherly or fatherly presence, without the slightest token of love, blessed only with her premonition, her need to love and be loved, she had recognized that same need in this man who was old enough to be her father (and who would doubtless take his place, although she wouldn't want to think of him as such), with whom she would create as soon as possible the family neither he nor still less she had ever known. With him, she would soon establish a haven so warm, so protected, so secure, that with only one exception—the friendship of Paul, the Dark Man's daily appearance—they would no longer feel obliged to maintain close relationships with other people, those social ties so many couples need to mask a joyless void at home, the inert silence of marriages unraveling because their reason for being, or for ever having been at all, is quite forgotten. As he listened now to his friend the diamond merchant, bound for Biarritz, in the contented calm of the Villa, nestled in that Haut-Soleil as yet unshaken by any of the winds of war, did my father realize what subtle bonds prompted him to open his arms so readily to strangers? He found it very easy to say yes, when Awiczi, alias Justin Case, repeated his apparently harmless question in a soft voice, just as he was leaving.

"May I send a few friends along to you?"

15

At first, Justin Case's friends arrived at the Villa at wide intervals, beginning in early 1940.

But word had spread through a small Jewish circle in Vienna, where Justin Case had made his fortune before living it up in Paris, in those extravagant years of late nights and pretty women. He had never really cared about his business in Vienna and would have much rather been a "crreatorr," a playwright, a conductor, a painter. His friends had all belonged to an intelligentsia that disappeared, little by little, into exile. One of these friends, a lawyer and fervent anti-Nazi, was Germain Bloch.

He'd waited until the last possible moment before escaping from Austria, after helping to set up a resistance organization to fight the Gestapo, but when the Nazis had put a price on his head, Germain Bloch had been forced to go underground and flee to what then seemed the safest haven, the French unoccupied zone. It wasn't sheer chance that led him to our doorstep. The arrival of "Monsieur Germain" threw the mechanism of solidarity into gear, and over the following months, and years, my father was sought out not only by the lawyer's friends but also by other men and women, distant relations of earlier refugees, whom he tried to resettle in town or out in the surrounding countryside, or to pass on to other similar networks, to "stations" in Les Causses, Le Gers, Les Pyrénées. He did all this with the help of the Dark Man, whose close ties to the local municipal administration provided contacts for the procurement of false identity papers, ration cards, and other necessities.

Most of those whom we children still naïvely called our "visitors" were only passing through Haut-Soleil, staying just the one night, sometimes two.

We'd barely begin to get used to these new faces before they'd vanish: two sisters called Edith and Judith, one of whom suffered from a stammer caused by her terror of nightfall; Abramovici, a bearded painter, a fatalist who loved to tell jokes and play pranks; Monsieur Krutz—whom we had to call "Cruse"—who arrived with a motherless baby whom he left under a false name at the day nursery in Montbeton. Fleeting and pathetic masks, silhouettes lost in the morning mist, scattering through orchards tinted violet by the haze, through rows of stunted fig trees, through brambles spangled with dew.

Some of these refugees stayed on, however, and grew accustomed to the world of the Villa. Of these men and women, Monsieur Germain and Dora were the ones who were most familiar to us. And so, when Monsieur Germain felt it urgent to report, with his exquisite politeness, that three of the boys had behaved in a manner "nott korreckt," and that their peashooter ambushes might provoke what the adults feared most of all (the interest of outsiders!), Father decided that it was time to initiate us into the many mysteries that puzzled us in our daily lives.

He made something of a solemn occasion of it, summoning us to his office, as though we were clients. We waited outside the door, on the upholstered bench usually reserved for distinguished visitors, where the lovely Madame Blèze had rested, a fragile, silken vision. We were seated in order of age and height, trying to repress our fits of giggles, divided between the fear of a scolding and the desire to find out what was going on.

Finally, the door opened. "Come in, children," murmured Father.

He wasn't wearing his stern "Statue of the Commendatore" look. Mother was standing at his side. She was smiling, as though to reassure us, and I suppose that she had advised him, with the persistent sweetness that imperceptibly influenced many of his attitudes, to speak "gently, above all on account of the little ones." Father had his arm around her waist, and standing before this couple who simply radiated tenderness, we guessed that we'd soon be forgiven for our peashooters and would then move on to infinitely more serious matters.

16

We knew what "the office" looked like, but we'd hardly ever set foot in it. It was a kind of sanctuary.

I'd had the privilege of observing it from my convalescent's sofa, but that had been a long time ago, and this time I saw it from a different angle, from the point of view of Father's visitors.

It was a large room with walls completely paneled in dark walnut, and the paneling was entirely covered with bookshelves. No matter where you looked, that's all you could see: books! Some of them were heavy, richly ornamented, bound in olive green or scarlet leather, while others were dog-eared, their gilt edges faded by time. The complete works of Alexandre Dumas, Racine, Corneille, even Rostand, stood alongside those of Bergson, Renan, or Anatole France, but there were also Rudyard Kipling and Paul Féval and the adventures of those swashbuckling heroes Le Bossu, Nez-de-Cuir, Pardaillan, and Lagardère. And Baudelaire, Sir Walter Scott, and Victor Hugo! And James Fenimore Cooper and Jack London, Montaigne and Saint-Simon. Cardinal de Retz rubbed shoulders with Balzac's *La Comédie Humaine*, Huysmans, Jules Verne, and Michelet. An incongruous assortment of books, and yet a faithful reflection of my father's taste for beautiful writing, in poetry as well as prose, in historical romance as well as philosophy. The Précis-

Dalloz collection alone took up several shelves with its thirty volumes of legal and fiscal information. Finally, in a place of honor, its pedestal set in a recess that broke the geometric rhythm of those endless rows of books, sat a darkened bronze copy of Houdon's famous bust of Voltaire.

My attention was immediately drawn to the face of that man, whose name I didn't know. I'd noticed the bust before, but it was only then that I was truly struck by his appearance. It was as though recent events and our summons to the office had given the statue a new dimension, and Father noticed my open-mouthed, wide-eyed contemplation of the great man's likeness. Pierre and Michel had adopted the same pose.

"He is called Voltaire," Father announced, anticipating our question.

"Why 'is called'? Isn't he dead?"

"He died two centuries ago," came the reply, "but he is still very much alive."

That was just the answer I expected, for it confirmed the impression I'd already received; to me the bust seemed incredibly alive, which both frightened and excited me. It was as though the man were sending us a message, but a message children our age found impossible to decipher. Laughing, staring down his aquiline nose at us, fixing humanity with his penetrating eye, his lips curled in a wry grimace, François Marie Arouet was saying to anyone able to understand him, "Well, what have you accomplished in your life that will stand the test of time?"

That smile, that huge, bony forehead, that cap perched so jauntily on that big head—they had such an effect on me that later I would occasionally sneak into Father's study when he wasn't there, to see if Voltaire was still "alive" and still taking an interest in us. Gazing down on children and grownups alike, this personification of intelligence silently imposed his will on whoever beheld him, putting all vanity in its place. One day, when I had left my childhood far behind, I would come to the conclusion that my father had placed the bust there with precisely that intention: he must have hoped—without cherishing too many illusions—that the contemplation of Voltaire's countenance would allow even the most stubborn individuals to become aware of their own narrow-mindedness, and even the hardest hearts to grow ashamed of their selfishness.

It was in this setting, in this realm of books that conjured up the invisible presence of Jean Valjean and Jérôme Coignard, Cyrano de Bergerac and Robespierre, D'Artagnan and Crainquebille, Belliou la Fumée and Quentin Durward, in this retreat that harbored the words of Pascal and Daudet, Péguy and Rivarol, that we were taught our most beautiful lesson of virtue and History.

Father spoke to us about the real state of the world, about France, and our little town. Speaking simply and to the point, he talked about Hitler, Nazism, the Occupation, the Jews, the Collaboration—in that order—and emphasized the duty of resistance and the fundamental concept of helping one's fellow men. Then he urged us to be discreet, prudent, and loyal.

"You are now, all of you, entrusted with a vital secret," he reminded us. "I hope I've made it clear that you must never betray this secret."

Great clouds of confusion were swept from our imaginations. So that's what Father and the Dark Man talked about in private! So that's what it was all about, those discussions, the comings and goings, those temporary house guests in their strange clothes, the evening visitors, the incompetent gardeners, the cleaning women who had no idea how to handle a broom, that Monsieur Germain who never spoke, and young Edith with her jet-black hair and mauve eyelids, who cried during the night.

Antoine and Juliette had nodded their heads while Father spoke to us, and we younger ones took that as proof that our older siblings had already figured out more than we had. Father had tried not to use any of those unusual words he liked to sprinkle around his conversation, but he hadn't been able to avoid them all, and since both he and our mother had encouraged and trained us in the art of open dialogue, we were all bursting with questions, especially we younger ones.

"Monsieur Germain is an Austrian intellectual," Father had said.

And we asked, "What's an intellectual?"

"It's someone who works with his head rather than his hands."

He'd said, "All Europe is in the grip of an epidemic of intolerance."

And we asked, "What's intolerance?"

"It's when some people refuse to let others have any opinions different from their own, or when they hate people with a different color skin. And when they're ready to kill them because of it."

He'd mentioned anti-Semitism.

When we'd asked what that meant, he'd told us it was the same thing as intolerance. He'd spoken of de Gaulle, and we'd asked him who he was.

"He's one man," Father had replied, "who was able to say no when everyone else was saying yes."

When we'd asked, "How do you recognize a traitor?" and, "How can you tell when someone's a collabo?" he'd told us, "It's not easy. But let me give you this advice: Always look people straight in the eye. Shifty eyes are never a good sign."

Finally, he'd spoken of our country, of our values.

And we asked, "What are values?"

He'd thought for a moment about that question, then heaved a little sigh that implied how difficult it was to arrive at a clear, simple, yet satisfying answer. After a while, he got up from his chair and held out his arms toward all those hundreds of his beloved books, in a sweeping movement that also embraced the bronze bust of the Sage of Ferney.

"Values? Patriotism? Why, they're all this, children!" He spoke with serene confidence, for the evidence was irrefutable.

No one spoke after that, and we were all united in the same

silence, a silence like the intervals of rest that punctuate a sonata.
A sonata, or a prayer.

Outdoors, it was so quiet you could have heard the soft footfall of a cat playing on the terrace. A breeze had sprung up,
gently rustling the poplar leaves, and you could tell from the
way the noise became fuller, more like a chorus of human voices,
that the wind was still rising and had reached the sturdier trees
with denser foliage, the oaks and larches. From down in the
valley came the intermittent sound of bells and the lowing of
cattle from the Barbier farm, where we went regularly to get
our milk and fresh eggs. The milk we carried back in the big,
unpolished metal can would still be warm from the cows' ud-
ders, and as we climbed back up the hill to the Villa, the heavy
sloshing of the rich liquid was part of the harmony that surrounded us.

We never stopped to think how lucky we were. It hadn't
occurred to me that this tranquillity, this peaceful haven, might
now be threatened by the decisions Father had made. Only he
and Mother were able to judge the risks they had taken. And
this wasn't the least of the reasons why he looked so worried,
and why I hardly ever saw him except with his brow furrowed
with care. Father and Mother had both tried to protect their
children, taking them far from Paris to watch them grow up in
the calm of a quiet province. There was a certain contradictory
aspect to our upbringing, for our parents were both protective
of us yet anxious to foster our independence. Both of them
allowed their boys to fight among themselves until the blood
ran, for example, but they'd lose sleep over our most minor
ailment. And now what had been generous assistance to home-
less friends when we lived in the unoccupied zone had become
illicit, rebellious activity with the arrival of the Occupation. Even
though he was devoted to the same cause, Paul had clearly
pointed out the danger.

"You understand, don't you, what you're letting your little
world in for?"

"Oh yes, I know," Father had replied.

Later, the Dark Man had suggested, "Don't you think it's about time to tell the little ones what's going on?"

"We took care of that yesterday."

"Not a moment too soon," grumbled the Dark Man.

"Don't worry, everything will be fine," added Father.

He found it somewhat ironic that it was he, the dyed-in-the-wool pessimist, who had to reassure his old friend. It was true that between 1940 and 1942 the entire southwest of France had become an immense haven for refugees. On the farms, the estates, the *métairies*, in the obscure little hamlets, in La Dordogne, Le Périgord, Le Quercy, L'Agenais, dozens of decent people had made the same fundamental gesture, the most beautiful of human gestures: they had held out their hands to the oppressed.

And for that sort of people, as for my father, no doubt, there was one phrase that said it all, a phrase he used one evening to stem the flood of thanks from a certain Horowitz, whose haggard eyes still reflected the horror of the Warsaw Ghetto.

"Don't thank me. It's only natural, it's the least we can do."

17

It was "only natural," and we children had to go on behaving naturally. But that meant we were being asked to play a role.

Keeping a secret means living in danger. Nothing must show. Classmates must not be told a single thing. The tantalizing desire to boast must be repressed. And most difficult of all, one must not act mysterious, like a conspirator.

I learn to live with these rules. When I'm asked questions, I have to pretend I don't know a thing. The teachers talk to us, and the students talk among themselves. The whole town is talking. Nobody's talking about anything else, actually: the Boches, the militia, the Vichy government appointees who've taken charge of the prefecture and the municipality. The town has split into several factions: those who accept and go so far as to assist the Nazis; those who remain neutral; those who are ready to resist.

One day Monsieur Furbaire asks me to stay after class for a moment, and questions me with surprising friendliness.

"Tell me, son, may I send someone to speak to your father?"

It's my duty to reply that I don't know what he's talking about. Furbaire might be a Spy!

"Ask him, anyway," says Furbaire before dismissing me. "He'll understand. And if your friends ask why I wanted to speak to you," he adds, "tell them I chewed you out for talking during geography."

This precaution reassures me, since it suggests that Furbaire wants to camouflage the real subject of our conversation because he's on our side. And I look straight into his eyes, just as Father had told us to. His eyes are an ordinary brown, and rather glassy, but I see that he's looking straight back at me without flinching. That's why I'm able to give an optimistic and full report to my father, who runs his fingers through my hair with a sudden dazzling smile.

"When you see your teacher tomorrow," he replies evenly, "you may tell him it's fine with me. This Furbaire is 'the right sort.' "

My father belonged to that generation of Frenchmen for whom these three simple words, for over fifty years, were enough to define a person's moral character. It didn't matter if he was of limited intelligence, arbitrary in his judgments, lacking in verve in the teaching of his classes in Histo-and-Geo, or so boring that more than a few minutes of his company would have you politely stifling a yawn—once you felt and knew that the man possessed both the moral strength that separates brave men from cowards and the integrity that refuses compromise with one's conscience. It wasn't unusual for these men to have received a secular education grounded in the humanities, to have survived the butchery of the First World War, and to have risen painfully on the social scale through sheer hard work, but they could also be found among those who had received a religious education, inherited substantial wealth, and were accustomed to sleeping on fresh linen every night. All shared the same conception of honor, the same disdain for crookedness, deceit, pretense. They were the sort of people of whom you said, "He's got principles."

And you didn't have to spell them out.

I'm so excited! Father entrusted me with a message for Furbaire. I had a mission to accomplish. I thought it would be too obvious if I just went right up to the teacher, at the moment when the rec bell rang under the metal roof of the playground shelter, echoing along the old walls of red brick and rough plaster. I thought of something cleverer than that, and at noon, when there was a great rush down the narrow main hall leading to the lycée's entrance, when the corridor is filled with the infernal din of the students racing to the dining hall and those rushing for their bikes (lined up in the shabby little park adorned with one palm tree and three catalpas) so they can get home in time for lunch, I ran smack into Furbaire, on purpose. He staggered, fell back against the wall, and grabbed my forearm.

"Why don't you watch where you're going?"

In the midst of the yelling and the racket, I quickly passed on my message in an earnest voice. "Papa told me to tell you it's all right."

He seemed to understand and let go of my arm, shouting, "Slow down, or I'll stick you with an hour's detention!"

I was proud of myself. I'd carried out my plan without a hitch. Perhaps my stratagem was superfluous, because from the very beginning of the Occupation, the entire teaching staff had adopted an attitude of defiance toward the invaders' authorities and their actions. The teachers willingly added the refugees' children to their class rolls, and to everyone's surprise, our insignificant Monsieur Poussière displayed a strong streak of initiative. The lycée became one of the main suppliers of false identity papers, the hub of various clandestine networks. Later, several assistant teachers and gym monitors, including the famous Red-Cheeks-except-in-the-Middle, would vanish overnight; rumor had it they'd taken to the maquis, putting into action the spirit of resistance that reflected the true personality of the little town.

It was a proud Huguenot town, which over the centuries had established a tradition of independence, had taken a defiant stand during the Wars of Religion, and had already tested its ability to reject all foreign bodies from its organism. It had gone against the grain for the town to take in all its refugees, most of them Polish Jews, with a smattering of Russians, as well as many Parisians swept along in the Exodus, and that had been going on for two years now. But the townspeople had gotten used to them, whereas the irruption of the Germans in their verdigris uniforms—soon followed by their lackeys, Frenchmen in civilian clothes or the uniforms of the militia—had triggered an instinctive reaction of hostility. It would be untrue to claim that the entire community showed the same pugnacity, but, on the whole, the town behaved with dignity.

I was unaware of all these things but enthusiastic about the new game I'd just had a taste of. I'd become a Secret Agent, an indispensable Courier! I was all the heroes whose exploits I'd precociously devoured in the books my father had permitted me to read. I was Judex and Arsène Lupin, Fantômas and La Flèche, I was Gavroche dying on the cobblestones at the barricades during the Paris Commune, I was Captain Corcoran, Roland de Roncevaux; I was Colonel Chabert—a character portrayed by a stocky man with an unforgettable voice, an actor called Raimu, whom we'd discovered in a black-and-white film, perhaps the first one to leave an impression on my imagination. I rarely received permission to see the movies shown in the large room hung with red curtains in the Théâtre Municipal, near Place de la Prefecture. The "big kids" enjoyed this privilege, but when my parents took Antoine and Juliette with them, and sometimes the "in-between" brothers and sisters, I'd stay home in the empty house, left in the care of Dora.

Before, I would have been scared stiff. Now I'd grown up a little, I knew what Dora represented, and I saw myself as a full-fledged member of the Resistance, so staying with Dora seemed to me part of the same adventure, and I told myself that I was there as much to protect her as she was to care for a little boy. The young woman was a native of Cologne, where her entire family had been massacred during a night of pogrom—but I didn't know that. She'd spoken of it only once, to my mother;

they were the same age, or just about, and my mother, whose heart was always open to others, had told her, "You're one of us now."

Dora had replied, in her uneven French, "Your kindness makes feel like crying, but I can no more."

We'd seen and heard little Edith cry and cry, hiccuping with fear as soon as night fell on our benevolent countryside, those hills where peaches and apricots grew so abundantly, those valleys that harbored only the diaphanous swirls of an evening mist. She'd continued on her way toward Perpignan, helped by her older sister Judith, and her sobs, which would change into painful rasping groans as the night wore on, had left us, the children of the Villa, helpless and aghast. Juliette had tried to take her in her arms, but Judith had gently intervened.

"No. No use."

We no longer dared consign such scenes to the Album. We didn't know the precise cause of the nightmare that tormented young Edith, but we'd vaguely understood that it had to be as terrible as whatever had burned away all Dora's tears. One cried endlessly, the other would never shed a single tear, and it was for the same reason, but poor ignorant souls that we were, despite our father's discussion with us in his office, we couldn't possibly understand the true extent of what was happening. Yet our freedom from care had been spoiled, for an invisible pall had fallen silently over the paradise of Haut-Soleil.

18

At the movies, in those days, the screen was filled with a whole crowd of people who had nothing whatsoever to do with the reality of our time, people who astonished their provincial audiences and tickled us kids no end as we sat hooting derisively in the dark, for we hadn't lost our sense of mischief.

There was a man with incredible teeth and a horse-faced grin, who played the fool to perfection: his name was Fernandel. There were handsome men with hair as white as snow, as white as the white in black-and-white films, but we imagined their hair was blond or red, because the actors were young and graceful, with names like Jean Marais, Pierre Blanchar, or Pierre-Richard Wilm. Others were less handsome, but more gripping as performers, thanks to their striking diction, singular appearance, and spectacular style: Louis Jouvet, Jules Berry, Alexandre Rignault, Saturnin Fabre, Michel Simon. There was one ridiculous stammering fatty called Gabriello, a name impossible to take seriously, and there was also Jean Tissier, a character who was sort of half man and half woman, with hair of a washed-out color, and a drawling, treacly voice that seemed to stretch out interminably, like taffy.

The women were no less unreal than their partners. Edwige Feuillère, of course, who'd inspired Juliette to put on the airs of a duchess and parade around like a well-bred ostrich; Suzanne Dehelly, a beanpole with an equally outrageous voice, who seemed to enjoy her domineering roles; Françoise Rosay, another "great lady" whom it was hard to imagine plunging her hands into the flour bin or a sink full of dishwater, because she was so obviously great and so obviously a lady; and Madeleine Sologne, a blonde with such long, lank hair, and such pale, hollow cheeks, that she seemed to be a chronic invalid.

There were other actresses who were quite different, however, "girls" rather than women, with teasing eyes and painted lips, thighs and breasts they managed to display without showing too much. They had the look of creatures most at home amid tousled bedclothes, who lived in hotel rooms, who were unhappy, and whom men loved to touch, to slap, or to kiss on their showy mouths. Most of them were brunettes, with hair as black as ink, as black as the black of black-and-white films, and their names were Viviane, Ginette, Dita, Simone, Lucienne. They made a stronger impression on me than the men did, simply because the black fabric and lace that covered their white bodies reminded me of the beautiful Madame Blèze, whose dark silk-sheathed ankles I'd secretly hoped to caress at least once.

That was the single connection I was able to establish between my life and those movies. Madame Blèze was the only person who resembled those actresses, those giant figures on the screen in the Théâtre Municipal. All the other men and women up there seemed absolutely inaccessible and unbelievable to me, and to my brothers and sisters as well. Those people wore tuxedos, evening gowns, lamé, spangles, jewelry; they smoked long cigarettes stuck in the ends of slender ivory holders; they were decked out in costumes of the Middle Ages, uniforms, or clothes from faraway places, from warm and exotic lands. And even when the stories were set closer to home, on docks, in ports, in bistros or train stations, the characters were still just as sleek, impeccable, and disembodied, gliding through a light not of this world. Contrary to all received wisdom, we didn't dream about these people, nor did we envy them. True, Juliette had identified with Edwige Feuillère for a while sometime ago, but she'd gotten over it. Now she and Antoine seemed to be looking elsewhere for inspiration, a change that hadn't escaped my parents.

It was simply that the people we saw every day—the local peasants and farmers, the teachers at the lycée, our classmates, parents, but also and especially the "visitors," who had subtly effected a profound change in the world of the Villa—were so different from those celluloid creatures that the make-believe bunch seemed not only marvelous but also grotesque, or even scandalous.

We couldn't believe in what we were shown on the silver screen, but that was what gave those movies both their strength and their fragility. They weren't based on any tangible reality. All the characters, the starring as well as the supporting roles, had been conceived and brought to life on a different planet. The idlers lounging around the tables of the Café Delarep maintained that these celluloid creations were cooked up in Paris, in the Capital, a mythical metropolis that seemed even more far-off than it had before, now that our area was becoming aware of the roundups and summary executions carried out by the occupation forces, as well as the Allied bombing raids and the activities of the Resistance. Just as we, up in the Villa, would finally come to grips with something completely unforeseeable.

19

Early one morning, when we hadn't yet finished our bowls of ersatz *café au lait* made with roasted barley, before we'd wheeled out our bikes to head down to the lycée, we heard strange noises in the garden. Metallic sounds, short cries, the thud of objects hitting the ground.

"It's swarming with Germans," said Michel, who'd been the first to reach a window.

"What?" exclaimed Father. "Stay right where you are, all of you!"

He rose and went outside through the kitchen door. We rushed to the window.

On the lawn where we horsed around with our rugby ball, armed and helmeted infantrymen were performing tasks in a rapid and well-organized fashion. There were no heavy armored vehicles visible on the graveled area right by the front gate, but we saw a motorcycle with a sidecar, and standing next to the seated driver, a high-ranking officer wearing a gray cap surveyed the activities of his men, who were busy digging up our lawn. Here and there, with a certain regularity, using short-handled shovels with large blades, they were cutting trenches in which they would then lie down flat on their stomachs, with their guns resting on the ground and pointing straight ahead of them. Positioned on the lowest and strongest branch of one of our big oaks, a soldier was studying the surrounding area through binoculars. His boots gleamed in the sparkling morning sunshine. The grounds of the Villa looked a mess, if not wrecked. The uniforms bustling all over, the shovels hacking up our lawn—ours!—and the brazen assurance with which all this was going on left us speechless.

We saw Father go over to the officer and nod curtly to him. The two men appeared to be conversing with composure and courtesy. It was obvious that Father knew how to talk to this kind of person, in this kind of situation.

"There are some behind the house, too!" Pierre called out, running back from the parlor–dining room.

He'd seen the same deployment of troops and activity through the French windows that gave onto the terrace.

"My God," exclaimed Mother, "the diamonds! Antoine, we've got to do something!"

Speaking quickly but precisely, Mother told Antoine—who was standing ready behind his chair while the rest of us listened silently—that Norbert Awiczi (a.k.a. Justin Case) had entrusted to our father a small suede pouch filled with diamonds that he preferred not to take along with him when he went on to Biarritz. It was doubtless meant to be a sort of security deposit or advance payment, intended to cover all the "friends" my father had agreed to take in on his recommendation. Since there was no safe in the Villa, the two men had dug a shallow hole outside one night and buried the treasure.

"It's at the foot of the third poplar on the right, as you're facing the Tescou River," said Mother. "Go sit down over there and don't budge."

After ordering the rest of us not to leave the kitchen for any reason whatsoever, she vanished quickly down the stairs leading to the laundry room and on down to the cellar below. There, among the hampers of vegetables, the bags of fertilizer, the gardening tools, was where we'd set up a living space for Dora, and it was there as well that all our secret visitors, those travelers of despair, would sleep for a night or two, in a kind of dormitory arranged with cots and straw mattresses. We heard her speak to Dora and discovered she spoke German quite well. But we were even more surprised by her decisiveness, her swift efficiency, and her cold-blooded desperation.

Returning to the kitchen, she locks the door to the laundry room stairs behind her. "Help me, children."

Together we push the big kitchen table with our wobbling breakfast bowls over against the door, and Juliette moves our napkins and the mulberry-twig breadbasket to hide the doorknob and lock.

Father enters the kitchen and turns to Mother. "The laundry room. The suede pouch."

"All taken care of," she replies.

He smiles, and his smile is only for her. He kisses her. Then, moved by the desire to give us the impression that he has everything well in hand, that our imposing father has the problem under control, he smiles at us in a different way, not as lovingly, more protectively.

"Go back to your seats," he tells us. "I've spoken with the officer, he's a captain, and you know that I was one also. He seems a decent enough sort to me. They didn't pick out the Villa for any special reason. There are men next door at Dr. Sucre's place, and more up by the water tower. In fact, they're all over Haut-Soleil. They're holding some small-scale routine maneuvers, but it would be better if you didn't go to school this morning."

"Antoine went off to sit under the poplar," Mother tells him.

"It would look strange if I went to join him," replies Father, "so he'll have to handle things on his own."

Father has remained standing and wants to tell us even more about the state of affairs at the Villa, as though to show us that we shouldn't let ourselves be upset by the profanation of our sacred territory.

"The officer and I have reached an agreement," he continues, "that the houses will be left untouched. Their exercise should be over within an hour from now, at the most. I only hope that the day workers won't turn up any earlier than usual."

And, in fact, it's time for our amateur gardeners to be arriving on the road from the valley, crossing the Barbier farmlands to climb to the fields under cultivation, shepherded by Monsieur Germain. All eyes are on Father as he thinks out loud. He changes his mind.

"No," he announces, "after all, we can't take the risk of them all landing like that, right in the lap of the Boches. We have to head off Monsieur Germain!" He looks around the table at us; he consults his watch. "Someone will have to nip down on a bike, taking the shortcut at Lovers' Lane. Your mother and I must stay here, since I'll have to stick close to this officer, while your mother must watch over Dora, the laundry room, and all that."

Juliette raises her hand. "I'll go right away," she offers.

Father refuses, shaking his head. "Certainly not a girl your age."

"But why?" she protests.

"Because," he replies, "just because!" He turns to the little ones. "Young children like you can speed around anywhere without anyone noticing. Do I have a volunteer?"

I've remained silent a few seconds too long, because I haven't dared confess my long-standing and irrational fear of the serpentine darkness of Lovers' Lane. Pierre and Michel have already grabbed their capes from their chair backs: they're ready to go get their bikes. Father, keeping it short and simple, tells the twins exactly what to say to Monsieur Germain. The two younger girls, Violette and Jacqueline, cross the hall with Mother to go look out the French windows in the parlor and try to see how Antoine is "handling things." I trail after them, a pitiful figure in the throes of humiliation. The Secret Agent has been exposed as a fraud. I'd burst into tears, if it weren't for my wounded pride. But I feel more and more ashamed: Judex is a coward, Gavroche has cold feet, Corcoran is Captain Chickenheart!

20

Antoine was sitting on the ground, with his right hip up against the trunk of the poplar, directly over the spot where the diamond merchant's suede pouch was buried.

Several yards beyond him, a young German soldier lay stretched out in a freshly dug little trench, his nose glued to the butt plate of his Mauser. The soldier flashed what was meant to be a friendly smile at Antoine and spoke a few words in German.

I'm not going to answer him, thought Antoine. Anyway, I don't know what he's saying to me. And I'm certainly not going to smile back at him.

He pored over a big book of recipes from the regional cuisine of Le Bas-Quercy, the only book he'd been able to find in the kitchen before heading out to the third poplar.

He'd thought that it would look more natural to sit under a tree with something to read, to study. It hadn't occurred to him that it might seem somewhat strange for a young man to be reading on the lawn, still damp with dew, at eight in the morning. On his way to the poplars, he'd passed several soldiers busy at their tasks, who hadn't paid any attention to him. His heart had pounded some, but not too much, and he'd quickened his step. The important thing was to get to the tree before some

German started digging there. He'd reached the tree without any problem and carefully counted down the line of poplars to avoid making any mistake. Since Mother had had enough time to explain that the hole Father and Justin Case had dug was rather shallow, Antoine had first trampled the soil beneath his feet to press down the pouch, but he hadn't felt any lump sticking up beneath his shoes, so after a few seconds of this stamping he'd sat down, determined to do just as he'd been told and not budge from his seat. Behind him, the soldier had finished spading up the earth and lain down just as Antoine was getting settled. I must be an idiot, was Antoine's second coherent thought. "If I don't want to make that guy suspicious, I'd better smile back at him."

He closed the cookbook. He was so alert and on edge that he hadn't been able to read a single line in it, and the words "truffle," "foie gras," "cassoulet," "lardons," "conserves," and "morels" had swum before his eyes until he'd felt nauseated. Putting down the heavy book, he turned toward the soldier and smiled, saying, *"Nicht spragen sie Deutsch."*

The soldier seemed to find this utterly hilarious, laughing helplessly in his little trench. Antoine turned back around and contemplated the landscape before him.

He was on a kind of observation plateau, a landing set between the first big playground on the Villa's lawn and the cultivable hillsides sloping down to the Barbier farm and the river. It wasn't an accident that Father had chosen this place to plant the seven trees that had come from a stand of poplars running along the banks of the Aveyron River, over by the village of La Française. He'd been finicky enough to insist that the nurseryman deliver seven trees of different sizes, so that, when lined up in order of decreasing height, each poplar might correspond to one of us children. And we had all, at one time or another in our childhood, cut our names in their bark with a penknife, adding a few cabalistic signs as the years wore on.

The row of poplars was one of our favorite places, where we

ate our snacks, weather permitting: bread rubbed with garlic, figs, Meunier chocolate bars—if the grocer had any left. From this vantage point, on a clear day, you could see the whole valley, which was called the Vallée du Tempé, and the hills beyond. It was a captivating panorama, vast enough to allow the imagination to roam across the blue slopes, the green fields, the trees of various colors, the emerald hills, but its dimensions were on a human scale, so that you could slowly begin to feel that this countryside belonged to you, that it was a part of your innermost life. When he studied the horizon off to his right, Antoine knew that behind the brown shapes marking the edge of the town lay the neighborhood of Sapiac, as well as the municipal rugby stadium, referred to by both players and fans as the Washbowl. Antoine had discovered the stadium and rugby when he was twelve, and he was still infatuated with the game. The stadium was called the Washbowl because of its shape, since the playing field was surrounded by a steeply banked bicycle track of ugly black tar. This circle was ringed by the tiers of seats in the stands, so the whole thing really did look like a washbowl, especially since it wasn't a very elaborate affair. It had been thrown together rather haphazardly, and whenever it rained, the water poured across the tracks to soak into the turf, a narrow square of sparse stubble that was almost always a quagmire, where the visiting teams felt as though they'd fallen into a tight trap, and sometimes a bloody one.

Antoine had made his debut there as a scrum half, a position of command in which he had quickly excelled. When he'd been promoted to the local team's junior division, he'd been proud to wear the official jersey of black and dark green, which seemed curiously appropriate to the place, with its brutal, tough-guy atmosphere. Antoine had also liked the Washbowl because it was a good place to meet girls. They went there not out of any interest in rugby but to admire the star players, the town heroes. After the match, the girls would stroll back into town with you. Walking your bike down the Rue Delarep with one hand on the handlebars and the other on a girl's arm, your hair carefully combed, your plus fours falling "just so" over the high-top shoes, you were king of all you surveyed. You'd stop at the Café Delarep and take part in the word matches refereed by the Stork, discovering the honeyed taste of Balto cigarettes, or the harsher flavor of Gauloises in their distinctive green pack.

Antoine had gradually begun to neglect his studies and had had a violent dispute with Father about this; there'd been a few more arguments since then, but we didn't know the details. Their relationship had grown strained, which is only normal during this period of adolescent adjustment, and although we never noticed, the strain had saddened both of them. I have no idea what feelings of pride, what sense of reserve, of dignity, or what desire not to upset the little world of the Villa led my father and his oldest son to resolve, each on his own, to keep their conflict secret. But one had disappointed the other—"I've got other plans for him besides strutting around as a provincial show-off!" Father had snapped at Pauloto—and the young man, aware of this disappointment, was rebelling against such over-whelming authority.

Now, sitting with his back against the poplar, Antoine had one of those flashes of insight afforded by a dangerous action. What he'd just done, what he was experiencing at that moment by remaining obstinately seated to protect the diamond merchant's stash while a German soldier with a gun lounged nearby, had forced him to take another look at himself. He was enjoying what had happened. He was well aware of the faintly comic aspect of the whole business, which might lead to a great story in our Album. But he also exaggerated the seriousness of the affair, imagining among other things that his brothers, sisters, mother, and above all his father, must be watching him from the house and praising his perseverance. Father couldn't help but be impressed, couldn't help but admire him, and this idea brought a flush to his cheeks. When he thought about his behavior during that past year, he felt disgust creep over him.

Nothing was as exhilarating as this feeling of surpassing himself. It was much more intoxicating than rugby. And, anyway, the Washbowl had been abandoned by its stars, who had taken to the maquis, disappearing without warning to avoid conscription into compulsory labor units. As for the hours wasted at the Café Delarep—that was what really made Antoine feel guilty and foolish.

The Stork drives me crazy, he thought. I can't stand those jerks anymore.

That tall, thin oddball was still boasting about his expertise in American jazz and seemed to wave this theme around like a flag, which was his way of "resisting" the Occupation. While his audience listened all afternoon to his descriptions of meetings (that had probably never taken place) with the most famous practitioners of the New Orleans style, he "resisted," and continued distilling his lewd tittle-tattle, his sinister hypotheses regarding the townspeople's hidden sex lives, for the monotonous pleasure of the bistro habitués.

He was the sort of man who makes people uneasy, who knows how to fascinate the gullible, and even, for a while, those who should know better. An artist of insinuation, a prince of negativity, one of those beings who seek out the little flaw in others, or, when they can't find it, invent one and develop it freely, thus flattering that portion of baseness, that taste for the sordid, that cozy little vice that slumbers in each of us. He was all the more pernicious in that he did nothing else, for he lived in an emotional void, with only his mother for company, a crippled old woman whose private income supported her good-for-nothing son. His remarkable appearance, however, along with his unbeatable glibness and expert knowledge of an arcane area of music, had given him a hold on the town's population of layabouts and failures, all those my father referred to disdainfully as "loose ends." People said that the Stork had thousands of jazz records at home, all obsessively organized, and that he knew all the song titles, playing times, and performers by heart. To gain admittance into his inner circle, you had to win his confidence or turn his head with flattery, because he was quite vain, of course.

"You should drop by my place one evening," the Stork had said in his deep voice. "We smoke eucalyptus cigarettes and listen to really great records."

"Sure, come on along," urged Barroyer, a dead-eyed hanger-on in flashy clothes, whose signal privilege it was to man the record player. "If the Stork likes you, you can help me wind up the turntable."

Antoine had declined the invitation.

He was seized by the sudden revelation that real life was elsewhere. He wanted to go away, to flee the Villa, and probably his father's domination as well. One of the elementary-school teachers, a guy named Henri with glasses and brown hair, knew how to make the trip to Spain, and from there—after an obligatory stay in Franco's prisons—on into Portugal and across the sea to England. Some of the gym teachers at the lycée also knew about the escape route. Antoine decided he'd talk to his father about it that very day, as soon as the Germans had left the property. And since he wasn't sure he'd be able to persuade him on his own, he had his third coherent thought of the morning.

"First I'll tell Juliette, and we'll both go see him in his office. She'll help me convince him."

Then he made a slight change in his plan. "We won't talk to him in the office, but here, under the poplars."

The stand of poplars, a symbolic meeting ground! Antoine had just discovered how certain places can inspire ardent hearts and determined souls. Fired by his new resolution, he saw the misty blue landscape with different eyes, and swelled with an emotion he would have liked to share with someone, but his only company was that idiot Kraut, who was now dozing with his cheek against his weapon, while a stalk of alfalfa fluttered gently over his motionless boots, whose gleaming leather had been splattered by our good native soil.

21

The orange-and-yellow jar.

On the west side of the Villa, anchored in the gravel that surrounded our house, was an enormous terra-cotta jar, the rim and top half of which were glazed in a bright yellow, while the lower half and base were a vivid orange, of a tint seen nowhere else in the region and which it pleased us to imagine had been dreamed up—along with the jar itself—in some faraway land of the Orient.

It seems that the jar was already there when Father came to take his first look at the acres of uncleared land he'd just bought and to decide on a site for the Villa; I wouldn't claim that the site was selected with regard to the precise position of this jar of unknown origins and extraordinary dimensions, but it's quite possible to think so, because the jar was, very simply, immovable. The brambles, flowers, bindweed, and couch grass that had grown up all around its base brought a supplementary touch of green, beige, and violet to the orange-and-yellow ensemble, and bore witness to how long the jar had been lying on the slopes of Haut-Soleil. Who had put it there, and when? Countless autumn storms and gentle spring rains had filled it to the brim, and although the gardeners often dipped out the dirty water within, they never managed to empty it completely because it was so deep. Someone would have had to get all dressed up like a sewer worker, with overalls and rubber boots, and climb down inside the thing. And so there was always a thick sludge in its depths, a glaucous liquid with a pestilential odor you could smell by clambering up the imposing jar.

As I was the lightest, the others would give me a leg up, and I'd manage to kneel on the rounded rim. I'd try to see the bottom, as though I were kneeling over a well, and would receive a horrendous whiff of that fetid stink, which I actually liked, however, without really knowing why. I wondered if there might be, lurking below, some dragon from the dawn of time, or else, perhaps, a drowsing Spirit. When I'd call out, "Spirit of the Jar, are you there?" the only reply would be the muddled echo of my timid voice.

When the sun beat down hard on summer afternoons, we'd play at clamping our naked torsos against the giant pot to feel the heat stored up by the layer of colored glaze. We'd almost burn ourselves. The circumference of the thing was large enough so that, by spreading our arms and legs and holding hands, at least five of us could form a human chain, a band of high-relief sculpture around the jar. We'd stay motionless for a few seconds before the cruel heat would force us to break the chain and crumple onto the gravel, which now felt ever so much cooler. At the piano, Juliette could be heard through an open window, playing the measures of a Diabelli or Chopin étude. She'd repeat the same notes several times, and I loved it when she wouldn't finish a piece but keep tirelessly repeating the difficult passage, because as she worked to correct her mistake, I was able to savor the ineffable pleasure of time standing still.

At those moments, I'd look at the orange-and-yellow jar that had just spread its warmth through my body and I'd tell myself that as long as the Spirit of the Jar reigned over us, as long as the jar remained in the same place, as long as it stayed rooted in the center of our childhood, then nothing really bad could ever happen to us.

22

Mother was sorting through the jars of potted meat from the butchered pig when two men in civilian clothes walked up to the Villa. We could see their black Citroën 11 CV at the end of the path, parked near the entrance gate, with the chauffeur's silhouette visible behind the steering wheel.

They wore soft felt hats and didn't seem to be in any hurry.

Spring had only just arrived. We'd forgotten the "army maneuvers"; the trenches the German soldiers had dug in the garden had been filled in a long time ago. Father had taken that episode as a serious alert, and drawn the appropriate conclusions. From then on, we had perhaps the same number of "visitors," "gardeners," and "governesses," but they no longer stayed with us any length of time. The Villa was still a refuge, but had become a way station rather than a permanent shelter. With Paul's help, Father made sure that every "visitor" who came to him was shuttled out to the farms as of the very first night. He hadn't been able to resign himself to seeing Dora leave, however, or Monsieur Germain, or his assistant Franck, an Austrian engineer, who could make vegetables thrive where they had no business growing, and there was a new addition to the Villa, a thirteen-year-old Jewish girl named Jannette. Her parents had left town one night, abandoning her with a neighbor, who had, quite naturally, handed her over to my parents, with the connivance of her teachers at the lycée. A placid, quiet girl with a pretty smile and a tendency toward bulimia, Jannette shared the bedroom of my two youngest sisters and rode down to the lycée with us on a borrowed bike. We'd been told to say she was a cousin from Le Dordogne.

Our family, once nine members strong, was now up to thirteen.

We had to feed all these people. The food shortages made things difficult, as the refugees couldn't risk going into town with their forged papers to apply for ration cards. We could count on produce from the farms, however.

There were three of them. Way off in a valley of Le Bas-Quercy was Le Jougla, the most distant farm, which belonged to the Dark Man. In the opposite direction was Saint-Martial, on the plain of the Aveyron, while La Carrière was on the hills nearest the town. Paul had also advised Father in the purchase of these last two farms, small operations involving livestock, corn, and a modest selection of crops. They were *métairies*, cultivated by tenants for a share of the proceeds, and Father lost money on them, but they allowed him to feed his little community as well as shelter all his "visitors." Father was careful to send a priest, who was willing to help in the deception, to make regular rounds to his two farms, so that people would see the priest on his bicycle and think he'd come to confess all these fugitives masquerading as Monsieur Bertrand, Madame Durand, Monsieur Fournier, or the Blanchard family, "Parisians" who'd come to breathe the good clean country air, and who naturally needed a priest occasionally to see to their spiritual health.

Going to Le Jougla was one of my greatest joys. The Dark Man would drive me there in his Phaeton, the black Juvaquatre that had led us to give him his second nickname, Pauloto. When we'd set out together for his farm, his mood wouldn't be "dark" at all, he'd be Pauloto again, a cheerful companion who whistled and sang the whole way there, constantly needling me with ironic comments.

"Once more the little city boy is off to see his fiancées," he'd say—a favorite opening remark.

There were several girls my age at Le Jougla. They lived in a hamlet comprising a little chapel, an old cemetery, four cottages, a stream chockful of reeds and trout crossed by an ancient stone bridge, and a tiny school attended by the children of all the country people in that small valley. The particular charm of the vale lay in the fact that it formed a kind of natural frontier, the border between the green plains of Le Tarn and Les Causses, with its white rocks, gravelly marl, its hares and partridges hunted by mongrel dogs, champion gobblers of bread and plums. Two civilizations or, rather, two cultures met there: one of peach and pear trees, of rich, clayey earth, so easy to work, and one of chestnut trees, goats, grapevines, Chasselas, fields of rye, and dry stone walls. You had to know the roads and paths very well to find this small valley; it was an out-of-the-way place, one of those countless little "backs of beyond" that nestled throughout the French countryside. The Germans never went near it. And I hope and imagine that even today it's still unspoiled, just as green and white, as peaceful and inaccessible, as pleasant and occasionally arid as it ever was, perfumed by its willows, lindens, sunflowers, and stable litter.

"You like those girls, hmm? You don't know which way to turn anymore," continued Pauloto.

The "little fiancées" at Le Jougla were named Marie, Lucette, and Sylvie. With them, I was at last bold enough to venture touching, kissing, groping about under their aprons, laughing crazily with them while we wrestled on the haystacks or the fragrant floor of the grain silo. I'd emerge from these encounters all flushed and rumpled, embarrassed but not ashamed, and Pauloto's family would laugh, taking me for what I was not—the "rascal" little Murielle had called me. But Murielle frightened me with her perversity, while my "fiancées" excited me with their frankness.

"Which one did you go off hiding with in the barn? And what did the two of you get up to in there?"

I didn't answer. The car sped across the hills, through several villages, past fields and vines, leaving the city far behind.

As he drew nearer to Le Jougla, the farm he had inherited from his father, Pauloto grew younger, first loosening his somber tie, then taking off his heavy black jacket, revealing the broad, cream-colored suspenders stretched taut over his well-muscled chest, and finally winding up in shirtsleeves by the time we were only a few kilometers away from his beloved valley. Through the car's wide-open front windows came the cawing of crows, the flapping of buzzards' wings, the scent of ferns and gorse, and Pauloto would urge me to join him in singing, at the top of our lungs,

> *Forward, march!*
> *The regiment*
> *Of mandolins.*

Then he'd start asking me more pointed questions, which amused me as much as it did him, since I knew, without having to ask, that he would never have breathed a word to my parents about my least little escapade. He probably felt that this part of my education at Le Jougla was rightfully his department, and that it would help make up for the stern moral standards my father tried to instill in us. Pauloto called him "the Puritan," and Father replied in kind, cheerily insulting him as "the Icon-oclast." Their deep complicity thrived on such contrasts, and Pauloto would exaggerate his own convictions on purpose for the simple pleasure of baiting his friend.

"You are some scamp, my boy," Pauloto would tell me. "Quite a terror! That's what you are, a regular little terror."

Then he'd burst out laughing. "Your father was also quite a scamp. Once upon a time."

Then I'd speak up: my whole childhood had been and would continue to be dominated, even obsessed, by our curiosity about these two men who gave such a strong impression of sharing great secrets. Of course, one of these secrets had been revealed to us: their organization of a network to help persecuted Jews. I was more fascinated than my brothers and sisters by the larger-than-life aura of these two friends, so I cherished the idea that the bond between my father and the Dark Man went back a long, long way, and that they knew a lot more than they were telling.

"Why do you say that Papa was a scamp?" I asked. "What did he used to do, 'once upon a time'?"

Pauloto would take off again. "None of your beeswax. You'd be better off feeling sorry about that business you were up to in the cornfield the other day with Hare-Brain!"

Among the band of children at Le Jougla was a real nut, a farm foreman's son, an awkward, flat-nosed, wild-eyed clown with carroty hair and bowlegs, who introduced himself to everyone he met with these words: "They call me Hare-Brain, and that's exactly what I am!"

He spent all his time trying to deserve the name he'd been called one day when he'd done something even more idiotic than the usual child's antics. For us, who so loved nicknames and filled the pages of our Album with them, Hare-Brain was a gift from heaven. And since I was the one who visited Le Jougla most often, I had the honor of recounting his exploits to my brothers and sisters.

I wrote: "Hare-Brain squatted on the ground, ate some goose shit, and said it tasted like licorice."

Or: "Hare-Brain jumped into the pond fully clothed, waving a fork, claiming he was going to spear a pike."

Or again: "Hare-Brain tried to climb the church steeple to play his trumpet, but he didn't make it and tore a hole in his pants."

But I certainly didn't write down what Pauloto was chiding me for: Hare-Brain and I had made some corn-silk cigarettes and had smoked them until we got violent headaches, puking and almost setting the cornfield on fire. That evening, still sick, I'd stayed in bed in Pauloto's house with a boiling-hot water bottle at my feet, my only medicine a glass of hot, sweetened wine. It was delicious, as wonderful as the previous September's adventure of crushing a vat full of Chasselas grapes with my bare feet during the harvest, before accompanying the pickers off to the wine press. The sloshing of the juice, the grape skins, the fruit bursting under the soles of our feet, the purple, red, and yellow spurts that stained our ankles—all this had left me with clear memories of breathless delight, and I prayed that the same orgy would take place again the following autumn.

I'd also acquired quite a taste for chicken noodle soup, for when the bowl was about three-quarters empty, a splash of red wine was added for a finishing touch. Then you put down your spoon and picked up the bowl to slurp in the mixture of bouillon and wine. That was called "*faire chabrot*," and when I got back to the Villa, I boasted to my siblings of having participated in this ritual, which I described in detail, like a traveler returned from a faraway land to tell of exotic feasts.

And I'd kept quiet about what Hare-Brain and I got up to with the pigs from the little farm's pigsty. Straddling them bare-back, one on the sow, the other on a large piglet, we whipped them with elder switches and made them gallop down an embankment along the road. Gripping the big animal's thick pink hide with my naked thighs, I rode the silly, submissive beast as it squealed and snorted. That time I'd gotten a real scolding from Pauloto, who was usually so indulgent toward my attempts to keep up with Hare-Brain's foolishness, his "harebrained ideas."

"Don't you ever do that again!" he'd told me, raising his voice.

He could make his words resonate and roll his *r*'s more intimidatingly than any of my teachers at the lycée. He had a beautiful deep voice, with a timbre that gave a special emphasis and meaning to what he said, as when a dramatic artist transforms a banal text into an epic tirade.

"We don't trifle with pigs around here," he'd added. "Especially not in wartime."

To impress this concrete truth upon me, this dominant ideology of an entire period and region, Pauloto had once again adopted the tone and manner of the Dark Man. And he was right, of course: the pig, an animal of infinite uses, was the mainstay of my family's provisions. And the reason Pauloto had driven me to the farm and back in his Juvaquatre was to deliver a whole pig to us in Haut-Soleil, a gift from the community at Le Jougla to the thirteen occupants and occasional "visitors" in the Villa.

The dead and already decapitated pig, wrapped in a tarp and tied up with a cord, was a heavy weight in the car trunk, where we could hear it jouncing and crashing about whenever we went around a curve. Pauloto had me sit beside him on the front seat. Did I provide a useful alibi for going through the city?

"If they stop us," he'd told me, "you start crying and calling for your mother."

But we didn't run into any military roadblocks.

"It smells," I told Pauloto.

"What's that?"

"The pig. It smells."

"No, no," he said, laughing. "That's your city-boy imagination at work. Think about your fiancées, instead. Which one did you kiss today?"

I'd kissed Lucette. She'd tasted sour.

"Pauloto," I asked after a moment, "why do you always make fun of me?"

He rumpled my hair with his right hand. "Just because. It's always fun to tease those you love."

We'd reached the Villa. With the pig safe in the trunk, Pauloto's car turned onto the gravel drive, and I felt all puffed up with importance.

23

Then we "fixed the pig."

The huge laundry room in the cellar had been cleared of everything except what was needed for the job at hand. There was a large deal table to which had been added two extensions supported by sawhorses of the same wood, reinforced with steel braces. In the four corners of the room, with its low ceiling and gray cement floor, freshly hosed down, galvanized metal basins had been placed in readiness, some of them empty, others filled with boiling water, still others with pickling brine. Things were set out neatly on the table: dozens of little pots of sulfurized paper, knives and pigstickers (long, short, broad-bladed or pointed), cheesecloth, kilos of coarse salt, a meat grinder that had been clamped to the table, several piles of folded dish towels, aprons of white or red-and-blue-checked twill, little stoneware jars, and old sheets.

The participants in the ceremony were gathered around a big woman named Maria, who had come to the Villa to help on this occasion. She was the wife of the *métayer* at La Carrière, one of our farms, and hailed originally from Castelsarrasin.

A few chairs and stools had been lined up along the walls of the laundry room, while in the fireplace at the far end a log fire burned under a heavy caldron of dark copper pitted by age. I watched and sniffed up the smells, entranced by the activity swirling around this dead animal, on whose silky, hairy rump I'd ridden only a few days before. I was again enjoying that same form of olfactory intoxication that had so affected me during the vintage, for in the air there was the smell of meat, fresh blood and fat, lard, but also herbs and spices, laurel and onions, celery, the smarting odor of pepper, and the tang of the brandy used to wash the bowels and organ meats.

The operation required two whole days, because each step in the preparation of the carcass took time. The viscera were removed and the body divided into sections, the different cuts of meat were trimmed, sausages were prepared—some fresh, some preserved—and pork pâtés were laid down in pots. We children weren't there during the entire lengthy process, certain aspects of which repelled me, such as the moment when the freshly severed stomach, bowels, liver, heart, and kidneys poured out in bloody hunks upon the table. At other times I was enthralled, as when the pig was shaved before its evisceration, or when it was plunged into boiling water, or cut lengthwise by the person called "the slaughterer."

He was Maria's son, and the two of them orchestrated the entire operation. The slaughterer was quite competent, proficient at killing animals with a precise knife thrust and cutting them into pieces rapidly and skillfully with a small handsaw. He was built like his mother. They had strong hands, sturdy arms, big, solid heads, and a blond glint in their hair that betrayed their distant origins, because they were said to have come from Le Piémont. The father had stayed home on the farm, for it seemed he didn't like butchering animals and preferred leaving this chore to his son—which no one found surprising—and his wife, which did cause tongues to wag a bit. Maria didn't talk very much, her son even less. We drank in every one of their words and gave their slightest order melodramatic dimensions.

"The basin. The salt. Time to prepare the court bouillon."

Spoken in the local accent by the impassible slaughterer (bending over his worktable, weapon in hand, dressed in blood-spattered blue overalls), these banal instructions echoed through the steamy laundry room, smoky from the lard crackling in the caldrons, like magical incantations we'd later repeat among ourselves while at play and during our games of mimicry.

Mother bustled around Maria and her son, helped by Juliette, Dora, and the women from the Barbier farm; Father kept out of the way, making an occasional visit, frowning and wrinkling his nose, which earned him jeers from the Dark Man.

"You find this disgusting? You're denying your origins! You're a peasant's son, don't you forget it!"

Father crossed the room to greet Dr. Sucre, who received a few jars of potted meat. Still dressed in white, with his bicycle clips as protuberant as ever at his trouser cuffs, Dr. Sucre had been expertly courted: he was given fruits, vegetables, and a few pieces of pork to ensure his silence. Father dreaded people's curiosity, their inclination to gossip or inform on one another, for Monsieur Germain, Dora, Jannette, Franck, and the constant stream of visitors had prompted questions from the neighbors, which had meant more pretense, more cajolery, more lies. Despite his natural aloofness, Father was thus obliged to deal with "Punchinellos and Harlequins," buffoons and featherbrains.

"Why do you call them Punchinellos?" I'd asked him.

To me, the word meant an ugly, hunchbacked, ridiculous person, and I didn't think little Murielle's parents or our other neighbors in Haut-Soleil were so laughable. Of course, I didn't grant them any of the love, respect, and admiration I felt for the white-haired man with the steady gaze who ruled our lives. His judgment was not open to question, but I wanted to understand how this book lover used every word. For quite some time now, he'd been taking infinite care to choose *le mot juste*, and infinite pleasure in teaching us the most unusual words, whenever possible.

"Words have weight," he liked to tell us. "Some weigh ten grams; others, a hundred kilos. You must know how to size them up. Each of you ought to carry inside yourself a tiny balance to weigh words before using them."

And he'd make one of his favorite gestures, bringing his hands up to his chest and holding them flat, as though they were the two pans of that invisible balance that we should carry in our minds.

"Why Punchinellos?" I persisted.

He'd led us to expect answers to our questions, since he was always encouraging us to ask them in the first place.

"That little boy is beginning to stand up to me," I'd heard him remark to Paul.

"I'm not surprised," his friend had replied. "Guess where he got it from!"

So Father answered me. "A 'Punchinello' isn't just someone ugly or ridiculous. It can also mean a person who is irresponsible, unthinking. Later you'll understand that most people you meet are *thoughtless* in their speech and actions. I didn't mean to imply that we're surrounded by idiots, only that none of us, myself included, thinks things over well enough, often enough, quickly enough."

"But, Papa," I said, "we can't always consider things so carefully."

"No," he replied, "but let me point out that that's exactly what you just did."

Our favorite part of fixing the pig was the greaves, which we also called cracklings. They were the residue in the bottom of the caldron where everything had been simmered, where the meat had rendered its fat, where hour after hour, day after day, the pig's skin, flesh, bones, and entrails had marinated in a mixture of herbs and spices, of pepper and even—added by a guest exhilarated at the relaxed, festive atmosphere of the divine beast's culinary toilette—a few drops of brandy. And after the women had finished with the cooking, there was an encrusted residue of meat and fat on the sides and bottom of the empty caldron.

You'd scrape off the cracklings and pack them into a little ramekin. You'd toast bread over the hot ashes of the same fire that had heated the caldron, spread the cracklings over this toast like butter, and bite into it with a voracity that would quickly change to prudence, because although the taste was succulent, it was also greasy, and very hot, so your snack would lie heavy in your stomach if you overindulged.

The effect, in that case, was awful. Your eyes would roll up, your head would swim, your whole body would suffer throes of disgust with the pig, its leavings, its smells. You'd rue the greediness that had landed you in this predicament, and you'd hang your head as the adults chorused laughingly, "The cracklings got you, the cracklings got you!"

This moment of ecstasy so brutally followed by an equally impressive repentance gave the signal for the big cleanup. The children no longer had any reason to linger in the dirty, smoky laundry room, so we'd use the outside staircase to return to the kitchen, where my mother, with Dora's help, had immediately begun putting away some of the freshly filled jars of preserved meat. It was during this last phase of the pig proceedings that we saw two men in civilian clothes and soft felt hats walking up to the house.

Mother instinctively recognized the bearing of men who know they have the power to do harm.

"It's the police," she told Dora. "Run!" Turning to us, she added, "Go warn your father."

Then she calmly covered the illicit jars with a white cloth and went outside to confront the two men.

24

She advanced toward them, still wearing her apron, and a yellow-and-white scarf on her head. Juliette and I were on either side of her. She took each of us by the hand, so that we three were like a frail human wall barring access to the Villa.

My other brothers and sisters had run down to the laundry room, where I supposed Father was organizing the escape of Monsieur Germain, Dora, and the others to the Barbier farm, through the hills and orchards in back of the Villa.

The first man had thin lips, a black mole on his cheek, and a big nose, the tip of which bent slightly to the right, giving him a comical look. He was smiling. The second man reminded me of someone I'd already seen, in Father's office when I was convalescing and silently contemplating the "Punchinellos" who came to consult him. He was short and chubby, and from beneath his velour hat poked out black locks of thick but lank hair, whose ends seemed to stick to his temples like soggy duck feathers. It was his hair that helped me to identify the "stuffed shirt," Monsieur Floqueboque. He wasn't smiling.

I've said that the two men were in civvies, but everything about their demeanor and their choice of identical clothing indicated that they wished to seem like members of an organization, a kind of army. The same long, belted raincoat of a putty-colored waterproof material; the same brown woolen trousers creasing over the same lace-up shoes, black leather wing tips with real soles, not ones made of wood like almost all the rest of us had; and always the same hat, which is what I think set the alarm off in my mother's head. Because these hats were hardly ever seen around that part of the country. When my father decided to wear a felt hat, he picked something less big and dark, something more familiar, whereas the felt from which these two men's hats were made had something foreign about it, as though the hats had been bought elsewhere, in a different city, so that all such men might recognize each other more easily. I who thought that terra-cotta jars (as well as the busts of great men) could talk, I heard this hostile hat say to us: "I know that I'm ugly, but I don't give a damn, because I'm not trying to be nice."

The two men come up to us and stop. Big Twisted Nose bows to Mother and says, slowly, with a very strong accent, "You have in your house a woman by the name of Dora Kümmer, a foreigner and a Jewess. She is summoned to appear at the city hall for a verification of identity. She should bring with her a small overnight bag."

"We have no one here by that name," replies Mother.

"Madame, we know what we're talking about," announces Floqueboque.

He immediately trots out that verbal tic of his I'd noted in the Album for the pleasure of my readers. "And I might add, we are not here by accident."

Then he falls silent.

"Gentlemen, who are you?" inquires Mother.

"We're the police," replies Big Twisted Nose.

I notice that Floqueboque doesn't "add" anything. I also notice that although he's using that self-consciously affected tone I'd already pegged for fake, Big Twisted Nose speaks with the local accent, which makes him seem less dangerous to me. Floqueboque gestures vaguely toward the Villa, over my mother's shoulder.

"Is your husband at home, madame?"

"He's coming," she replies.

It looks as though the two men don't dare force the fragile barrier before them.

I can feel my mother's warm hand in mine, gripping my fingers, to reinforce our defiant posture and her determination to bar their way. Big Twisted Nose seems ill at ease. Hesitatingly, as though it's something he must do, although unwillingly, he says, "Madame, just fetch that woman and we won't bother you anymore."

"You're not bothering me at all," answers Mother, in a voice that might seem calm to the two men, but in which I hear a note of frailty, of timidity. "However, we have no one here except the members of our family."

In his unctuous and self-satisfied tone, Floqueboque insists, "And I might add that we're here only to deliver the summons. And I might add: a small overnight bag, that's all."

Behind us, I hear my father's step on the gravel. Relief floods through me. Not that I don't have confidence in my mother, whose impassiveness has astonished me, whom I admire for standing right in the middle of the path, flanked by a girl and a little boy, to defy two men in putty-colored raincoats who could easily barge past us to the Villa. It's just that I'm sure things will take a different turn now that Father is arriving on the scene. A line of poetry by Victor Hugo, often recited by my mother, springs to mind, for it has made a deep impression on me and will be close to my heart throughout my childhood: "My father, this hero with so gentle a smile."

Without turning around to watch him join us, I know that at this very moment he's smiling, which will reassure us all the more in that he so rarely smiles, preferring to wear, for his little domestic circle, the severe expression that has earned him over the years all sorts of patronymic abbreviations from us, his impertinent audience: "Pessimo," "Mysterioso," and even "Misanthropo."

Catching sight of him, Floqueboque takes a step forward. Big Twisted Nose tips his ugly hat, and I have the impression he's recognized him. Moreover, Father addresses this man first, ignoring Floqueboque.

"I believe we've already met. You're Pallombière, isn't that right?"

"That's correct, monsieur," replies the man.

I notice that he said "monsieur," while Father called him simply "Pallombière," and I can sense some kind of difference between them that will grow more pronounced as they speak.

"At the Hôpital Saint-Hippolyte, that's where," continues Father. "We were there together when the reserves were called up a few years back. I was a captain in the reserves, your commanding officer, I believe, and now, if I understand correctly, you're in the police?"

Big Twisted Nose shifts from one foot to another. "No, I'm not really in the police, I'm working for City Hall, in the registry office."

"What were you, at the time? A corporal?" asks Father.

"Uh, yes, Cap—uh, I mean, monsieur."

Mother intervenes, trying to sound naïve. "But you just told me you were from the police."

"Well, yes, it's almost the same thing," says Pallombière.

Father, as though judging Pallombière temporarily neutralized, now turns to Floqueboque. "It's not at all the same thing, and you, Monsieur Floqueboque, with your exquisite sense of administrative propriety, will hardly be the one to contradict me on this. How are you? What have you been doing since last we met? You're a municipal employee now? What authority brings you here, and how can I help you?"

The little boy is unable to appreciate how these few sentences have been modulated by subtle variations of tone, and how a dose of flattery has counterbalanced a pinch of irony, with an overall sprinkling of courtesy and firmness, while hovering constantly in the background is my father's air of superiority, although he doesn't overdo it, since he knows how easily mediocre people can take offense at this, and how important it is in this instance to tread lightly around the adversary precisely because

137

of his inferiority, so as not to risk irritating him, but rather to bolster his self-satisfaction, his sense of the importance of his position.

Neither am I able to discern, on Floqueboque's homely face, the equally numerous and contradictory signs of vexation and vanity, his desire to force the issue coupled with his caution and restraint before this man, whose prestige in the town he is well aware of, and his realization, if only thanks to the respectful attitude of Pallombière, his local stooge, that the latter has already backed off, leaving to him the responsibility of what will be the failure of their mission. Floqueboque is a "stuffed shirt," but he's both spiteful and resourceful. And if my father were at leisure to bend down and explain to me what's going on, he'd give me another of his lessons in human natural history, somewhat along these lines:

"The stuffed shirt belongs, of course, to a vain, pedantic, and ridiculous species . . . The stuffed shirt is incapable of seeing himself clearly when he displays to others the attitudes that characterize him, or of listening to himself when his opinions or the tone in which he voices them betray the limits of his intelligence, but he is still a creature to be reckoned with, since his weakness blinds him enough to allow him to make his way shamelessly through life, brushing aside those who behave more discreetly, and thus less effectively. And, after all, his pedantry is grounded in some knowledge, a motley assortment of information and references that permits him, there again, to survive or even thrive amid less noisy and peremptory but therefore less enterprising animals than himself. Never underestimate a stuffed shirt. He is a pedant, not a dimwit. It would never occur to him to get down in the dirt to taste goose droppings, like Hare-Brain at Le Jougla. On the other hand, even after mature thought, he can't help confusing goose shit with licorice, just like that imbecile playmate of yours, in the same way he takes every stranger for a fool, every powerful person for a guiding light, and every humble soul for a victim."

I don't understand all this yet, but I have an inkling of what's going on here, thanks to that close attention to the weight of words Father so hopes will help direct us in our lives. As he had told us to do, I watch Floqueboque's eyes, and am almost pleased to find them so shifty: here's at least one person I can easily identify as a traitor.

"May I inform you, monsieur," announces Floqueboque, "that I have placed my administrative experience at the service of what I believe to be the right cause, and I might add that it is the cause backed by the real representatives of the nation. The New Men. And I might add that in so doing I believe I am rendering a tangible service to our country."

"That is certainly true," replies Father, "but may I ask you to show me a warrant, a document that might justify your visit here—and its purpose?"

Floqueboque suddenly loses patience. "We have already explained all that to your wife. A small overnight bag will be sufficient. Simply produce this Dora Kümmer, the Jewess who is living secretly with you. If her papers are in order, she may return to you tomorrow morning."

"I asked you to show me your warrant."

Floqueboque takes a paper from his raincoat pocket, unfolds it, and waves it in my father's face. "But here it is, what else did you expect! What we're doing is perfectly legal, and, I might add, entirely in keeping with our judicious collaboration with the Third Reich."

"I don't doubt it," replies Father, after slowly perusing the document. "Since we are not hiding anyone here, I'm perfectly willing to see you in my office to discuss this with you, but nowhere on this summons do I see it written that I must allow you access to all of my home and property."

Turning once more to Big Twisted Nose, who'd been lost in silence and boredom, he asks, "And what do you think about all this, Pallombière?"

Big Twisted Nose laughs shortly, in rueful admiration, and I hear him say what had occurred to me a few minutes before. "I think, monsieur, that if someone was hiding in your house, while we've all been standing around out here talking, she's had plenty of time to beat it. That's what I think."

He automatically punctuates his last words with a "fuck" worthy of my little classmates' best efforts, as though wanting to make sure he appears in his true light, to underline the difference between himself, the local guy caught up in an undertaking over which he has no control, and the transplanted "Parisian" with the overblown verbiage and suspect ambitions.

"Well, you're right about that," admits Floqueboque with a short sigh of irritation. "Goodbye, monsieur; we will meet again."

Father motions to us to go up to the Villa.

"Although you came here without an appointment," he says to the two men, "I shall escort you to the front gate."

Father explained to us later that he hadn't accompanied them simply to keep up an appearance of politeness, but in order to check on the surrounding area, on the paths and intersections of Haut-Soleil visible from that vantage point. What he saw was hardly reassuring: there were two other black Citroëns just like Floqueboque and Pallombière's in the neighborhood. Men in civilian dress had entered several yards and were patrolling along the edges of the bramble thickets.

About fifty meters from our Villa, by the intersection with Lovers' Lane, Father saw an abandoned bicycle with twisted handlebars, its front wheel still spinning in the air. It was the bicycle of someone who must have been intercepted and knocked down, someone who'd tried to evade a roadblock. It was easily recognizable, from the wicker basket attached to the rear baggage rack, as the bicycle of Monsieur Germain.

We couldn't figure out how Monsieur Germain had come to be there. Logically, he should have gone across the slopes down to the lower road along the Tescou, escaping toward La Carrière, where he knew he would be hidden by our tenant farmers. How had he gotten completely turned around, why had he come uphill, up Lovers' Lane to Haut-Soleil, where he'd been trapped in a neighborhood swarming with plainclothes policemen? We decided that there must have been other roadblocks near the river that had forced Monsieur Germain to take the uphill path. Father made a remark that explained nothing, but said everything: "It was the only thing he could do."

But Dora, Jannette, and Franck had had no difficulty walking to the Barbier farm, the one closest to our property, accompanied by all the people who had helped us "fix the pig." So why hadn't Monsieur Germain stayed with this group? Something must have happened that we didn't know about.

Father just shook his head. "It was probably the only thing he could do."

Father usually wore espadrilles, trousers of white or light gray flannel, and a casual cotton jacket over worsted shirts with soft collars, thus presenting the composite picture of a gentleman farmer, a tennis player relaxing after practice, or one of those debonair British tourists he'd seen in the Basque country before the war, whose studied negligence he'd admired and imitated. This austere man, with just a hint of starchiness in his manner, took something of a coquettish pleasure in no longer wearing clothes that reminded him unpleasantly of his former business career in Paris. It was another way of saying: I am a free man, hidden away in my sacred Villa, willing to listen to everyone's woes and to dispense advice to all comers, but I will dress as I please, like a man who has withdrawn from the world and shaken off the tyranny of appearances.

One day he even pushed that nonconformity to the point of arriving in old shoes and a white cloth cap with a green sun visor à la Suzanne Lenglen to pick up his oldest daughters after their First Communion, to the absolute astonishment of the bourgeois congregation and the suppressed indignation of my mother, who took their children's religious education more seriously than he did.

His friend Paul had congratulated him. "You're as much of a heathen as I am!"

But the moment it became clear that Monsieur Germain had disappeared, Father changed into more formal attire. He dressed quickly: starched shirt, tie, black shoes, and a pin-striped, single-breasted jacket.

He went down to the city hall, where the Dark Man was waiting for him, along with a few officials who were on their side. Together they tried to obtain Monsieur Germain's release. They had to go to the Caserne Doumercq, where they were given the runaround for a while before learning that the little group of prisoners had been taken by truck to the station. There they were informed that a train with locked and sealed doors, carrying the men and women rounded up during the day, had set off for a camp near Font-Romeu, in the Pyrénées.

Later we discovered that this human shipment had been sent by other trains to two other camps, but outside of France this time, camps with names unfamiliar to us.

"Never forget, children," Father told us heatedly, "never forget that it was the French police, that it was French officials who put Monsieur Germain on the first train."

Then he shut himself up in his office.

As for us, clustered around our mother, whose eyes glistened with tears, we thought sorrowfully of Monsieur Germain, and then we turned our thoughts to our own Antoine. He'd joined the Resistance off in the mountains of Vazerac, along with Henri, the elementary-school teacher, just as he'd vowed to do one day, under the poplar tree. Father had given him his permission without a second's hesitation, to the surprise of Juliette and all of us younger ones.

25

At La Carrière one day, where the twins and I had gone with a message for a certain Monsieur Durand, a young man I'd never seen before came out of a barn to meet me.

"My name's Diego," he announced.

He was tall and thin, with hazel eyes and a swarthy complexion; a lock of dark hair fell over his forehead. His lips were delicately curved, like two flower petals, but he had the face of a condottiere—bold and insolent, handsome, romantic, marked by audacity, or even madness. It was a kind of apparition: emerging from the shadows to strike a pose in the center of the peaceful barnyard, Diego carried a double-barreled shotgun slung across his shoulder and sported two full cartridge belts crossed over his chest. Even though our farm and the area around it were never visited by German soldiers, I interpreted this disdainful refusal to keep out of sight as a sign that he belonged to the Resistance, and saw in his proud flamboyance the mark of an unusual character.

He had the bearing of a professional horseman. This was the only flaw in that slender body, that sleek silhouette: legs so bowed that this graceful creature seemed somewhat clumsy when he walked. His twisted ankles, muscular thighs, and the peculiar rolling gait that immediately betrays a horseman seemed to indicate that this Diego, despite his youth (he couldn't have been more than eighteen), had spent his entire life in the saddle. To dispel any doubt, he wore tall riding boots of a faded red mahogany, an unusual color out of harmony with the landscape, as were the cream-colored riding breeches of closely woven whipcord, stained with mud around the knees. I hadn't seen a single maquisard since the morning we watched Antoine set out on his bicycle with Henri. They'd left early, their knapsacks laden with provisions and warm clothes. I'd tried to imagine what a person would look like, once he'd reached the forests and mountains, the caves, the barns and shelters that were home to these men whose dangerous existence I so envied. Well, I had a winner in Diego: he was the best-looking maquisard I'd ever get to see, even if he didn't call himself by that name.

"I'm a partisan," he told me. "I belong to the Perelski demolition team, in the Pamiers commando unit."

I didn't understand why he was telling me such confidential information, but I was flattered beyond measure that he'd crouched down in front of me to speak of such extraordinary things: demolition, commando unit, partisan!

I felt bold enough to question him. "What do you do?"

"I work by night."

"D'you know my brother Antoine?"

"I don't see anyone," he replied. "Nobody but the guys I work with at night."

"And what do you do at night?"

He leaned closer, staring at me with a green glint of defiance in his eyes, and smiled, as though he wanted to cast an even stronger spell over me. Slowly, in a low voice, he said, "We blow up things. We're specialists."

I was bowled over, almost thrilled to death.

Some machinery and parts stored at the Ville-Bourbon railroad station had been destroyed, and much of the town had heard the explosions that had helped slow down the transport of German war matériel. Another night, the electric power station at Verlaguet had been attacked, and sabotage had later taken out the high tension lines at the Chaume bridge, once again in the middle of the night. Such actions came with increasing frequency as 1944 wore on. From overheard snatches of conversation between Father and the Dark Man, we knew that people called "the Allies" had landed in North Africa, that decisive events were occurring on the Eastern Front, and one evening we had watched as Father pointed out on a giant atlas the progress of one side (the good guys) and the retreat of the other (the bad guys).

There had even been some excitement in the town. The pharmacy of a collabo on Rue Marcy had been blown up; the windows of a shoe store on the Rue Fraîche had been shattered. Reprisals, denunciations, arrests, and deportations had followed apace. We'd talked about these upheavals that had changed the face of our town, banished its peace and quiet, and now here I was, face to face with someone who had perhaps helped perform these exploits! I couldn't get over the shock, and still couldn't figure out why he'd decided to tell me all this in the middle of the barnyard.

"Diego!"

Behind us, a man somewhat older than my unexpected hero—a small man with a stern, impassive face, wearing a tight bomber jacket—signaled to him to return.

"We're leaving!" he shouted.

Before standing up to go, Diego put his hands on my shoulders, pressing lightly against the back of my neck.

"Tell your father you saw me," he told me quickly. "Tell him: Diego is here."

Then he straightened up, and I watched this handsome lad walk back to the man who seemed to be his leader. They disappeared around the corner of the barn, heading toward the path that led through sandy wasteland and undergrowth to an old stone quarry.

I was admiring the retreating figure of my romantic "partisan" when Pierre and Michel ran up to me. "What did he say to you? What did he say?"

"Nothing," I told them.

Back at the Villa, I gave my father a detailed account of my meeting with the young man in the mahogany-red boots. And I repeated for him the words "Diego is here."

He thanked me, kissed me on the forehead, and made me swear not to tell anyone else anything that the young man had said to me.

That evening, when the Dark Man arrived at his usual time, Father took him aside. They did not settle down in the two blue chairs in the parlor, where they always sat when listening to the wireless, twisting the knobs, tuning in the crackling, fuzzy broadcast of news that sometimes raised their spirits, sometimes left them downcast, while we occasionally tried to follow their arguments or understand their comments.

Father ushered the Dark Man into his office, where they remained closeted all evening. I told myself that I'd been right: there really was another, greater mystery about them. And although I longed desperately to know more, I got the feeling from their studied inscrutability, their sequestration in Father's office, and the whispering we heard begin the moment the door closed behind them, that this time we wouldn't learn a thing about this new secret.

26

Outside the lycée, on the stony little square where students waited for the school bell to ring (the older children trading cigarettes, while the younger ones swapped marbles), we told all sorts of stories about the Germans.

It was said they would give away cakes in the town, and that these cakes, like the sugared almonds that came with them, were poisoned. No sweets offered by an officer—still less by a soldier—were ever to be munched, sucked, or swallowed. They were arsenic, rat poison, cyanide! It was also rumored that a parachute drop of English arms had landed in the woods above Fau, and everyone clustered around Bonazèbe, who claimed to have found a scrap of parachute material during a family outing in that area.

"If you're so smart, show it to us," said envious voices.

Bonazèbe was an uninteresting child, a somewhat pale, thin boy in a close-fitting woman's jacket with a fur collar that had been altered by his mother. He'd never been the object of the slightest attention, in either the lower-school or the upper-school playgrounds, but now that he was believed to be the owner of such a rare fetish, he had become so boastful that finally the more aggressive boys knocked him down on the rough ground, pinned him by the arms and legs, and went through his pants pockets.

"Here it is!" shouted the one who'd found the bit of cloth.

Passed from hand to hand, it wasn't any bigger than a hankie, and seemed to have torn edges.

"This stupid thing is just junk," his attackers scoffed.

Off they went. I asked Bonazèbe to let me see it for a moment, this scrap that had unleashed so much envy. It was gleaming white, and when I held it in my fingers the texture felt soft, pleasant, like silk. Where had it come from? England? In what unknown factory filled with the babble of foreign tongues had it been made?

"Me, I believe you," I told Bonazèbe. "I'm sure it's real."

Bonazèbe smiled gratefully. He told me that while on an outing with his parents, he'd found a large piece of parachute, the size of a bed sheet, wrapped around a clump of thorn bushes at the foot of a chestnut tree. His parents had been afraid to return to town with such a compromising article, however, and had kept only the little square that Bonazèbe had let me touch.

"If you want," he told me, "I'll take you to that place to-morrow. We'll cut ourselves a bigger piece. And then we'll be able to trade for all the marbles and shooters we want!"

When I mentioned Bonazèbe's exciting proposition to my parents, they forbade me to go wandering around in the Fau woods.

"This isn't a game," said Father, almost harshly.

He had a preoccupied, worn-out air, as though the problems and incidents that had piled up over time had just come to a head.

While we were at school that afternoon, a German aide-de-camp from the Waffen SS had turned up at the Villa, driving a black Mercedes sporting wire wheels, a shining radiator grille, and a black-and-silver flag. The Obersturmführer had explained to my father that his superior officer, a major general, was thinking about moving into our house. He'd had enough of living in the Grand Hôtel du Midi in the heart of town, which had been serving as the headquarters of the occupying forces for more than a year, and he was looking for quieter lodgings, where he might—as he suggested to his aide-de-camp—"be awakened by the birds." After some investigation, including numerous and varied inspections in the surrounding area, it had been decided that the Villa du Haut-Soleil would fill the bill.

"With your permission, I'll return in a few days with my superior so that he may judge for himself," the officer had said.

He spoke polished French, imbued with flawless courtesy. He had informed my father at the outset that he was aware of his reputation as an eminent jurist from Paris, heeded and respected by all. If the project was to be carried out, there would be no question of disturbing my father's normal office routine, still less of evacuating the Villa. The aide-de-camp was simply proposing the temporary use of one floor of our house, for his commanding officer alone, just until he felt somewhat rested.

"You understand," he'd said, "the Brigadeführer detests promiscuity."

"Meaning . . . ?" Father had asked.

"The company of the other officers, monsieur! Working all day, monsieur! Well then, to sleep in one's workplace, to spend the evening with the same men with whom one has toiled all day long—this is extremely tiring! And the city, monsieur, with its noise . . . whereas here . . . the birds . . ."

"If I understand you correctly," Father had replied, "my home has been requisitioned."

The first lieutenant had protested in accents of outraged sincerity. "Do not use that word, monsieur! Not that word! Not as one officer to another."

Because he had immediately let my father know, when he introduced himself with a bow and a clicking of heels, that he knew my father to be an officer in the reserves, and that this point in common overrode considerations of nationality and conflict, thus allowing the avoidance of all misunderstanding.

"Among officers, monsieur, things must be frank and aboveboard."

"Of course," Father had replied.

The Mercedes had driven away.

For the first time since the end of the unoccupied zone, my father felt unable to shake off the apprehension that oppressed him.

Until then, he'd always managed, with his wife, to control the events that had disturbed our daily life at the Villa. The episode of the military maneuvers on our lawn, Floqueboque's attempt to arrest Dora, the disappearance of Monsieur Germain, Antoine's departure to join the maquisards—none of these things had disturbed his serenity. He had seen these incidents as sporadic crises, for which he had always found a solution and which did not profoundly affect what he called "the course of things." And even when he'd been powerless to remedy a situation, as in the case of Monsieur Germain (whose absence weighed on him, for he had felt responsible for the safety of his silent "gardener"), he had nevertheless decided that this did not bring into question the way his little world turned, his children's education, his wife's happiness, his reading, his friendship with Paul, or even the proper functioning of his secret network of "visitors."

Faced with the unexpected, he would exercise a mixture of fatalism and rationality that allowed him to keep on course without showing any sign of doubt or dismay, which he knew might have upset our carefree climate of laughter and games, that close family atmosphere he so cherished, which gave him the strength to overcome the underlying pessimism that had too often ruled his thoughts. He had succeeded in battling his sworn enemy, Anxiety, thanks to the love of his wife and the seven chattering little creatures growing up in their care who had claimed every moment of their life together. He possessed that solidity of character suitable to clear-eyed skeptics, that moral resilience acquired through repeated trials by fire—in this case, the sudden, premature death of his father, and his own survival of the bloodbath of the Great War.

When my oldest brother had come to tell him, with trembling voice and wavering gaze, of his wish to leave for Spain and then England, Father hadn't made any objection.

"Naturally, Antoine," he'd said. "I approve."

The young man had been left speechless. He'd steeled himself for a firm, even violent rejection of his proposition, which would have provided the pretext for a fresh critique of his fecklessness, his poor scholastic record, his dubious acquaintances in town. Having unsettled Antoine by immediately accepting his proposal, Father was then able to modify the youngster's plans without offending him by seeming to influence such an important decision.

"Listen to me carefully," Father had told him. "You're so young that I shouldn't let you have your way, but if I were your age and in your position, I'd have the same impulse, and I'm proud of you. But things are moving more quickly now. The Allies are everywhere poised for reconquest. Within the next few months, you'll see them getting down to the job of liberating France. The trip to England is long and difficult, and you risk arriving in London after the Free French Forces have left to come back here. It makes more sense for you to join the Resistance and use the remaining time right away, and right here."

Father had immediately gotten in touch with Henri, the elementary-school teacher, and Antoine had been able to leave the Villa with Henri to go off and live his adventure, but Father knew he was close by, somewhere in the hills beyond the river, and he felt that once again he had managed to remain in control of the situation. As for the "visitors," who were still just as numerous in spite of sporadic alarms and the raid that had swept up Monsieur Germain, my father continued to safeguard their comings and goings. He anticipated a few more seasons of difficult times, true, but just as he'd predicted the coming world-wide catastrophe several years in advance, he now expected to see this tragic episode come to a close, and felt that he'd managed to keep disaster from striking his own hearth and home.

And now he was being forced to deal with the most delicate, the most dangerous of situations. We were going to be saddled with a general of the occupation forces, in the very midst of our daily life, in the absolute heart of our family circle, and there was no possible way for Father to head off this development. Although he was stunned by the prospect, he tried to hide his dismay.

"But, Papa," said one of my sisters, when Father felt obliged to break the news to us, "he hasn't the right to come live with us!"

"It's our house," I insisted, "our house!"

"He hasn't the right," replied Father, "but he has *his* right, he's laying down *his* law, and it's the law of might makes right."

"Yes, but in our house?" persisted Juliette. "Really, Papa, the Villa!"

"But Dora, and Franck, and Jannette," chorused the twins, "what will they do?"

"This officer isn't going to eat at our table, is he?" demanded Juliette.

Juliette had pronounced the words "the Villa!" à la Duchesse de Langeais, one of Edwige Feuillère's roles; although she no longer imitated that actress's intonations, she still lapsed occasionally into her "great lady" mode, and her cry, "the Villa!" had seemed like an unconscious parody of some dialogue from a movie in which a beautiful aristocrat in similar circumstances would have protested, "The château! They simply mustn't touch the château!"

Father decided to put an end to the discussion. "Don't worry; leave everything to your mother and me."

He hadn't answered our questions. Until that day, the country's invasion and the occupation of the town had seemed, to our childish or adolescent minds, if not somewhat abstract, at least difficult to grasp. We'd continued riding our bikes to the lycée, playing in our wonderland on the grounds of the Villa, and Juliette was still taking her dancing and piano lessons, still teasing Diabelli from the ivories and wafting him out the windows, so although we saw lots of uniforms in the town, they appeared to us more like a blot on the landscape than an inexorable tyranny.

People spoke of attacks and bloody reprisals, but we hadn't actually seen any of this. We'd been spared. We were close to the action, personally involved, since the Villa was used as a hiding place for Jews, yet we persisted in feeling ourselves exempted, immunized. The secret of the "visitors," which we children had been asked to help protect, had been integrated into that endless game-playing, that universe of make-believe, that inability to see reality clearly that constitute the privilege, and the weakness, of happy childhoods. Struck by our amazement, Father understood that all those recent alarming developments hadn't disturbed any of our certainties: our home was our home, and they could very well occupy the whole town, the entire Midi, all of France, but the Villa was still the Villa! And no foreigner was going to dare set foot in it, period.

Father told us again, however, that we were mistaken, that we had to try to understand, and we finally came around to the idea that there were limits to freedom, that there was another law, one more powerful than those "rights" we'd had the illusion of deserving to enjoy, since we'd faithfully performed our "duties."

This "might makes right" business bothered me.

"Papa, tell me, why are the Germans stronger than we are?"

I saw him stifle a gesture of exasperation. His face became a mosaic of complex and changing expressions that I was too young to decipher, a mixture of resignation and a lightning-quick awareness of history, of Europe's past, but there was bitterness as well, the wish to struggle against the feeling that all is vanity, the scars left by the quiet despair that can seem like wisdom. But since my question could have only one answer, one of those answers children don't want to hear ("Because that's how things are, that's all"), Father sent me back to my notebooks, my toys, and my bread-and-butter sandwiches. And we wrote in the Album, "There is no answer to the question of why the Germans are stronger than the French."

With a superior smile intended to seem diabolical, the Dark Man broke his long silence. "I see an incredible advantage for us in this."

Surprised, Father looked at him inquisitively. He respected Paul's intelligence, but he'd rarely found himself lagging behind his friend when it came to ideas. He knew Paul had more peasant cunning than he did, that he was closer to life, to things of the flesh, to animals, to hunting, to the land. He'd admitted to Paul his feelings of helplessness, his dread, his worries about what lay in store for their "visitors." He didn't see how he could suddenly interrupt the operation of this network he'd created to deal with the pressing refugee situation.

"Once this general of yours moves in with you," announced Paul in the mocking tone he often used, "then you're all set, you'll have nothing more to fear from Vichy, Floqueboque, the cops, the Gestapo, denunciations, or surprise raids. Sonova-bitch! Think about it! A real lucky break. Just like that, your property will become un-touch-a-ble!"

"You think so?"

"I even think, old chum, that your kiss-my-ass Brigadeführer won't be able to believe for a single instant, with him living under your roof, that you could possibly be running an under-ground railroad for Jewish refugees!"

"You think so," repeated Father, this time without even a hint of a question mark after his words.

"Well, dammit!" exclaimed Paul. "You sound as though you've never in your life played any poker—just bridge!"

The two white-haired men, the Puritan and the Iconoclast, as they liked to call each other, considered every possible advantage they might draw from the coming requisition, seen in this new light. After a few hours of serious thought, enriched by their views on the various war fronts around the world, they wound up having a good laugh about the whole thing.

Then they tackled an equally worrisome subject: Diego.

27

In Paris, in the mid-1920s, a tall Argentinian beauty held court in her mansion on Boulevard Malesherbes, near Parc Monceau. Her slender figure, bedroom eyes, porcelain skin, studiedly naïve voice, and lively intelligence turned the heads of men who came ostensibly to see her husband, but had eyes only for her.

Her name was Consuelo Barzillievi. The husband was Russian, Armenian, Iranian—nobody really knew. A shady financier rather than a respectable banker, he was a heavy, powerful man with a pug nose and a hard-hearted manner, who shaved his head and wore a mustache. Passing through Buenos Aires one time, he'd bought himself the prettiest society belle around and set her up in Paris as window dressing, a decoy, a come-on. It didn't bother him at all that married men and bachelors alike found her enticing, and that she had a few affairs on the side, because he'd assiduously corrupted her so that she would shamelessly exercise her talents as a seductress, her flair for intrigue, her skill at blackmail, and her ability to enmesh her victims in a web of guilt. Husband and wife had made an arrangement; they respected the terms of a contract that may even have been openly drawn up by Barzillievi and stashed in a safe, like a precious gem.

People called her "the lady in ocher," because she chose to

dress herself almost exclusively in yellow or earth tones, wearing face powder of a pink verging on ocher, with lipstick in the same tints, which set off the lovely, pure, liquid green of her large eyes in a striking, almost scandalous manner. And since malicious gossip soon had it that she was a man-eater, devouring victims of all ages and social status (as long as that status was high, and the financial standing as well), some people had baptized her "the Ochress." She was unusually tall, and when the habitués of her salon crowded around her, her domination of them became almost farcical. The Ochress presided over a circus that teetered on the brink of the ridiculous. The only thing needed to strip this woman and her husband of all pretense was an eye with that diamond sparkle described by the Cardinal de Retz: the unerring gift for seeing the truth.

This is just what happened during a reception at the home of an associate of Barzillievi's, when my father (who was still single) spoke a few words of reproof to Consuelo. He had already seen her many times in her home on Boulevard Malesherbes, and like everyone else, he knew her reputation. He had conceived an unreasonable aversion toward her that had finally led him to lose his temper.

"You are undoubtedly aware of your attractiveness, madame," he'd told her, "but have you considered the grotesque aspects of this constant social playacting? Do you think that the simple fact of being a lovely woman authorizes or excuses so much fakery, so much effort devoted to such a sordid end?"

The Ochress hadn't blinked. Holding her ground, she'd presented the same smiling, reserved expression, the same regal sang-froid.

"Who are you to judge me?" she'd calmly replied.

He'd turned on his heel and left the room.

The Ochress wasn't just a pretty face peddling her charms for the benefit of a wheeler-dealer husband. I mentioned that she was both intelligent and spirited—and this stern man's insulting words had stung her to the quick. She did not report the incident to her husband, and as it happened, there had been no witnesses to their brief exchange, during which they had both spoken without raising their voices. She decided to find out what she could about my father.

She'd learned of his success, his independence, the position he held within the business world, and the respectful silence that would fall during board meetings when it was his turn to offer an opinion or reconcile conflicting arguments. But she had also discovered—for her network of informers was efficient and far-flung—that he enjoyed the company of women, that his mistresses never held his interest very long, and that he'd already had quite a number of them. She'd decided to see him again and to seduce him, for she suffered from that fateful inclination of the heart that drives creatures accustomed to having their own charming way to devote all their energy, passion, and the strength born of their wounded pride to winning the love of the one person who has shown them contempt or indifference.

But since she was clever, and as the campaign she had undertaken had stimulated her wits and multiplied her strategic skills tenfold, she understood that, in this kind of battle, sensuality cannot be used as a weapon but must come rather as a last bouquet, so she had first to win over her adversary through the riches and ingenuity of her mind. Consuelo Barzillievi first approached my father on a purely intellectual level, through the twists and turns of literary conversation. He had seen the trap but had taken the bait, lured by her flattery and the challenge to his misogyny.

She came to their rendezvous discreetly made-up, determined to play down her beauty, to show that she wasn't a high-class whore but someone who could be loved, or at least valued, for her qualities of judgment, her gift for maieutics, her appreciation of the poetry of Baudelaire and the theories of Spinoza. Since she had a wide range of interests and kept up-to-date, she brought the spice of the latest intellectual fashions to their discussions: Nietzsche, l'Art Nègre, the Surréalistes.

"Have you noticed," she asked him one day (flirting with him, but at the same time perfectly sincere), "that I've changed color for you?"

Ocher had completely disappeared. She was dressing in gray, pink, black, or garnet-red, depending on the season or her mood. All this went on for quite some time. Then he gave in, and they became lovers.

Consuelo hadn't interrupted her frenetic social activity, so she was now putting on two shows instead of one. Love made her possessive, while her lucidity made her destructive, for she was clearheaded enough to understand that this man would never forgive her her past, and she felt that, all in all, she was better off trying to debauch and debase him because they could never build anything lasting between them; she was depressed because she was now more aware of her true position, her husband's cruelty, other men's greed, and the cynicism of the times, while her suffering was heightened by the stimulating play of intelligence between her lover and herself, and his influence as an unattached man; she was unable to break with him, for she craved a noble and redeeming passion with my father as well as a life of wealth and vice with Barzillievi, and she was all the more hysterical because her lover wasn't asking her to choose between them, but was himself reflecting on how low he had sunk in this affair, and would soon begin to draw away from her, thirsting for purity, unconsciously seeking to change the direction of his life, experiencing more and more often the same revulsion that had led him to insult this woman in the first place.

They repeatedly broke off and patched up their affair, and then he shut the door on her for good. Never again would she be part of his life, for he had found the girl who was to become my mother.

The Ochress tried to pursue him. He had left Paris on his honeymoon. He gave instructions to Paul, the confidant and friend with whom he had shared a few wild, youthful years when Paul had stayed with him in Paris, trying vainly to adapt to life in the capital.

"Go see her. Placate her. Explain—and if you can't explain, console."

Paul followed his instructions to the letter, and even somewhat beyond. In fact, he'd been literally asked to clean house, because Consuelo wasn't the only one. In what Paul and my father would later call their "former life," love and the traces it leaves—its load of responsibilities, moral debts, guilt, reproaches, strong pressures or loose ties—had been of great importance.

Paul made the rounds of the "ex-girlfriends," settling accounts, from the most simple (the material) to the most painful (the sentimental). A handsome, magnetic man, Paul was witty, sexually vigorous, and able to breach the most impregnable defenses. He had his own brief fling with Consuelo, who gave herself to him out of spite, perversity, a taste for revenge, and a wish to weaken the fraternal bond between the two men, while Paul might have seen this adventure as the most definitive way of breaking all ties for his friend. But she'd gotten her hooks into him, and as he later admitted, he'd been deeply infatuated with her.

He told my father everything. Time passed. One day, each of them received an elliptical letter on ocher paper, in the same handwriting, unsigned, with the same message: "It's not impossible that one of you has given me a child: a boy. I've named him Diego."

The two men had no doubt that the same perfidious missive must have been sent to several other correspondents throughout France and the world. And that was the last they heard from the Argentinian beauty with whom they'd spent those torrid nights in their younger days.

Much later, during the darkest moments of the war and the Occupation, they learned that Barzillievi had fled with his wife to a suite in the Hôtel Régina, in Nice. Then the man had disappeared, and the woman, now on her own, had moved on to Menton, Beaulieu, Monaco, and the Italian Riviera.

Had Diego made his way up from there? What dangerous journey had brought him to the maquis of southwestern France? What had Consuelo told him? She had to be at least forty years old by now. Should they contact Diego? What good would that do? Who knew what was going on? What did they themselves know about this spectacular "partisan" with the same flamboyant attitudes as his mother? And what did Diego know? Hadn't she lied about the whole thing just to make them suffer? But, in that case, who was Diego, and why had he given that message to the little boy: "Tell your father that I'm here"?

So they mulled over all these questions during evenings at the Villa, bathed in a kind of nostalgia for a vanished past, for which they now felt—at home once more with the land, the trees, the pastoral calm of their native soil—no regret, but an indulgent affection, tempered, however, by the difficult realities of the present situation and the feeling that, despite themselves, they now had a new responsibility to bear, one very close to them both.

28

Juliette left the Villa the day the SS Brigadeführer moved in. She was eighteen, and so beautiful that she stood out from all her classmates. She seemed beyond the reach of boys her own age, Antoine's friends at the lycée, who sought in vain the privilege of walking at her side, of wheeling their bikes together along narrow Rue Delarep. Juliette didn't observe these provincial rites. Whenever she thought about her ambitions, she'd begun to feel increasingly restricted, hemmed in. She would have liked to dance, act on stage, travel the world with a ballet company, a chorus, or a theatrical troupe, or, better yet, be a soloist, be applauded, recognized, famous! When the longing to experience love began to trouble her virginal body, she became even more secretive.

She'd succeeded in outgrowing that phase in the relationship between mother and daughter when they seem perpetually at odds, when an unspeakable jealousy slips into the darkened room of adolescence like a shaft of light through the blinds. They'd become allies once more, like two childhood friends or two big sisters, and Juliette confided in her mother, who spoke to her husband again about their daughter's frustrations.

"In any case," he said, "it's time for her to leave."

"Why?"

"Because I don't want her here when that officer and his staff move in with us."

"But what are you afraid of?" asked Mother.

"I don't want to run any risks. Juliette is too pretty, and those soldiers have been on their own too long."

Juliette was sent to live with a female cousin of Paul's in Toulouse—the big city! So near and yet so far, so different from our little town. Toulouse, with its large theater, its capitol, its cafés with their colorful terraces, its movie theaters, its avenues with their wide sidewalks swarming with pedestrians, its splendid wisterias and hundred-year-old plane trees; so many unknown faces, so many things to learn and discover . . . She had the impression she was leaving for the ends of the earth, a different life, while her parents felt that the Villa was emptying out, since Antoine was already off in the maquis. Only "the little ones" were left.

The German officer was tall, pale, taciturn, and sure of himself. He had a long, bony face, hollow cheeks, a cleft chin, ears set close to his head, and he wore his hair cut so short and trimmed so high up his neck that you couldn't even see how blond it was until he took off his cap, with its black band sporting the little embroidered death's-head, the famous emblem of his corps. We also noticed the runic SS on the collar of his tunic, and around his neck the Iron Cross, with silvery edges that flashed when he moved.

"You'll say hello and goodbye when you're spoken to, and nothing more," Father had told us.

He'd assigned three bedrooms on the ground floor to the remaining children (three brothers, two sisters, plus "Cousin Jannette"), abandoning the upstairs floor, including Juliette's former bedroom, to the Brigadeführer and his aide-de-camp. He thought this arrangement would make it easier to keep an eye on their activities. He'd explained to us that everything would go on just as before, except that Dora, who was still helping Mother with all the cooking and housework, would no longer talk, just to be on the safe side. As a result, we'd have to get used to speaking to her as little as possible, and were to act as though she was mentally deficient.

"We'll say that she's seriously retarded. We must hide her German accent at all costs, and remember, even if the officer never sets foot in the kitchen, there are still his chauffeur and his aide-de-camp."

The Romanian chauffeur spoke fluent French. He was a dark, round young man, quite ordinary-looking. When he arrived each morning in the black Mercedes, we'd be busy getting our bikes ready, since we left the Villa at the same time as the officer went off to his HQ. From the very first day, an inviolable routine was established: the chauffeur would back the car up to the Villa so that he could set off again down the gravel drive without losing a moment. Then he'd open the car doors and wait, standing right by the vehicle, saying a few words to us in an effort to be friendly.

"The Romanian has been 'requisitioned,' too," Father had said. "He's not a bad sort. His country has been occupied, like ours. But he works for them, he wears their uniform, so keep your distance."

The officer would come down the stairs, followed by his aide-de-camp, who moments before had brought him a cup of coffee prepared in the kitchen by Dora, in her role as a mute half-wit. Father would be pacing up and down the front hall, waiting for the Brigadeführer. At first we took this behavior for excessive politeness, and were surprised and humiliated by it, but we soon realized what Father was up to, because his rule was not to let the officer out of his sight from the second he returned to the Villa in the evening to the moment when he left the next morning "to go to work." Father didn't want him to have any opportunity of speaking to anyone else, or of snooping around in the secret life of the Villa. The two men would exchange a few polite, harmless remarks in French. Each one kept his distance, observing a kind of formality that had been tacitly adopted.

"Ah, monsieur!" the officer would say, "many birds, this morning."

"Yes," Father would reply, "they're very numerous at this time of year."

"Oh, I wanted to tell you, I won't be dining in my room this evening. Back very late."

"Very well," Father would say.

And it was understood that Father would wait up for him, no matter how late the hour. They would nod curtly to each other. Father would step aside to let the aide-de-camp open the door for the officer, and the two Germans would then go down the three front steps and walk a few yards to the car, where the Romanian awaited them. Sometimes the officer would pause on the threshold and look over at us, as we awaited the Mercedes's departure and Father's signal to get on our bikes and set out for the lycée.

The officer would then point in our direction. "The children," he'd announce, as though he were drawing up an inventory.

He never made any comment or spoke to us directly; he might just as well have said in the same tone: "The trees. The chestnuts. The gravel. The bicycles."

We'd stare at him.

A short scar ran from the end of his top lip across his left cheek, a souvenir, most probably, from a saber cut received during a duel fought when he was a student. His long eyebrows arched over lids that seemed stretched to the sides, covering half the eyeballs and their light blue pupils. Those hard, hooded eyes and the way the lids slanted upward gave the German an air of severity, as well as a vaguely Oriental look. He neither frightened nor fascinated us, but he disturbed us more than we would have liked to admit.

First off, we couldn't figure out a nickname for him. None of the possibilities we discussed won unanimous approval, so none could be inscribed in the Album. If Antoine and Juliette had still been there, perhaps they'd have come up with the right adjective. Deprived of their influence, however, and left to our own devices, we felt impoverished, and I saw clearly what a void had been left, first by Antoine's departure, then by Juliette's. Our father, for example, no longer used any of those rare words he'd once enjoyed helping us discover. The Album was the poorer for this, and our contributions less frequent. We'd certainly tried to find a nickname for our "guest"—Scar, or Skull, or Panzeros—but nothing seemed adequate, which left us blocked by this enigma: a man who could not be nicknamed. So we called him the Officer, or the German.

We were also bothered by the stiffness of his features. Our father's face had always seemed severe and intimidating to us, but although there might have been a certain resemblance between the two men—they were both just under six feet tall, with the same erect posture, the same masks of adult composure and self-control, the same ability to impose their will on others—one of them seemed to us all light and warmth, while the other was cold and dark. True, we cherished the one and knew nothing of the other, but filial devotion alone was not enough to explain this feeling of difference. Was it because of that black tunic with the high collar, that SS Panzer jacket enveloping his body like a carapace and setting off the pallor of his skin, or was it because of everything we didn't know but could suspect about the journey that had brought him across the continent, from the Russian front to our Villa, with everything he'd seen and done, and the orders he'd given—was it because the four years he'd spent at the head of his elite division had slowly frozen his face, removing all trace of tenderness from his eyes, and stripped him of his humanity?

Finally, I was even more upset by his very position in the heart of our daily life. I couldn't accept the fact that every night he slept, at the same time as I did, in a bedroom on the floor above ours. That a human being so foreign to my family should turn up just like that and go off to bed each night in my house bothered me no end. What does he dream about, I wondered, up in Juliette's room?

When I thought of my parents, my brothers and sisters, each one nestled deep in sleep throughout the night, all under the same roof, I imagined that, even though we didn't dream the same dreams, they still had something in common. I'd see my mother or father in my dreams, just as I met characters from the books I read, or animals and people I'd see in the town or out in the countryside. And so I never doubted that my father, mother, brothers, and sisters would likewise find me popping up in their dreams. Knowing that I could stroll around in my mother's dreams had always been a comfort to me, bolstering the notion that a communal spirit watched over us and our happiness—the Spirit that I'd sought in the depths of the giant orange-and-yellow jar.

But the German officer's dreams? What were they like?

Surely the birds, horses, fire and water, women, dogs and children, swords and ships, dragons and fortresses in his dreams were not like those in mine. Their shapes, their colors would be different. I was convinced that people's dreams could leave their bedrooms to go hover amiably around other sleepers. I was afraid that the officer's dreams, which I suspected were blacker than ours, would escape from the floor above, slipping down the staircase to push open my door so that his birds, his swords, his fears might attack my slumber.

Suddenly, a more terrible thought struck me, and struck hard: What if he'd brought me into his own dreams? He'd been living with us for almost a month. Who could say whether or not, little by little, the inhabitants of the Villa hadn't wandered into his dreams? And what if I were already promenading around in one of them? And if so, what was he doing with me?

What was I doing in the dream of a man who commanded other men whom my father, my brother Antoine, and Diego were fighting?

I wake from this nightmare in tears. I get out of bed. There's a light at the end of the hall. Frightened and curious, I tiptoe toward the light. There, in the front hall, on the parlor sofa, I see my father, wrapped in a blanket. He's asleep. His chest and legs stick out at either end of the blanket, so I can see he's not in pajamas but is still wearing his trousers and a woolen shirt. He has chosen to camp out at this key spot, this intersection between the staircase to the upper floor and the corridors leading toward the kitchen and the children's bedrooms, as well as to the cellar door.

And I tell myself that he's not there simply to keep an eye on any possible inopportune comings and goings. I see that he has resolved to stand guard over my dreams. Then I kneel down to kiss his hand, freckled with age, still lying on the back of an open book.

29

The request was first presented by the aide-de-camp, who spoke
very good French.

"The Brigadeführer would like to hold a little ceremony here,
so I've come to ask if we might use your dining room on this
particular occasion."

Father knew that he couldn't possibly refuse and that, even
if he did, they could easily proceed with their plans despite his
opposition. In fact, he took this polite overture as a sign that
his attitude of discretion and formal courtesy was paying off.
The Dark Man's prediction had come true. During the day, after
the Mercedes had carried its cargo off to HQ in the town, my
father was able to go about his work, deal with the flow of
"visitors" to the farms, and follow over the wireless the slow
and inexorable collapse of the armies of the Axis and the Third
Reich on all fronts.

"*Andromache perfumes herself with lavender*," soon followed by similar messages, had told him and the Dark Man
that the long-awaited main Allied offensive had begun at last.
This was in June. The landing had just taken place. My father
never mentioned this extraordinary event to the SS Brigadeführer during their two daily encounters—when the German
left in the morning and returned in the evening—but he had

noticed the officer's preoccupied air, and from certain remarks dropped by the Romanian chauffeur, and even by the aide-de-camp, we understood that the "requisition" was quickly drawing to a close. The worried looks of those three men were in sharp contrast to the enthusiasm that now filled the faces of my parents, who did their best to conceal their joy.

"Not one word, not one sign of celebration or provocation," Father had warned us, because, up until the last day and the very last minute of that occupation, he would continue to dread the destruction of his fragile creation, his world of innocent children and defenseless women, through a lack of caution or tact.

We kept quiet about our excitement, but news of the landing had swept through the town, including the playground at the lycée, provoking smiles and excited conversations. The Dark Man no longer came to the Villa in the evenings, so as to leave my father at complete liberty to keep tabs on the Brigadeführer's movements, but the good news led him to visit us during the day.

"You see," he rejoiced, "it's the beginning of the end."

"Perhaps the Allies will be pushed back to the sea," observed my father.

"Still the same horrible pessimist!"

"It's one of my faults," admitted Father, "you know perfectly well, it's my way of trying to avoid misfortune."

The weeks preceding the Allied landing had seen a resurgence of Resistance activity, an increased number of attacks, and people talked about the exploits of partisans operating higher up on the map: in Périgord, Limousin, and Quercy.

"You know what we call those areas when we're among ourselves?" the Brigadeführer asked my father. "We call that region Little Russia."

"Why?"

"Because the terrorist resistance there is as tenacious, and the terrain as difficult, as they were during our Russian campaign."

The officer was sitting in Father's office. After his aide-de-camp had made the initial request, he had insisted on coming himself to reach an agreement. And for the first time he'd spoken in more than just monosyllables. The aide-de-camp was present to serve as an interpreter.

"Ah, monsieur, Russia! That is my very worst memory . . . But let's talk about how things will be organized."

"Let's do that," agrees my father.

"We're having a kind of farewell party. My division will soon be leaving to reinforce our armies in Normandy. My comrades from the other units, who will be remaining here, would like to celebrate our departure."

"When will you be leaving?" asks Father.

"Frankly, I don't see any reason why you shouldn't know: tomorrow morning."

"Ah!" says Father.

"This pleases you?"

"Pardon?"

The aide-de-camp presses the point: "The SS Brigadeführer would like to know if your 'Ah!' expresses a sigh of pleasure."

"The SS Brigadeführer," replies Father, "may put himself in my place and ask himself how he would react to such news."

Once Father's reply has been translated for him, the officer flashes him a smile that raises his upper lip and seems to extend the scar higher on that usually impassive face, whose moods my father has learned to read.

"Diplomatic, monsieur, very diplomatic!" he says in French. Then he returns to his native tongue and his aide's services as an interpreter.

"The SS Brigadeführer would like to inform you that we will be twenty officers all told tonight, including ourselves. We will bring everything: food, drink, dishes. You will not have to do a thing. He simply requests the use of the dining room and the rear terrace. It will be hot, and the evening air will be refreshing."

My father doesn't reply, and the two soldiers take his silence for consent. They stand up. As Father prepares to accompany them to the door, the Brigadeführer says, without using the interpreter, "I must warn you, there will be heavy drinking. No one will be hurt, but I advise you to lock the doors of the other rooms."

Father watches them leave, his brow furrowed with anxiety.

Twenty minutes later, without warning, as though the decision has already been made and everything has been organized well in advance, irrespective of Father's response, the carnival begins.

A parade of armored cars, driven by ordinary soldiers wearing the uniform of the Wehrmacht, delivers case after case of liquor and champagne. Next to arrive is an army field kitchen, a canteen truck that parks on the gravel drive, a verdigris-colored vehicle with two smoking chimneys on its roof, its motor chuffing out noisy black clouds of foul-smelling exhaust. Cooks fling open the doors, folding back metal shutters to reveal two small stoves and a counter on which will accumulate dishes, silverware, platters, and tureens. The cooks converse among themselves, but without haste, efficiently, in brief bursts, and in a satisfied tone. Various auxiliaries in boots and forage caps set up a short double line of dwarf privet shrubs in steel-banded wooden jardinières to serve as a kind of "guard of honor" a few yards long that will lead to the front steps of the Villa when the guests emerge from their cars. There is a rehearsal, then a second, then a third, until everything goes smoothly according to protocol. In the meantime, armed guards in helmets have taken up position at the front gate and along the driveway.

After bicycling back from the lycée, we sat until sunset on the gravel, at a front corner of the Villa, fascinated by this practical illustration of a word we'd heard the officer use several times, but the full dimension of which now came as a revelation: *organization.*

The day before all this activity, Father had taken in the Bernhardt family, a Jewish couple and their child. The husband was a lawyer, the wife was an antiques dealer, and their little boy

Maurice was my age. They'd spent the night in the cellar. It had been decided that they'd set out again the next morning, after most of the inhabitants of the Villa had left for the day, but the sudden arrival of so many vehicles, soldiers, cooks, aides-de-camp, drivers, and other military personnel had made any departure to the farms impossible.

Father considered the situation: with the three Bernhardts in the cellar, Dora and Franck sleeping on camp beds in the basement laundry room, and our "Cousin Jannette" sharing my sisters' bedroom, there were six Jews under our roof illegally. Plus five children (the twins, the two girls, and me) and their mother. And all these had to be concealed or protected! For a brief moment, Father lost heart.

He sat on the sofa, which he no longer bothered to move back every morning to its usual place in the parlor. His head hanging, his shoulders slumped, he told himself that he'd been blindly optimistic, unseeing, and that step by step he'd brought his little world to the brink of catastrophe. There'd been no recent news from Antoine, and the stepped-up activities of the Resistance meant his oldest son was in even greater danger than before. Juliette was far away, and he'd been surprised to find how much he missed her lively intelligence, her sweet disposition, and her affection. Finally, there was his constant uncertainty over Diego, from whom he'd received no sign since that one message I'd brought; Diego, whose real identity was a mystery and whom he wanted to see at least once with his own eyes . . . All these worries weighed him down like too many logs piled in the carrier strapped to a woodcutter's back: he felt his muscles stiffen, his body sink into the pernicious exhaustion that can lead to abandoning all effort.

There was more: the Bernhardts had brought terrible news. They'd fled from Bayonne, which had been hit by a wave of roundups and denunciations, and they'd learned that in the neighboring city of Biarritz the diamond merchant Norbert Awiczi, our amusing "Justin Case," had been hurled through a window to his death. Two men from the Gestapo had thrown him from his room in the Grand Hôtel du Palais, and his body had landed on the wrought-iron spikes of the fence enclosing the hotel grounds, by the sea. Never again would we hear him call our father his "dearr frriend," and Father, sickened at this disappearance of another close acquaintance from before the war, never even remembered the little pouch of diamonds the two of them had buried at the foot of the poplar tree.

Instead, since one death inevitably reminds us of others, my father began to brood once more over the fate of Monsieur Germain. In spite of all his efforts and his constant appeals to the fleeing refugees themselves for any information they might have, he'd never learned what had happened to our dignified and gentle "gardener," the Viennese intellectual who had shared our lives for two years. Father still hadn't managed to find out the names of the camps where the train carrying Monsieur Germain and his unfortunate companions was supposed to have gone, and the truth hadn't yet dawned on him, because at that time there wasn't any way of knowing the truth.

"Don't worry, dearest, this will be the last of our trials. Tomorrow everything will be better."

He looked up. Kneeling before him was a young woman with light hair framing her delicate face, and a gentle, sensual manner.

As she spoke, she gazed at him with all the love in her heart, a love formed of gratitude, respect, and admiration, but passion and tenderness as well, so that, despite the difference in their ages, my mother's behavior toward him truly seemed like that of any woman in love, and yet her love was too great to be encompassed by a single role, a single definition.

That love went out to him with the strength of other instincts, dependent not simply on desire or the uniqueness of the harmonious bond between man and woman, but on those unexpected elements that seem like magic, completely beyond the realm of reason, and about which Proust wrote that it's best not to try to understand them. Father sometimes liked to think

174

that he was taking the place of the father his wife had never had, but did he even see, in that particular moment, how she enveloped him in a maternal solicitude, speaking to him in the same tone, caressing him with the same patience, and enfolding him in the same indulgence she used with her "little ones," and did he recognize, in the words she'd just spoken, the accents he'd noticed several years before, when, as they had both bent over the bed of their little boy hovering between life and death, she'd sung and murmured tirelessly, for hours and hours, the music of her devotion, the melody of her consolation?

He tended to be affectionately ironical about her "little girl" reactions to things, and it probably satisfied his pride somehow (or perhaps confirmed the prejudices of his generation and the dominant culture of the previous century, for he had been born just as that century was drawing to a close) to see his wife as an impulsive and fragile bird, and to fear she might be over-whelmed by the difficulties she would face if something should happen to him and she was left on her own. But what he was forgetting in those moments was the strength that had allowed this woman to weather the trauma of a shattered childhood, the composure and resolution she had shown several times when the Villa and its world had been in danger. Such forgetfulness never lasted long, and although he hadn't always been able to see the firm set of her jaw in the tender oval of her face, or the determination behind her limpid smile, that night she had only to urge him gently to take the necessary precautions (assigning various tasks, telling the children to carry messages between the world upstairs and the people hiding in the cellar, keeping the bedroom doors closed), and remind him that their ordeal would be over in the morning, when they would be free of their un-welcome guests, and so, thanks to his wife, my father recovered the steadfast frame of mind he had so briefly lost.

She had enabled him to vanquish his discouragement with renewed confidence and a tranquil sense of purpose.

30

The shutters had been closed well before nightfall, but the ever-industrious twins had managed to enlarge a gap between two wooden slats with their penknives, so we were able to watch the officers arrive in their caravan of cars.

Most of them wore black instead of gray-green, and all were resplendent in boots and dress caps, ribbons and medals. The skulls, eagles, oak leaves, sigla, chevrons, emblems, sabers, lions, arms brandishing swords, Gothic SS, swastikas, the colorful badges or strips of braid denoting each man's special branch in the army (orange for the *feldgendarmerie*, golden yellow for the cavalry, red for the artillery), all these decorations embellished those impeccable tunics with sparkling silver buttons, those tight collars, those stiff epaulets, those tailored sleeves, those gleaming shoulder belts. Gloved and close-shaven, the guests gathered on the gravel, chatting among themselves, and the strangely similar faces of this courtly group all wore the same smile.

Watching them, we children didn't feel any particular hatred or attraction. A shiver of fear coursed through us, though, at the idea that these men had come to drink the cases of wine and champagne we'd seen piled up earlier, and that they were going to do this in our house, in our dining room, and that they might "break things." We were intrigued by their air of family resemblance. They all looked like brothers, despite the differences of age, size, and weight, and when I remarked to my own brothers, "That one there is as fat as the Barbiers' pig," Michel replied, "It doesn't matter, they're all alike."

Was it the uniforms, the little death's-heads with the empty eye sockets and grinning jaws, or the silver-pommeled daggers in the leather sheaths hanging from their belts that gave them that identical appearance, or was it perhaps above all that self-confident expression, that affectation of superiority we'd noticed in our resident SS Brigadeführer, which had won him the only nickname we'd found even remotely satisfactory: General Arrogaboche?

Later that evening, Father opened the door to our room and came over to my bed.

"You must go down the back stairs," he told me in a low voice, "and through the garden to the outside door of the laundry room. Knock and let them know who you are. Go inside and tell the Bernhardts that they can take what they want from the food supplies stored down there. Your mother and I forgot to tell them this, so I'm afraid they won't dare touch anything and will be terribly hungry tonight."

In my pajamas and slippers, I went outside by way of the little terrace adjoining our large room—the one with four beds—and did as Father had asked. I wasn't frightened, for I'd seen the officers come in the front door on their way to our dining room, so I was convinced that nothing would happen on the other side of the house. Especially since, at this point in the evening, they'd already been drinking for some time.

"Sit down with us for a minute," said Monsieur Bernhardt, after I'd delivered my message.

"Are there many of them upstairs?" his wife asked.

Their son, Maurice, was a skinny child with brown eyes, curly hair, and pale skin. Wrapped in a dark blue blanket, he stared at me silently.

"About twenty, I think."

All three of them were huddled together in a single mass, perched on the edge of their camp bed in the darkness of the cellar, and I realized that they were afraid. They'd rummaged up some apples and cheese in the storage cupboard, there were lots of cookies in tins, and they'd gotten some water from a tap in the basement, in the big laundry room where I'd seen the pig "fixed" several months earlier. But they weren't eating anything and they barely drank at all, passing around the glazed pitcher to fill some tin mugs, like those we'd used on our summer picnics under the poplars, in more innocent days.

"And what are they doing?"

"We don't know," I replied. "I think they're eating and drinking. Papa told us that their food didn't look tasty at all, but that so far they haven't made much of a mess."

Night had fallen. The only light the Bernhardts had allowed themselves came from a flashlight they'd balanced on its steel handle on the floor. I wanted to say good night and return to my room, but I sensed that my presence comforted them, especially little Maurice, who was still silent, but seemed less anxious than he had when I'd arrived.

"It's time for bed," his father told him.

The Bernhardts laid their son down in his trousers and heavy black sweater, completely dressed except for the clogs they'd carefully placed beneath the cot; then they drew the blue blanket up to his chin.

"Close your eyes and go to sleep," they murmured.

Little Maurice would obey, then open his eyes again within ten seconds. He kept looking at me, as though the small boy before him, in his pretty pajamas and bedroom slippers barely damp from the evening dew, were the buoy to which he clung to avoid sinking into the ocean of approaching night. He kept rubbing his eyes more and more often, and I found myself telling him, "It's all right for you to go to sleep, you know, 'cause my papa's taking care of everything. There's nothing to worry about."

178

Spoken with a certain pomposity (because for the first time in my life I had the exhilarating impression of dominating a child my own age, and of possessing a power that my elders had been able to exercise freely over me, until now), these few words had no instantaneous effect on Maurice. His parents thanked me with a silent nod, and after a few moments the boy did seem to find the repose he had so fiercely resisted with a determination that I knew only too well, and which had quickly made me feel close to him. I was a sympathetic witness to his struggle against the unknown, and thanks to Maurice, I'd just experienced the feeling that one of the twins had expressed in another context a little earlier, in speaking of the German officers: "They're all alike."

And I told myself that Maurice and I were alike, which troubled me, because I didn't know whether I wanted to remain the same person who'd always thought, I'm different from other people, or whether I ought to rejoice in the common identity of all lives, deriving a kind of assurance from this truth, an increase in wisdom. I wondered if it was emotions like these that led to the threshold of that phase I constantly heard so much about, the adventure of "growing up."

Above us, despite the distance that separated the dining room from our refuge in the cellar, we could hear a dull thumping, followed by cries and cheers that turned into singing. There was nothing martial about the songs, which sounded light and frivolous. A single voice, more youthful than the rest, carried the verses, while the others came in as a chorus on the refrain.

"Come, I'll go with you to the door," Monsieur Bernhardt told me.

His wife stayed next to her sleeping son and blew me a kiss. When we reached the first basement level, Monsieur Bernhardt looked up at the ceiling.

"What are they singing?" I asked him. "Do you understand German?"

"Of course. Just let me listen for a minute."

Dora appeared in her bathrobe to join us from behind the thin makeshift curtain of oilcloth that afforded her some privacy in her living quarters. She couldn't stop talking. The role of the mute, retarded housemaid she played during the day made her eager to chatter, to confide in someone. Monsieur Bernhardt managed to stem her flood of words. Then Franck, the engineer-gardener, emerged from the same area of the laundry room, and if I hadn't been completely engrossed in the songs and noise overhead, I might have been able to figure out that Franck was sharing Dora's bed. But I was too preoccupied by what was going on upstairs, and by the spectacle of those Jewish refugees lifting their faces toward the ceiling, whispering in their native language, the same language spoken by the officers on the floor above us. I could tell from their expressions that they recognized a familiar melody.

"What are they singing?" I repeated.

"Oh, nothing, it's always the same stuff," replied Monsieur Bernhardt. "They're very rustic songs, you know, full of forests and peasant girls. They're singing 'Rosemary,' and 'Monika,' and 'Westerwald.' This song goes,

> *In the meadow*
> *Grows a pretty little flower*
> *And her name is Erika.*

Dora unlocked the door to the laundry room and held it ajar. "Go back to your room now," she told me. "Quickly!"

Monsieur Bernhardt gave me a hug and a kiss. "If everything goes well," he said, "we'll be gone before you get back from school tomorrow. We may not see each other again, but I give you a kiss from Maurice, my little boy."

The blue-black sky was spangled with stars. It was a mild night, a long, fragrant, lovely June evening, ripe for indolence and sensual abandon. Reddish-orange lights burst off on the dark horizon over the Tescou Valley; there was a distant crashing and booming noise. A Resistance attack? A bombardment? The explosions were clearly coming from the area around the station and the military depots, which was where they had been concentrated for the most part over the last few months.

I was walking cautiously beneath the spacious terrace when I heard voices overhead. The French windows of the parlor-dining room opened as several officers came out for some fresh air, or had they been drawn by the far-off din of the explosions? They spoke in short, clipped phrases; their voices were tired and hoarse, and I didn't understand their words. One of them coughed, a brusque, moaning cough that ended in violent spasms, and I saw his vomit splatter on the grass in front of me. There were mocking laughs and exclamations; someone applauded. The men kept singing, however, and now the songs were more military, the tone more strident. Drunk or sober, bass or high-pitched, every voice was belting out the current refrain, repeating it to the point of exhaustion. If Monsieur Bernhardt had been with me, he could have translated the "*SS marschiert*":

> The SS are marching
> In the enemy's land
> And they're singing
> The Devil's song.

Standing paralyzed beneath the terrace, I felt sickened at having seen that man throw up, and fascinated by this song that seemed so simple to remember, a tune so catchy you couldn't help feeling like marching in step or clapping in time.

Then the mood was broken by other cries, shouts that sounded like orders. I heard many footsteps and realized that most of the officers had come out onto the terrace. I thought I recognized the voice of our "guest," and after he spoke, an atmosphere of departure suddenly replaced the sounds of ca-

181

rousing, breaking the spell that bound me: I was able to move again, and ran back to my room. Pierre and Michel were waiting for me, standing by the windows, peering through the shutters at the bustling activity among the chauffeurs and aides-de-camp who'd spent the evening bivouacking around the field kitchen.

"Where were you? What took you so long?" asked the twins.

"They're going," I told them.

"Yeah, we know. We watched."

The bedroom door opened.

"So there you are," said Father. "Everything went well?"

"Yes."

"Good. Now back to bed. You must get some sleep."

Engines backfired, men shouted commands, doors slammed, steps hurried along the gravel, motorcycles growled, wheels spat up dirt and pebbles as they crunched along the driveway. I fell asleep very quickly, as though stupefied by the wine that others had drunk.

The next morning, after enjoying the breakfast coffee that had been prepared for him as usual by silent Dora, the SS Brigadeführer left the Villa. The requisition was over. The Romanian chauffeur and the aide-de-camp waited in front of the Mercedes, which carried two steel footlockers in its open trunk. Both men's faces were inscrutable, impassive. Their commanding officer was wearing battle dress and had a parka of black leather thrown over his shoulders. He had retained his cool composure, while my father had abandoned neither his courtesy nor his reserve.

"*Auf Wiedersehen*," said the officer to Father, standing at attention as he saluted him.

"I'm not so sure," replied my father.

"Oh yes," insisted the officer in French. "We will meet again, monsieur."

Then he stepped into his car and was gone. Father hadn't understood what the German had meant with that last remark.

He went to the front gate to watch the car and its motorcycle escort drive away down the hill, away from Haut-Soleil. Then he walked slowly back to the Villa, raking the gravel with his foot, smoothing it out. It was as though he wanted to erase even the tire tracks of the Mercedes. Inside the Villa, the dining room had been hastily cleaned. There were still shards of broken glass lying around, and empty bottles abandoned in their ice buckets, bottoms up. The floor was stained with grease and spilled wine, the chair backs were dirty, and the room reeked of that sour and vaguely fetid smell that nightclubs have when you visit them by day. As if in apology for this botched cleanup job, a bouquet of gladioli had been left on the kitchen table.

There was something strange about the bouquet. It was too thick, the flower stems were sloppily cut, and the whole thing was clumsily wrapped in kraft paper, which gave off a sulfurous odor. Under the bouquet, attached to the wrapping paper with an ordinary straight pin, was an envelope with no name on it.

"It's certainly for the mistress of the house," said Father, handing the envelope to Mother.

"If you say so," she replied, opening it and withdrawing a card that likewise was addressed to no one. Her entire body flinched when she'd deciphered the few words written in German. There was only one sentence: "I have no doubt the Jewess in the kitchen will quickly recover the power of speech." It was signed by the SS Brigadeführer himself.

My father considered the German in his mind's eye: that vaguely Oriental gaze, the pent-up pride, and that little twitch of the upper lip, by the scar. Father wondered if the man had wanted to leave him this message to let us know that he hadn't been fooled, that he'd quickly seen through Dora's disguise, recognizing in the mute housemaid "the Jewess in the kitchen," but that he'd preferred to overlook the deception in exchange —who knows?—for a month and a half of sleeping amid our trees and birds. Father was also afraid that the German, who'd emphasized that "we will meet again," had left instructions with his counterparts in the Gestapo for them to come search the house again. That was why he decided to send Dora, Franck, and "Cousin Jannette" away immediately, at the same time as the Bernhardts, because he feared what he called a "delayed action."

Then, since he was a thinker and naturally came up with all sorts of hypotheses for a given problem, figuring that there was rarely just one completely adequate answer to any question, Father considered the idea that the SS Brigadeführer had wanted to display a certain sadism, and had left the note on the table in the hope of causing trouble, of disturbing our daily life at the Villa with the ambiguity of his cryptic message.

Finally, since he'd been brought up with a love of panache (he could recite for us by heart the great "No thank you" speech from *Cyrano de Bergerac*), and since he liked to believe that the pleasure of making a handsome gesture can tempt even the most unlikely people, my father wondered about the real personality of the man who had lived upstairs in his house. And then he smiled, hoping that his amusement might be mirrored by a faint smile on the face of the general at that very moment, as he led his tanks back across France and into battle. But this illusion was to last only a few days, because my father soon learned, as we did, that during the Germans' march to the front in Normandy, it was a regiment from the Das Reich Division —to which our officer belonged—that had burned an entire town to the ground near Limoges, incinerating its 642 inhabitants: men, women, and children.

And for years afterward we'd wonder if he'd been one of the twenty officers who'd gotten drunk in our dining room, singing their bucolic ditties: Sturmbahnführer Dickmann, whose first battalion had left our little town the same day as our SS Brigadeführer. And we'd wonder if the clear, high voice that had soared above the others to praise the lovely forest of Westerwald had belonged to this mass murderer, whose name would remain forever linked to the name of a certain village, a name fraught with grief and horror, a name that rang like a death knell: Oradour-sur-Glane.

31

The last image I remember from that period is the sight of four pairs of legs swaying beneath dense foliage, under the bright green parasols of the acacias on the main square.

You can see them from far away. The whole town has come by to look. Nobody, really, dares to approach them. People keep their distance. No one says a word.

They're four maquisards who were hanged early that morning from the strongest branches of the two biggest acacias on the square, right across from the Café Delarep, in reprisal for an attack carried out during the night against the German forces. More than a month has passed since the Allied landing in Normandy, but up in the north of France the armies of the Third Reich haven't yet lost enough ground for us to start talking about their defeat, and down in the south, where we are, attacks and counterattacks are on the increase. The repression is growing savage. They're burning houses and farms, sending people to concentration camps, torturing them, shooting them, burying them alive.

It's July, and the weather's very hot. It's summer vacation, so we don't bicycle down to the lycée anymore, and Father has asked us to stay as close as possible to the Villa and its grounds. Our Jewish "visitors" are safely sheltered on the farms.

The rumor has reached all the way up to Haut-Soleil, passed on by the neighbors, or little Murielle, or else the Dark Man, the eternal bearer of news from the town. "There are four hanged men on the square."

My father hesitates. Paul has spoken in a low voice. Father looks at us: the twins, the two girls, and me. He thinks of his two oldest, his absent son and daughter. We're young, but it doesn't take him long to make up his mind. It's his duty to take us along with him.

"The children should see this."

We depart on our bicycles, leaving Mother at the Villa. We've heard what the Dark Man has said. We know exactly why we're following our father down into town. And so, when I pass by the prison at the bottom of the long hill, for the first time I pay no attention to its massive, frightening walls of dirty gray stone. The prospect of "going to see the hanged men" has erased all other emotions in me, replaced all other fears, and although I see from my brothers' somber faces that they share my apprehension, I'm moved as well by a curiosity that is neither unhealthy nor impatient.

I've understood from my parents' tone that this is an obligation, like the end-of-trimester composition or the awards ceremony at the Théâtre Municipal, when we go to get our beribboned prize books and some classmate trots down the red-carpeted center aisle to receive the Prix d'Excellence that I haven't yet managed to win. We children know we're "going to see the hanged men," but we don't know why our father has decided that we should.

We're unaware that he's doing something just as important as when he recommends this or that book to us. We're unaware that, throughout his life, he has championed two rules of conduct: experience as the sole criterion of judgment, and the value of learning by example. But we do know, as we pedal in single file behind his large form, perched on the bicycle of our still-absent brother Antoine, that his presence at the head of our little group brings a special meaning and gravity to the expedition.

When we arrive at the square, he has us get off our bikes and walk over to a white stone bench on which the youngest among us may stand, to see over the heads of the adults.

There are two men on each of the two biggest acacias. Between the trees there's a wooden park bench with iron armrests, where passersby usually like to sit. On the other side of the street is the terrace of the Café Delarep, but today there are no tables, chairs, or customers; the café has closed its doors and pulled the metal shutters down over its windows. A kind of rectangular no-man's-land has thus been created all around the trees and their gruesome burden. An invisible line surrounds the four dangling corpses with an impassable barrier.

People keep arriving, most of them on foot, wearing caps and hats, but they take these off when they get their first glimpse of the bodies swaying gently, heads bowed, arms hanging by their sides, toes pointed toward the ground. I think I recognize the Café Delarep's chief stalwarts in the crowd. There's the Stork, who has wiped that sarcastic look off his face, surrounded by a few of his toadies, all as dumbfounded as he is. The leading citizens, the merchants and patrons of the sports team, seem chastened before the naked spectacle of death, and everything that these four hanged men in civilian clothes represent in the way of past courage. The regulars of the aperitif hour stand abashed before this heavy sacrifice. The loudmouths, always ready with a little vulgar gossip, have grown humble. The more sensitive souls are torn between mute indignation and an urge to flee this nauseating sight. A few women—less numerous than the men—make the sign of the cross over their blouses.

Respectful voices furtively pronounce the victims' names: "André, Michel, Henri, and another André."

Everyday names, ineffably ordinary, names heard on the playground, on the field at the stadium, at the fair on the Allées Malacan, on the Rue Delarep at noon, when girls try to catch your eye, on the railroad-station platform, on the farms at threshing time, or during the grape harvest. Names that, when spoken reverently, one by one, become synonyms of martyrdom.

Only after moving away from the silent center of their attention do the inhabitants dare talk once more, but in a hushed manner, in low voices. With my brothers at my side, I submit to this stillness that so astonishes us in the heart of town, ordinarily bustling with shouts and questions, orders relayed by the café waiters, the rumbling of a few gazogene-powered cars, the noisy passage of an armored convoy, the clicking of the spokes on the wheels of the vélo-taxis, and the chirping of sparrows drawn to the bread crumbs tossed by a few lounging idlers.

From where I stand on the stone bench, I can't see their faces. The shade cast by the tree leaves hides their features, while the sagging position of their heads makes them even more anonymous. One of them is wearing a short-sleeved shirt of a washed-out blue; another has on striped pants; the third is in white; the fourth is still wearing a jacket. They seem young, but hefty, well built. Since the acacias aren't tall, and as the men have been hanged low and close to the trunk, just where the branches begin, their feet almost touch the sidewalk. Struck by their rigidity, I wonder what would happen if someone were to cut the knotted ropes that tie them to the trees; would they perhaps remain standing, turning into statues?

"Children, we're going home," announces Father quietly.

We obey, and slowly remount our bikes to start back through the part of town called La Capelle. It's a long, tiring climb, and about halfway up, there's a little intersection where we usually pause to catch our breath. If you turn around at that point, you can see all of the main square and surrounding area: the town hall and municipal buildings, the café in the background, the beginning of the Allées, and the general post office. Today, however, none of us children wants to observe this ritual, and we would willingly have continued panting to the top of the slope if Father hadn't given us the signal to stop.

"Turn around," he commands us in the same calm voice.

Again, we obey. The acacias are already far away, and it's impossible to distinguish the bodies of the hanged men from the dark mass of the trees. We can just barely make out how the crowd is constantly dispersing, then re-forming with new arrivals, creating a slow-motion fluctuation that when seen from this height reminds me of the drifting shadow of a cloud floating over my favorite valley.

I'm thirsty and bathed in sweat. I sense Father's presence in our midst. He seems to be waiting, without giving us any instruction this time, for us to decide for ourselves when to look away from this sight. Silently I ask myself: What should we write in our Album tonight? What words will we find to describe this? One last time, I look down at the little square speckled with black spots, the gawkers gathered around that empty rectangle in whose center stand the dark green balls of the acacias, screening the corpses from our eyes. In this miniature provincial landscape, trivial and unpromising, like a naive painting, everything finally seems to have stopped moving, and I wish a violent storm would arise and rinse away these deadly colors. But it isn't going to rain, the town is bone-dry, the air is stifling, and Father gives his last order: "Home!"

Twenty-five days later, the town was liberated.

III

Going Up to Paris

32

I rang the bell to Madame Blèze's apartment. She opened the door.

"Madame," I said to her, "I've come to caress your legs."

With a vacant look, she gestured automatically for me to come in, as though she hadn't heard the words I'd been bold enough to say.

I'd hoped she would look as she had a few years earlier, dressed in that black suit with the tight skirt, her legs sheathed in smoke-colored silk, her eyelashes overloaded with mascara, high-heeled pumps on her feet, a round hat set upon her gleaming, fluffy curls. But she was wearing a scarf around her hair, a faded peach peignoir with mauve flowers, and slippers. I'd dreamed of finding her as she'd once seemed to me, exotic and seductive; now she looked like a dull, everyday housewife.

"Who are you, my boy, and what exactly do you want?" she asked me absently.

Then, turning her back to me, she knelt on the parquet floor, trying to close a battered steel trunk crammed so full of clothes and miscellaneous articles that the lid popped back up each time she tried to fasten it down.

"Well, since you're here, come help me," she said, without bothering to turn around.

I knelt beside her, placing my hands on the rebellious lid.

"Perhaps, with two of us, we'll succeed," she remarked.

She seemed completely preoccupied with closing this trunk, and I figured she wouldn't pay attention to anything else until she'd managed to fasten the huge clasps on either side of the thing. I wasn't very pleased with this situation, which wasn't at all what I'd expected, but I reasoned that at least I'd won the first part of my bet, since I'd gotten into Madame Blèze's apartment, and as my buddies downstairs in the street hadn't seen me come back out of the building, they'd probably begun to envy my luck, admire my courage, and fantasize about the unspeakably lewd adventures I was having.

It had all started during one of the Bals de la Libération.

People had begun organizing these public dances after a certain period of transition and uncertainty. There had been scattered gunshots during the first few days, until the Germans pulled out for good. Then the Forces Françaises de l'Intérieur and the Francs-Tireurs et Partisans had staged parades through the town, followed by memorial ceremonies for the heroes who had taken apart a German column that had tried to go through the center of town on the last day of the Occupation. The first black-and-white film of the Allied Forces had begun appearing on newsreels. Then came the long-awaited return of Antoine and Juliette to the Villa. We learned that Paris had been liberated, and there was much more news, in words and images always presented at that exciting moment before the feature film began, when stirring martial music told us that world events were about to unfold before us, and we would see jeeps (which we'd never heard of before) carrying GIs (another first) wearing helmets that were quite different from the German ones, less rough, angular, and aggressive, more rounded, and these smooth-faced men would let themselves be kissed by people in the streets of the Capital, as they handed out little flat objects that the lucky recipients then took from their paper wrappers and stuffed into their mouths, chewing ecstatically.

August was over; September had arrived, warm and heavy with all sorts of promises. I felt as though my entire life had been made new again, for now I was old enough to make plans, to look forward to the vintage season, when I'd trample the Chasselas grapes with my bare feet and play around with my "fiancées" at Le Jougla, and soon we'd be going back to school, where I would finally cross that invisible barrier into "the big kids' playground." We questioned Antoine eagerly, but he was modestly reluctant to tell us about his few months spent in caves and on farms with the maquisards.

"Did you kill someone? Did you kill any Germans?"

"No. I didn't kill anyone."

Actually, because of his youth, he'd helped mainly with communications and provisioning. We were also delighted to hear, through the open window of her "liberated" room, our Juliette tackling Scriabin and Diabelli on her piano again. She'd made some progress with her teacher in Toulouse.

"If only I could go study in Paris!" she confided to Mother.

For a while we would hear sustained bursts of gunfire deep down in the valley. This dry, brutal sound marked the summary executions of traitors or murderers, carried out by a "purification committee." And although our father had taken us "to see the hanged men," he did not allow us to go observe these firing squads at work in the Barbiers' field, with an audience of a few farmers or townspeople who'd bicycled out to watch.

"That's not the right way to bring them to justice," he'd say.

And then the Dark Man would start shouting at him: "The bastards must pay! You know perfectly well it was inevitable! How can you allow them to get away with what they did? They had it coming!"

"Why should I condemn one crime, then turn around and excuse another?" Father would reply.

They'd returned to their ritual discussions after the evening meal, and with the same vehemence, each one happily egging the other on for the simple pleasure of having a good argument. Unbeknown to us, they'd checked with everyone they knew and all their networks, they'd asked at every farm seeking news of Diego, fearing to learn that the easily recognizable figure of the guerrilla fighter in boots and riding breeches had been seen hanging from a tree before the Germans had left—but nothing came of their inquiries. So they abandoned their whispered conversations about this reminder—no sooner here than gone—of their younger days.

And now that the greatest dangers seemed past, their conversations were no longer so shrouded in mystery; more and more often we found ourselves allowed to sit in a circle around their armchairs, to follow these duels in which humor and witty caricature were mixed with political and literary references.

Above all, however, we were attracted by a spectacle that we knew wouldn't last out the autumn: the so-called Bals de la Libération.

Although they went by this rather grandiose name, they were really a series of neighborhood parties held in broad daylight at street intersections or traffic circles, sometimes organized overnight, and more often by the residents themselves than by any municipal authority. A kind of stage would be set up, where a skimpy band of accordionists would take their places, and when no musicians were available, loudspeakers blared music from a phonograph. Garlands of multicolored paper were hung up, along with the decorations for the July 14 Bastille Day dances, which hadn't been held for several years. Shopkeepers would improvise a refreshments stand, while people danced in the streets and on the sidewalks in the late-summer sunshine, in an atmosphere of joyous reunion. Near the center of the festivities, there would almost always be a caravan of gypsies, whose expressions, habits, and costumes intrigued us enormously. Around their bizarrely colored van you could have your fortune told, or buy nougat, boxes of magic powder, and individual cigarettes. It was there, on the sly, that I smoked my first Naja, which tasted of pepper and honey.

We'd go to the ball on our bikes, led by Mother and our father—who seemed to have abandoned his customary aloofness, to everyone's surprise, for he shook hands and chatted with his fellow citizens, deigning to make small talk with the "puppets" he'd so often disparaged. But he would never stay long. He had really come to see if the atmosphere was "suitable," so that he might confidently leave his band of girls and boys in their mother's care. After raising a convivial glass of muscatel, he would slip back to the Villa to shut himself up in his office, where he and an accountant would labor over the books kept during the years of the Occupation. We had no idea that the farms and their upkeep had just about ruined him.

I liked watching the dances as much as I liked taking part in them. I envied my oldest brother when I'd see him twirling girls around, and sometimes he'd swing them overhead, crouching down for them to land on his back or on his upper thighs, in those syncopated, acrobatic moves young people his age had picked up in no time after their first exposure to swing through newsreels showing the latest dance craze in liberated Paris. The Stork had provided a few of his most precious records. He bragged of how quickly a friend from Marseilles had managed to get him early hits played by the Glenn Miller and Benny Goodman orchestras. He didn't dance, however, and seemed neurotically shy in front of the young women out on the improvised dance floor.

I joined the throng of dancers, trying to imitate Antoine as well as to assuage my growing need for contact with other people's bodies, my desire to claim my little share of love and rejoicing. The signal for dancing couples to change partners would be given by a drumbeat or, if there was no drum around, by a strident blast on a bulb horn. Children would dance together, and I held little Murielle tight, as though the street parties and their customs had allowed me to exorcise my longtime fear of my perverse girl-next-door. But she brought my newfound enthusiasm up short.

"You don't interest me anymore," she announced, pushing me forcefully away.

A gangling man with slicked-down hair, a red nose, and a

drooping lower lip stood on the stage with a Basque beret draped rakishly over one ear; although he had no shirt on, he wore a white wool jacket and a bow tie as he warbled "*La Romance de Paris.*"

> *Who knows if love will last through tomorrow?*
> *Sometimes one finds happiness in sorrow.*

"What's the matter? You don't want to anymore?" I asked Murielle, upset by her reaction.

She made a nasty face and answered me in a strong accent that dragged out the final *e* on her words.

"Nothing's wrong. You were-eu a lot more-eu funny when you didn't want it. Now that you do, I don't want to anymore-eu."

She walked off in the middle of the dance and left me standing there. Whom could I have asked to explain my little neighborhood Carmen's "*Si tu ne m'aimes pas, je t'aime*"? Pauloto, the Dark Man, wasn't there to decipher, with cynical and blasé laughter, the capricious twists and turns of the female mind.

Far from discouraging me, this rejection increased my longing: I did "want it," and before the afternoon was over I meant to win a kiss, a wave, or even just a smile from a woman. I ended up back at the foot of the stage with two classmates from the lycée, the self-effacing Bonazèbe and the priceless Pécontal, alias Short-Ass. We were intoxicated by the shrill cries of the women dancers whose bare legs swung high over their partners' shoulders, by the heady smell of the white wine from the nearby refreshments table, by the sight of all those grownups entwined in each other's arms, by those lingering kisses, by the men's strong hands around the women's waists, sometimes even cupping their buttocks, and by the haunting refrain:

> *It gives the hearts of those in love*
> *A chance to dream, blue skies above.*

The scent of jasmine and withered grass, wafting up from the riverbank close by, added to the sensuality of the atmosphere.

"I'm all excited!" shrieked Pécontal.

"Me, too!" chorused Bonazèbe and I.

We started trying to top one another with different boasts and challenges. Pécontal told us he'd shown his penis to his girl cousin the day before, behind the gypsy wagon, and that she'd touched it. Bonazèbe swore he had a romantic "rendezvous" with the baker's daughter after the ball, and that she would definitely touch his. Our excitement grew with each burst of braggadocio.

"And me, I bet you I can touch Madame Blèze's legs," I announced, to my own astonishment.

The dance was being held on a corner of the Allées Malacan, at the edge of the neighborhood where the lovely modiste lived. We were only a few minutes' walk from her apartment.

"You can't do it!" they sneered.

The bet was on. We took off, after telling those in charge of us that we were going to "stroll over to the main square." My two acolytes were unaware that I'd been waiting for this chance, hoping for this excuse. For some time, I'd longed ardently to see once again the lady who had awakened my sexual feelings, whose memory had stirred me one night—quite recently—as I slept, flushed and dreaming a new kind of dream that had ended in deliciously moist embarrassment.

Climbing the stairs to Madame Blèze's apartment, I thought I could still hear the taunts of my two "excited" companions. They'd promised they'd wait for me downstairs. As my heart pounded away, I repeated to myself the phrase I'd decided to say as soon as she opened the door. A feeling of danger goaded me on. I'd carried messages on my bike during the Occupation. I'd listened one night, motionless beneath the terrace at the Villa, to the songs of the SS. I'd heard the sinister bursts of retributive gunfire in the field at the bottom of the hill. I'd listened to

Antoine's stories about his nights on guard outside the entrance to the caves of the maquisards. Life was nothing but danger, fear, trials, obstacles, explosions, sensational events! But ringing the doorbell of the beautiful Madame Blèze was the most thrilling adventure of all.

33

The lid of the trunk refused to close. Madame Blèze seemed to consider the problem, then gave me a quick nod as she made up her mind. Without makeup, her face seemed young, pale, with hollow cheeks and tired, reddened eyes. There was still something about her that set her apart from the local women, however, a different way of playing up her charms—her pouty, coaxing expressions, her quivering chin, and her too rapidly batting eyelashes, like the wings of dragonflies I would chase through the garden at the Villa.

"I'm going to sit on it, with all my weight," she said, "and as soon as you think it's closed enough, snap those two locks shut."

She stood up and settled herself squarely on the metal trunk, her hands placed flat on the cover at her sides, while I remained kneeling before the trunk, so I was looking straight at her legs, which were within kissing distance. Even though Madame Blèze wasn't all decked out in her alluring dressy black suit, this sudden proximity banished my disappointment and rekindled the feverish excitement of my dreams. I felt the same temptation as before.

"Is it closed?"

"Ah . . . I'm not sure."

"Well, at least try! What are you waiting for?"

Her idea had worked, and I easily closed each latch and then slipped its padlock through the ring. But I did this slowly, savoring the intimacy that had been established between us, consumed by painful anxiety over what was to come. The front panel of the peach-colored peignoir had slipped to one side, revealing more flesh, the slender shins, the beginning of the knees. I would have liked to remain at the feet of that lovely lady for a long time, feasting my eyes on the skin of her legs and the material of her peignoir, which I also wanted to feel, and that disturbed me, although it shouldn't have.

Because I loved the material as well as the flesh, just as, a few years before, it had been the black silk of her stockings as much as the legs they enclosed that had aroused my curiosity. If I hadn't been so thwarted by my own ignorance, I would have caressed her through her clothing; as an adult, I would not have desired her, had she been naked. But I was unable to make up my mind and carry out my pretentious wager with my friends: "I bet I can touch her legs." There they were, right there; all I needed to do was stretch out my fingers—just my fingers, not even my whole hand. I didn't dare, though; fear triumphed over eagerness.

"You can get up now," she told me.

I obeyed. Madame Blèze remained sitting on the trunk. I stepped back. For the first time since she'd opened her door to me, I was able to notice my surroundings. Much of the furniture had been removed from the room we were in; the rugs had been rolled up, and hatboxes of various colors had been piled on the floor. In the middle of the room was a bergère with bronze and pink cushions, and a dainty table on which stood an empty vase with a long neck, a beautiful thing of deep purple glass embellished with opaline flowers and intertwined plants. A few pieces of newspaper were lying on the gleaming parquet floor.

"You see," said Madame Blèze, as if she'd just glanced around the room with me, "you see, I'm leaving."

And she gave a harsh, bitter laugh.

"Where are you going, madame?" I asked.

"I'm going back to Paris. Have you been to Paris?"

I shook my head. She was still sitting on the trunk, and I was standing facing her, with the bergère and the table behind me. She seemed to have lost that sluggish, vacuous appearance that had so struck me when she'd let me in her apartment, as though some of her natural coquetry and verve had been restored by her success in finally closing that enormous trunk, over which she might have been struggling by herself for a good while in her bare little apartment. Her solitude and apparent weariness were no less pronounced, however, and I noticed that even though she'd been surprised to see me, she was now loath to have me leave.

"What's your name?" she asked.

I saw that I would have to answer, despite my fear that word of my outlandish prank might somehow reach my parents, and however friendly and reassuring her tone, I was afraid that she might keep asking more and more pointed questions.

"I didn't quite catch what you said to me when you rang my doorbell. Why did you come here?"

In a flash, I see how deep a hole I've dug for myself. My two randy chums waiting outside (and probably wondering what's taking so long) and my own initial sensual excitement are now the last things on my mind. I don't say a word, but Madame Blèze isn't easily put off.

"Answer me," she insists, gently but firmly.

I decide to lie. I can feel my cheeks burn, as they always do whenever I betray the truth.

"I came to say goodbye to you from my parents."

Her smile isn't very reassuring; it seems suspicious and naughty. "Oh, really? And why did they send you instead of coming themselves?"

"Uh . . . They're very busy."

Her smile broadens, becomes more mystifying, seems about to explode into laughter.

"You're lying," she tells me. "That's not very nice. I heard perfectly well what you said to me a little while ago."

It's as though she were playing with me, amusing herself, if only for a moment. In that same frail and cajoling voice that had captivated me when I saw her sitting in my father's office, crossing and uncrossing her legs, when I listened to her simpering and complaining in the same breath, Madame Blèze speaks the words I had hoped not to hear, since I'm now just as ashamed and embarrassed as I am terrified of my future punishment, when all this comes out—for I've no doubt she'll go "squeal" to my family.

"You're lying!" she repeats. "You told me you'd come to caress my legs."

Before I can protest, she wriggles her shoulders and lets out a deep, throaty laugh. "Well then," she says, "why don't you do what you came for? Come here."

When I hesitate, she holds out a hand, fingertips bright with polish, inviting me to come closer. Once more I feel a sense of danger, the desire to do something forbidden.

"Come on," she murmurs.

I take two steps toward her. Docile, torn between uneasiness and the promise of a pleasure I've often dreamed about, I reach out cautiously for one of her legs.

"You're allowed to touch," she assures me, "since I say so."

Timidly I draw my hand up over her ankle, grazing the softness of the peignoir, and as my fingers glide slowly over the young woman's skin, I don't dare look into her eyes.

She's wise enough to have sensed my qualms, however, and with the same hand that brought me to heel, she grasps the tip of my chin and lifts up my face. Her fingers are cold and bony, guided by a hidden strength.

"Look at me," she says, with a certain brusqueness. "Don't be embarrassed: do like all the others and look at me."

Taken aback by those last words, but under the spell of her command, I look at Madame Blèze. She begins to smile, when her face suddenly contracts in pain, while, at the same instant, big tears spill from her eyes, making me think—I don't know why—of the transparent drops of liquid glue I like to dribble decoratively over the covers of my school notebooks. This latest unexpected turn of events is the most surprising of all; shaken, I draw back my hand, which had reached the young woman's knee under her peignoir. Her tears keep falling, disfiguring Madame Blèze, who sobs wretchedly, burying her face in her hands. Once again, as when I first entered her apartment, I have the feeling I'm no longer of the slightest importance to her. I can't believe that I'm the one causing her so much sorrow.

Disoriented and completely baffled by such unsettling extremes of behavior, I beat a retreat. In my haste, I bump into the little table behind me. The empty vase with the long neck falls to the floor and breaks. Then I hear Madame Blèze's weeping turn into a scream of shock, a piercing sound I fear may rouse the whole building and cause crowds to gather in the street.

"The Gallé! He's broken the Gallé!"

What is she talking about? What is a Gallé? I've obviously just done something more reprehensible than my efforts to touch her legs, because she keeps shouting this unknown name ever faster and louder in mounting hysteria.

"My Gallé! He's broken my Gallé! My Gallé! My Gallé!"

My sense of duty overcomes my panic, and instead of fleeing, I crouch down to collect the broken pieces of the vase lying on the parquet.

"But it's not that bad, Madame Blèze," I say, trying to put a stop to her screams. "It's nothing, it can be fixed!"

To prove my point, I hold out to her the fragments of the neck of the vase. There are only two; the rest is intact. I'm sure the object can be repaired, and I keep telling her this with passionate conviction, but since crying is contagious, I can no longer contain the tears building up inside me. I've made a very stupid mistake—several, in fact. My inability to face the next

205

five minutes of my life and to take control of a situation that I can't even begin to understand makes me regress to that childhood I never should have left in my attempt to satisfy my budding sensuality. Sitting cross-legged on the floor, holding the broken vase, I weep, my head hanging, waiting for I don't know what punishment: the appearance of my father, the shrill blast of policemen's whistles, or the tumultuous arrival of dancers from the street party to mock and condemn me. Nothing happens, though, and Madame Blèze has stopped shrieking. There is silence once again. Looking up, I can see that she's still sitting motionless in the same position on her trunk.

"Go away," she tells me in a faint voice. "Go on, go away now. It's over. I'm not mad at you."

Then she stands up and undoes the scarf that was wrapped around her hair. When she shakes her head vigorously a few times, her curls tumble about her shoulders, as soft and black as they were the first time I saw her. Now I look at the tearstains on her cheeks, her breast heaving beneath the open neck of the peignoir, the eyes that seem to gaze beyond the little boy, the ruined Gallé, the untidy apartment, and even beyond that small town where she doesn't belong and where she has spent—in what circumstances, at the cost of what compromises, sacrifices, obligations—four years of loneliness, of clandestine or abortive love affairs, of pettiness, humiliation, privation, and she has already left, for she sees herself tomorrow, on the narrow platform of the little railroad station where sneering men will ogle her one last time, that svelte "Parisienne," before she vanishes with her delicate veils, her distress, her many secrets, and her hatboxes, and then I find this woman moving, beautiful, worthy of being loved, extravagantly admired, and embraced, and I would like to tell her I'm sorry, to give her my thanks, but I know in my heart that she is now and forever beyond my reach.

"Go away," she repeats.

And I do, still numbly clutching those two broken pieces of the Gallé.

34

Around that same time, but a little later, Sam came into our lives.

He was a young teacher of French and Latin who was so homely that he was both ridiculous and endearing. He reminded us of a bird in one of our *Fables de La Fontaine*, "the heron whose long beak sits atop a long neck." There was something of the grasshopper about him as well. He swam in clothes too large for his flimsy body; he had a pointed nose and owlish, protruding eyes that seemed to stare fixedly from behind his glasses. Sam's true singularity, however, lay in his voice. The first time he addressed our sixth-grade class, a little wiseacre whispered, "Hey, you'd think it was a girl talking."

The timbre of his speech contained not a single deep note, and when he impatiently tried raising his voice to make himself better heard over the inevitable racket provoked by his incongruous looks and bearing, he sounded like a soprano having her throat cut. His protuberant Adam's apple bounced up and down like a crazed yo-yo each time he tried to exercise his authority over some rebellious dunce in the back of the class. This verbal crescendo, along with his glottal agitation and rolling eyeballs, gave such an impression of extreme tension and high-pitched irritation that you might have thought he lived in a permanent state of utter indignation. After a few more days of observation, the little smart aleck, whose initial opinion had been echoed by many others in the class, added a fresh assessment of the newcomer: "This chicken's only half-baked."

Sam had delicate, pink, hairless hands with abnormally long nails that seemed to preoccupy him greatly, since he often studied them with almost finicky absorption. Over his vast forehead hung a glossy lock of hair that looked artificially arranged. A person like that was easy prey for caricature and wisecracks, but Sam was soon to surmount the handicap of his ugliness through his sparkling intelligence, his sense of humor, and his generosity toward his students. After only a few weeks it became clear that he spent more time than the other teachers helping pupils who had difficulties with their work, that he had a gift for spotting and nurturing each boy's special talent or vocation, and, that thanks to his teaching skills and the imaginative ways in which he explained the mysteries of a dead language or the subtleties of a living one, he was able to win over to literature and the humanities the most obtuse of boys, the worst ignoramuses, and even the little hayseeds fresh from struggling with their ABCs in village schoolrooms.

He loved idiotic puns; he encouraged us to express ourselves and had us act out short sketches drawn from Courteline and Labiche; he introduced us to poets largely unknown at that time and place, such as Cocteau, Desnos, Apollinaire; he brushed away the cobwebs of boredom our previous teachers had spun around authors whose genius now shone brightly: Corneille, Racine, Boileau, La Fontaine, du Bellay, Ronsard. It wasn't long before "going to Sam's class" had become an eagerly anticipated pleasure, and although at first we had participated in the cruel jokes and allusions made about him, we wound up defending him in the halls of the lycée and doing battle with those who dared suggest there was anything wrong with him. We called him Sam from the very first day; we'd never before encountered a first name like that, one so uncommon, so casual. Those three

simple letters fitted him perfectly, however, because he was comical and unusual. He took his teaching seriously, while seeking
constantly to astonish and amuse us as we learned.

"My name is Sam Palmiran," he announced to us by way of
an introduction, "and I'm not going to waste my time asking
you to call me 'monsieur,' because I know you'll all call me Sam
behind my back, which doesn't bother me, because I'm very
proud of the name my mother gave me. So call me Sam, even
if that doesn't sit too well with the academic higher-ups who
run this place."

As far as we knew (and that went for our elders as well), this
was the first time we'd been allowed to call a teacher by his
given name, just as though he were a friend or relative, and we
were so enthusiastic about it that the news soon spread throughout the playgrounds and neighboring classrooms. It wasn't long
before Sam acquired a reputation as an avant-gardist, and his
colleagues—who were mostly older than he was, as well as
hidebound by the traditions of the times and the limitations of
our antiquated establishment—might have become jealous if
they hadn't also been won over by this singular young man's
love of teaching and devotion to hard work. His entire life
seemed to revolve around those he called his "dear students,"
never once forgetting, even when they'd performed abysmally
in both effort and discipline, to put the adjective "dear" before
the word "student."

And when his fellow teachers went home after work to their
families or their usual routines, in the small town that had
returned to the cozy rhythms of its prewar days, Sam left the
lycée on his bicycle to make the rounds of the "private lessons"
he'd kindly decided to give those children whose performance
he hoped to improve. It was hours before he'd return, late at
night, to his bachelor quarters, a room he rented in the home
of a married couple, both doctors, on Rue des Sarrazins. There
he'd have a couple of rusks, a few grapes, and a shot of Heptyl-
Bourdou, a medicinal brew with a slightly alcoholic taste that

left him vaguely tipsy, and perhaps temporarily blunted his awareness of his destitute surroundings. Then he would go to bed, spending the night in insomnia, reading Gide, Martin du Gard, Giraudoux, Mauriac, when he wasn't correcting the papers (propped up on his knees) of his "dear students," the dearest of whom—his "carissime," as he soon called him—was me.

As a matter of fact, he'd taken a liking to me from my very first excursions up to the blackboard, when I'd surprised him with my flair for reciting poetry and my penchant for histrionics, which I seemed to develop as I grew older. He'd been impressed by the doggerel verses I'd composed, on the advice of my father, to enliven a routine homework assignment. He moved me up to the front row. He'd become my new hero; I'd already forgotten his ugliness, and saw only his zeal, his sense of humor, the effort he put into teaching us. In his classroom, I was always happy and eager to learn. I considered his physical anomalies rather picturesque, and while he irritated me with his exaggerated propensity to fawn over my slightest achievement, I was captivated by his original way of talking, his style.

People referred to him, at the time, as a "free spirit." My father wanted to see this strange bird with his own eyes. His friend Paul had already started winking suggestively as he passed on the local rumors, in this town so enamored of strength and virility, about the young man with a woman's voice and an excessive interest in little boys. The gossipmongers of the Café Delarep had found a fresh subject for their off-color musings. We decided to invite Sam up to Haut-Soleil for Sunday dinner.

He wore a double-breasted suit in an imitation Prince-of-Wales check, a suit so ill cut and ill proportioned to his slender form that, as Father watched him arrive, he murmured with a smile, "But he's Foottit—without Chocolat!"

He seemed to approve, however. We'd long since gotten used to Father's decided taste for eccentric characters, which he'd passed on to us. How many of them had already traipsed through our lives? Igor Tolstoy and his saber, Justin Case with his pouch of diamonds, Dr. Sucre wearing his bicycle clips, even Father's favorite sparring partner, the Dark Man, with his pig-smuggling Phaeton. By comparing Sam to Foottit, one of a famous pair of circus clowns from days gone by, Father had added Sam then and there to our private world of pet names and symbols. I was reassured, because I'd been afraid my "teach" wouldn't meet the rigorous standards of my family and the Villa, since I'd gathered from the students' vulgar jokes and the sly looks of the adults that Sam was not "like other people."

> *"Here are fruits, flowers, leaves and boughs.*
> *And take my heart as well, for it beats only for you,*

ladies!" declaimed Sam, reciting Verlaine with dramatic fervor.

From a basket attached to his bicycle's baggage rack, he had taken a mixed bouquet that had probably cost him half a month's salary. He placed it at the feet of my mother and Juliette, who burst out laughing and then applauded the bow that closed his performance, for he waved his arm around his head as though he were doffing and flourishing a felt slouch hat in the manner of a sixteenth-century marquis.

"So far, so good," remarked Michel, the twin who was always ready to comment dryly on events with a few choice words.

After the usual generalities, we sat down to dinner: tomatoes and Quercy sausage, leg of lamb with flageolets, cheese, and floating island for dessert. Sam tackled his food so voraciously that Father exclaimed, "Good Lord, one would think you hadn't eaten in ten days!"

The ensuing silence suggested that Father had come closer to the truth than he realized. Sam kept up a running barrage of compliments on Mother's cooking, and each time he praised her culinary skills, he added a flattering remark for Juliette, as though endeavoring to charm the women of the household and so curry favor with his stern, white-haired host, who was observing him, sizing him up—at first circumspect, then won over, for it was hard to resist our dear loony-bird's chatter and little ways for long.

It was clear from the beginning that Sam was happy among us—as though he'd waited a very long time to be welcomed by some group or another—and he expressed this happiness by stepping up the pace of his jokes, dithyrambs, and hyperboles. He seemed to have found himself a family, and for our part, we adopted him just as spontaneously. The twins watched him devour the leg of lamb, and followed, wide-eyed, the acrobatics of his lower lip, or his curious way of keeping his left hand closed in a fist on the table with only the thumb sticking up, not to mention the endless voyage of his Adam's apple up and down his scrawny neck.

Father decided to put his guest's literary knowledge to the test. The two men began a contest of quotations, feeding each other cues, a match in which the words of Victor Hugo came cheek by jowl with the *Contrerimes* of Paul-Jean Toulet. It was an astonishing dialogue between two such contradictory beings: the one amused and stimulated by his guest's pirouettes—and the other anxious to win the respect and esteem of his host. Only Antoine seemed unimpressed by Sam's pyrotechnics.

"Your little brother has told me that you play the piano," said Sam to Juliette after dinner. "Perhaps we two could give a small concert."

"Willingly," she replied. "But we'll have to go upstairs to my room."

Sam chuckled throatily.

"As long as your mother and father see no impropriety in my crossing the threshold of a girl's bedroom!"

Father couldn't help hooting with laughter. "I really don't see any danger!"

Sam took the reply in good part, as though he expected as much. Rising from the dinner table, he announced with regal disdain and bravura, "We'll leave the door open!"

He had come for Sunday dinner but stayed with us the whole day. First he went upstairs with Juliette, where we heard him tinkling out idiotic operetta tunes on the piano.

> *"I'm a gentleman," I informed the duke,*
> *"And would make a good match for your daughter fair."*
> *But His Grace begged to differ, with a stern rebuke,*
> *And fixed his eye on me with a disapproving air.*

Juliette would pick up the song, convulsed with laughter, because Sam's high voice was already perched at heights almost unbearable for the human ear. Later Sam took the younger boys and girls out into the garden for a session of hide-and-seek enlivened by forfeits and punctuated by time-outs during which he made us chant after him, with increasing speed,

> *Oh, you can't*
> *Oh, you can't*
> *Oh, you absolutely can't*
> *Squish an ant!*

Or a little bit of Offenbach:

> *What a tremolo!*
> *Presto, presto!*
> *Largo, largo!*
> *Pizzicato, pizzicato!*

Or snippets of rousing verse from all over, snatches of Dumas, Corneille, whatever sprang to mind:

> *Array him once more in his white uniform!*

Or:

> *We shall meet again at the Tour de Nesles!*

213

And:

> *We were just five hundred strong, but help was on the way . . .*

With these bits of bombast, Sam dramatized different moments in our games, victories by one side or another. We pounced on all his sallies and repeated them later, after his departure, to make them a part of our family vocabulary. We had discerned in Sam the same proclivities we loved in our parents: a taste for literary quotations, allusions, and words requiring explanations that blossomed into anecdotes and true stories. And even though Father later carefully pointed out to us, with his fine sense of judgment, what was superficial and scattershot about Sam's education, we had to admit that this strange bird was a charmer, and we resolved to invite him again for Sunday leg of lamb.

That first day he stayed for supper and even later, until the Dark Man arrived for his daily conversation with Father and found "the Oddity," as he was instantly to baptize him, busy teaching my sisters one of La Fontaine's fables in a version that had gone haywire:

> *A jay puts on his hack and bed*
> *Feathers a moulting sheacock ped,*
> *Thinking this will he a bandy*
> *Way to play the dack-a-jandy.*

Giving Father a look of commiseration, Paul loudly announced, "Here you are, joking around with this clown, when you should be concerned with the state of the world!"

He'd decided to join the "Friends of the U.S.S.R." Father disapproved violently, because he remained a fierce individualist, convinced that people are blind to the lessons of History. In the rapidly chilling Cold War climate that followed the Nazi capitulation and the division of the world into new opposing camps, the two friends had found an inexhaustible subject to nourish their vital arguments. Where my skeptical father saw the birth of a new totalitarianism, the Dark Man spoke of glorious tomorrows. One name kept turning up in their discussions, a man whom the youngest among us quickly identified as the bogeyman of the new era just dawning: Stalin! A fabled name, two syllables that sounded—depending on how Father or Paul pronounced them—like a threat or a promise.

35

As the seasons and semesters went by, Sam's Sunday visits became so routine that there was no longer any need to send him an invitation.

He would arrive a few minutes before dinner, always bearing a present (a fancy cake, some cut flowers, a box of chocolates, a pack of colored pencils), earning himself a "Sam, you shouldn't have" from my mother, which he answered with a "My pleasure, madame." There was always one of us youngsters around to trumpet the news of his arrival before he'd even gotten off his bike.

"We'll have to set another place at the table! One for Sam! Just one!"

Then Sam would mutter peevishly, pursing his lips into a massive pout, "Thanks so much."

Because he knew what nicknames had been bestowed upon him by us children: the Freeloader, the Sponger, or Our Friend Ozoire, after a character in a novel who was always getting himself invited to stay for dinner, according to Father. Sam realized, however, that we meant no harm with our teasing, and between our family and Sam the Unusual, Sam the Bizarre, the "confirmed bachelor," the effeminate loner, there had sprung up an affectionate and entirely unconventional bond based on mutual understanding and shared intellectual interests. Later, during our school vacation, he even spent several days with us in a house we rented in Hossegor, near Biarritz. With us children he played the role of a kindly tutor, helping ease the difficulties of studying dead languages, encouraging us to read and take pains with our writing, accompanying Juliette at the piano, going over the texts for the coming *baccalauréat* exam with Antoine, who had succumbed in the end to the Oddity's singular charm. Sam was an explorer as well, for he took us out to the movies more often, and to the theater, which was one of his passions, taking us on the train all the way to Toulouse so that we could see works that were "up-to-date": plays by Sartre, Giraudoux, Anouilh.

That was one of his favorite expressions: "I'm going to give you a little taste of something up-to-date," he'd say. "It'll make a nice change from all those classics your father shoves down your throats."

For he enjoyed parodying the famous literary quarrel between the ancients and the moderns, reproaching Father (with the utmost unctuosity) for what he called his literary conservatism, while Father made fun of Sam for his "fads." When Sam mentioned Cocteau, my father brought up Diderot, and trotted out Molière to face down Sacha Guitry. My father's taste in literature stopped well before Proust, whereas Sam swore by him, as well as Gide and a few other more recent novelists.

"But, monsieur, how can a man of your learning fail to appreciate such works?" Sam would fume, with that look of perpetual indignation on his thin, pop-eyed face.

"That's enough, Sam," my father would reply. "Stop your preaching."

Sam would blush and preen, doing his offended-coquette act. He took real pleasure in their pretend arguments and fully understood—from having silently observed the great political debates between Father and the Dark Man—that discussion was an exercise indispensable to my father's health; that dialectics,

like maieutics, were as invigorating and enriching for him as
listening to symphonic music is for some people. And arguing
about cultural matters with this quinquagenarian born in the
previous century allowed Sam to play a part in our lives, gave
him the feeling of being accepted, of being just like everyone
else, when all his life he'd been mocked and rebuffed, enduring
that perverse segregation provincial society could still inflict, in
those days, on people who were too different, lonely souls with
hidden and hopeless desires.

Our trips to Toulouse for a taste of "up-to-date" cultural life
(and for a taste of the spectacular iced coffee and whipped-
cream concoctions served on the terrace of the Grand Café
l'Albrighi) introduced us to the apartment on Rue Nazareth that
was Sam's real home. His elderly grandmother lived there, and
he joined her two or three times a week, traveling by train from
our little town. He was one of the "Toulousains," a slim con-
tingent of teachers in our lycée who would return to the big
city, if their schedules permitted, at the end of the school day.
Sam's life was divided between his room in town and his grandmother's home in Toulouse. We knew nothing about his mother
or father, and he kept so stubbornly silent about them that it
was impossible not to feel even more curious about his real
nature, and his mysterious solitude.

There were shadowy sides to the personality of my teacher
and friend that I didn't understand. Like the rest of the town's
inhabitants, I took part in the jokes made behind his back, I
listened to the cruel things that were said about him, and was
amused to notice with my brothers that, while on vacation with
us, Sam would change his clothes only in private and had never
dared show himself in a bathing suit.

"Maybe there's nothing at all underneath," one of the twins
had suggested.

And although we giggled at that remark, we knew we couldn't
repeat it in front of our parents, who had adopted a protective
and tolerant attitude toward Sam. Woe to any stranger who

might make fun of "the Family Friend" in front of them! I was
ashamed to have laughed at the mean things people said about
him, because although his features and gestures were almost
grotesquely strange, and his voice was that of a castrato, and
his clothes were so big that they made his clumsy body seem as
though a brisk puff of wind might scoop him up from the platform of the Matabiau railroad station and sail him over the
pink-tiled roofs, like the scarecrows in the cornfields of the
Garonne valleys, I had recognized in him the pure, trembling
soul of a frustrated artist, and had seen that he was a creature
with "tenderness enough and to spare," as my mother said, with
the keen intuition of her own sweet nature.

In any case, I loved him—discreetly, because I could tell that
the outside world had singled him out, mistrusting him because
he was different, but I also felt a secret admiration for his cosmopolitan spirit, which opened so many new doors for me:
"The Theater!" "Writing!" "Gérard Philipe!" "Picasso!" I felt
compassion as well, for one couldn't help feeling sorry for him
when he set out down the Villa's drive on his bike, heading
back to that tiny room in town where nothing awaited him but
the ghost of his own childhood, and the dizzying sensation, as
he gazed into his mirror, of his own helplessness and fatigue.

For Sam was exhausted, drained, old before his time. Something was wrong with him, something hard to pin down, a
congenital weakness that drove him to collapse fully clothed on
his bed as soon as he got home, to recover the energy he'd
squandered so extravagantly in clowning around, making us
laugh, loving and making himself loved by his "dear students,"
his "carissime," and this family that brought him so much happiness, but for whose sake he tried too hard never to be boring
or disappointing, and gave so much of himself! Then he would
have coughing fits, even spitting up a little blood. He'd feel his
legs give way beneath him, or his hands lose their strength and
grow numb.

His head would spin. He'd take off his glasses. He'd think,

Take a deep breath: breathe, Sam my boy, and get a grip on yourself. Time would pass. The little Jaz alarm clock on the wobbly bedside table ticked off the minutes of emptiness and despair. He thought back over his day. He'd run around too much with the children on the gravel, waved his hands and arms too much in the discussion with Monsieur and that Dark Man who looked upon him, Sam knew, with a pitiless eye, and he'd had too many helpings of custard at dessert—why was he so compulsively greedy? Now he was sure he was going to lose that dessert. He'd opened a window to let in some bracing fresh air, and a breeze wafted in the fragrance of wisteria, along with the dusty smell of streets after a light rain.

He felt better. The ceiling had stopped shifting and cracking. He adjusted his glasses. His hands and legs were back under control. He stood up. He was able to think about the children of the Villa again.

"I must speak to their father tomorrow," he told himself. "I can't wait any longer. I must find the courage to tell him what he doesn't see. It's going to tear me apart, but I have to tell him."

36

We'd finished our meal. The radio was playing:

> *Tico Tico par ci*
> *Tico Tico par la*

Sam wasn't dancing to the rhythm of this new hit tune, however. He looked very serious, and after the coffee things had been cleared away, he finally spoke to Father. "Monsieur, I should like the opportunity to discuss an important matter with you, in private, if at all possible."

My father raised his eyebrows. He was used to Sam's inflated way of talking, his convoluted phrases intended to make everyone smile. Father had noticed the young teacher's inability to say even the simplest things without extravagant circumlocutions. When Sam asked what time it was, Father was no longer surprised to hear him inquire, "Might you be able, dear sir, to inform me of the result, albeit only temporary, of the unwinnable competition in which the big hand is even now engaged with the little one, on the object strapped to your wrist?"

Now, however, Father detected a serious note in Sam's request, and the complete absence of that comic style he found rather amusing. In addition, and for the first time, he thought he heard in the young man's words something resembling a deep timbre, an almost normal tone of voice.

"Come with me to my office," he said.

There Sam squirmed in his chair, then seemed to swallow hard, and brushed back a lock of hair with a too perfectly manicured hand. Although he was shy, he was no coward, and preferred to get straight to the point.

"Monsieur," he said, "the time has come for you to leave this town."

Father listened attentively to Sam, taken aback by both his words and his resolute attitude.

"I . . . don't know how to say this to you, but I think you should move your family back to Paris."

"Tell me why, Sam."

Sam's thin voice still quivered with determination. "Because, monsieur, you have children who are worth more than the education they're receiving here."

"Including the education you're giving my youngest son?" intervened Father, with a touch of irony.

"Yes," replied Sam, who was growing more confident. "If you please, I would ask you not to interrupt me, because it's very hard for me to say this. Painful, even. But it can't be helped. I worry about them and about their future. Just consider them now with me, will you? Let's take a look at them together. Juliette has been stifled for years, like a bird in a cage. She's gifted, a promising musician, a success at whatever she puts her hand to. She's dying to try her luck at developing her talents, and normally, at her age, she would already be on the stage, before the public."

Father listened to him in silence.

"Antoine," continued the teacher, "your oldest son, will easily pass his second *baccalauréat* this year, but then what? You know what temptations lie in wait for him. He needs a focus for his ambitions, he needs to look higher and farther than the terraces of the Café Delarep. What will you do with him here? And does he even know what to do with himself?"

Father nodded in agreement.

"As for the other children, the twins, Jacqueline, Violette, and finally your youngest son, they're waking up to life, to literature, the arts, the sciences. Everything is in a ferment for them now. In Paris, all paths will be open to them. Here they risk languishing without fulfilling the promise within them. I can see how their eyes shine when I take them to Toulouse, and how eagerly they listen to your lively arguments with your friend Monsieur Paul, when you speak of world affairs. I feel that your children may do amazing things, if they're given the opportunity to pursue their respective vocations. They're capable of astonishing you, and themselves as well. You don't have the right to keep them away any longer from the great institutions, the great schools of Paris. Paris, monsieur, think about it! The Capital! Paris and its museums, its concerts, its theaters, its libraries! Paris, monsieur!"

He fell silent. It had been a long speech, and he seemed out of breath, but at the same time he'd warmed to his theme, and at his evocation of Paris, that prestigious capital in whose light deserved to bask the little creatures Sam had dearly cherished for more than a year, his emotion had so overwhelmed him that he'd lost control of his voice, winding up his tirade in a kind of shrill spasm that might have seemed ridiculous, but deserved respect and consideration.

"Calm yourself, Sam," said Father, with infinite gentleness.

He gazed across his desk at the eccentric young teacher with the owlish eyes, this Friend Ozoire he'd often enjoyed teasing (but whose moral integrity and pure devotion to his children had never been in doubt), this "Oddity" who had come today to tell him out loud things he'd been unable to face but which had secretly worried him for a long time now. He admired Sam's frankness and wished to tell him so, but Sam wasn't finished.

He raised his hand for silence. "Please excuse my presumption, and allow me to add something else."

In a confessional tone, with tears welling up in his eyes behind his glasses, Sam slowly continued. "It's very hard for me to say all this to you, because your departure will break my heart. Yes, it will, there's no other way of putting it, my heart will be broken. You have adopted and accepted me just as I am. Thanks to you and your family, my days are less empty and my nights less haunted. When I come to the Villa, when I spend an evening with you, I feel as though I were . . . like everyone else."

There was one more admission. "Last, I love your little boy. To me he represents the child I never was, and the child I'll obviously never have. I would have liked him to become my disciple."

The young teacher paused for a moment, hanging his head to conceal the tears that had begun trickling down his pale cheeks.

"I know that the second the boy leaves the lycée and this town, I'll lose my hold on him and no longer be able to influence the development of his mind, the way I would have liked to do. It doesn't matter! His future is more important than my affection for him, and my selfish satisfaction."

"He's a disaster at math," remarked my father, in an effort to relieve some of the seriousness and unhappiness of the moment.

Sam laughed derisively, almost condescendingly, in front of this white-haired paterfamilias. "But, monsieur," he said, "being a disaster at math is of no importance whatsoever! None!"

Father regretted having made such a commonplace remark and felt at a disadvantage before the young man. He was touched by his intelligence and disarmed by his candor and insight.

"But you, Sam," he said, "where are you in all this? You're so young! If you sincerely believe that Paris is the be-all and end-all, what are you waiting for? Why don't you go up to Paris as well, and teach there?"

"I can't leave my grandmother," replied Sam immediately.

"Really, Sam," observed Father, "she won't live forever."

Sam waved away these pipe dreams with the back of his hand.

"My place is here, monsieur," he said, with the bitterness

born of lucidity. "I'm one of those little provincial monstrosities who are better off not exposing themselves too often to the brilliant sunlight of the Capital."

Like all people who live in the provinces, he'd given "Capital" a big "C," thus managing to slip back somewhat into his familiar verbal folderol.

Father decided not to press the point. "In any case, Sam, I thank you for your advice."

"You're quite welcome," answered the other man as he rose from his chair.

Forgetting to perform his usual comical bow, he stepped spontaneously toward my father, who had crossed the room to him. The two men embraced. Leaning on my father's shoulder, Sam silently buried the rest of his sorrow deep within his heart.

At the age of fifty-seven, after returning to the countryside he had left once before, where he had thought to put down his roots again for the last time, my father felt obliged to think over the young teacher's words. He had been all the more struck by them because, even before Sam had forced the issue, Father had been more and more preoccupied by the problem of his children's future. He had wanted to protect them from the world conflict he'd felt was inevitable, and had in large part succeeded. Now that peace had returned to replace the uproar and terror of war, now that the "little ones" were growing up, the prospect of having to do everything all over again—to travel back along the same path!—seemed unavoidable.

He paced back and forth along the terrace overlooking the seven poplars he had planted out of pride and love, and the hills of fruit trees sloping gently down to the fields and the river, this landscape so conducive to reverie and to the composition of a few literary essays he'd long dreamed of writing and had hoped to complete in his semi-retirement, since at fifty-seven, for men of his generation, he could be said to be in his twilight years. But his children's future was once again determining his own.

Something was urging him on and would overcome all resistance mounted by his laziness, selfishness, and fatigue.

Because he said he was lazy, when he belonged to a tenacious generation that respected effort and discipline, a generation said to be made of steel, a generation that had survived two world wars, that had been born before the turn of the century into a world of handcarts, and had just learned that nuclear fission could reduce the planet to a desert of ruins and ashes.

Because he said he was selfish, when throughout his life he'd opened his arms and his home to orphans, outcasts, misfits, and the lonely.

Because he said he was tired, when within the space of a month, he would sell everything he owned, close his office, and acquire an apartment in Paris, where he would endeavor to pick up the slender threads of his prewar livelihood, forced to solicit and court new clients like a young beginner, and when he had finally done all that, he still had to organize the moving of his wife and children, books and furniture, so that his little world, astonished and bewildered, disoriented by such upheaval, might once more be humming along cheerfully by the first day of the coming school year.

3 7

We left the Villa, the garden, the trees, the little town and the countryside, in two separate groups. One group traveled by train, the other by car, in the Peugeot 403, known as the Family Peugeot, with a luggage rack full of suitcases on the roof.

I went with those who took the train.

Those who left by car related that at the last minute, when they were rolling down the gravel drive toward the wide-open entrance gate, all the passengers turned around for a last look. Even Father kept his eyes mostly on the rearview mirror instead of watching out for the turn coming up ahead of him. No one said a word.

"The jar!" cried Mother.

The movers had carried off everything except the enormous orange-and-yellow jar, the immovable object of mysterious origins that I had thought to be the guardian of our happiness and the peaceful order of our universe. It sat in solitary splendor in the middle of the gravel, unchanged. The years and the seasons had left no mark upon its shape and colors, no more than had the passing Germans and their nocturnal carousing.

"Leave it," said Father, although he'd slowed down and put the car into neutral, and seemed unable to cross the threshold to drive off down Chemin du Haut-Soleil, which would lead him to the main road, which would take us to the highway, which went all the way to Paris.

"Leave it," he repeated. "Where we're going, we'd never find any place to put it."

Then someone else cried out, probably Antoine, "The suede pouch!"

Mother and Father exchanged glances. They'd forgotten Justin Case's little bag of gems, buried one night by the Jewish diamond merchant and my father beneath the poplars, a treasure intended for the needs of Jewish refugees. In the end, Father had decided against using the contents of the famous pouch. Justin Case, the humorous and picturesque Norbert Awiczi, who died in exile, thrown by the Nazis from the window of a palace on the Côte Basque, would never return to claim his property.

"Leave it," said Father once more. And he added, "That money belongs to no one. It's just fine right where it is."

Then he put the car into first gear and drove away, abandoning the pouch, along with everything else, beneath the loam of the hillside, with the ghosts of vanished martyrs, illusions, memories, and regrets, and when he'd found the strength to look into the rearview mirror again, the vision of the big white house with its green shutters and red-tiled roof had disappeared.

38

Those who took the train were driven to the station by the Dark Man, who had rarely ever deserved his romantic, gloomy nickname as much as he did that morning.

He grumbled unintelligible words, sprinkled with a few curses, and had clamped a fat yellow Boyard cigarette between his lips to spew enough smoke to hide his anger and distress. He was furious with his friend for having decided to take the momentous step of returning to Paris; he already knew how much he'd miss their private evenings together, the fraternal understanding they had shared, which had brought them triumphantly through the dangers of the Occupation, had saved them from making some big mistakes, and had protected them from foolish self-delusions, thanks to their unflagging sense of critical irony. The Dark Man's peasant pride prevented him from agreeing with Father's reasoning.

"Is it truly as degrading as all that to pursue an education in a provincial town? What do you think you're going to find back there? Your children would have been perfectly well off leading their lives right here, and they could always have decided for themselves, later on."

Father had wanted to argue, but Paul hadn't let him get a word in edgewise.

"And can you really see yourself, at your age, dealing with Parisians, those pathetic bastards, those crooks? You're simply going to go to pieces, my friend, you're going to lose your soul! Here, with us, you're right at home and you can do as you please. Back there, you're going to have to start all over again from scratch. Sonovabitch, you're putting on a hair shirt!"

"Stop," Father had whispered.

His friend's rage was at its height. "It's that little eunuch Sam who conned you into this! That znob! Well," he griped, "do whatever you want. Your children will always be welcome to tramp their city shoes through my cowpats and breathe the smell of my vines and my farmland."

He'd suddenly abandoned the argument. He sensed that my father, as always, had carefully considered both sides of the question, and that he hadn't made up his mind without understanding how great a personal sacrifice was involved, so the Dark Man accepted his decision and gave way before such selflessness.

That morning, however, on the station platform, the handsome, weather-beaten face of this stubborn man—whose voice, words, and sheer physical presence had played such a role in my childhood—reflected a sorrowful irritation that ran counter to our excitement and impatience. For although we were nervous, somewhat dejected, and ignorant of what lay in store for us, we were also eager to discover new horizons, proud of "going up to Paris," curious about our unknown future and its promises. We were both terrified and thrilled at this turning point in our lives.

"Give me a hug, my boy," the Dark Man said to me, clasping me to his broad, strong chest. "And watch out for those little Parisian girls. They're more dangerous than your fiancées at Le Jougla."

We heard a piping call, Sam's unmistakable voice. "Children! Children! Juliette!"

He arrived at a run. He seemed to have trouble covering the

few yards that still lay between us, as though his body were somehow not dense enough to cleave its way through the morning air; his white, short-sleeved shirt with its too pointy collar flapped about his rickety shoulders. He reached us flushed and out of breath, with tears in his eyes, both joy and desolation written on his plain face.

"Well, here's the znob," fumed the Dark Man, stepping back to have a clear view of the gushy display about to enfold us.

For he had labeled our Freeloader a "znob" the first time he'd met him. We children had learned what the word meant from our father, but had understood that this meaning could vary, and that although it was a term of contempt when used by the Dark Man, it became a flattering title for the young teacher of literature from Toulouse. Because when we gently made fun of him, trying to imitate his affected ways, his quotations and allusions, he'd raise his voice to announce (as much to us as to the Dark Man, whose confidence and esteem he would have clearly liked to win): "Snobbism is a vehicle of new ideas—even if they're only minor ones."

We'd fall silent, disarmed by such peremptory self-defense. But now, at the moment of goodbye, both words and pluck failed Sam.

Juliette, who had been placed in charge of our little band until our arrival the next day at Gare d'Austerlitz, remarked upon his discomfiture: "Poor Sam, you don't look too well."

"It's because I feel torn, my dear girl," he replied. "I take pride in seeing you all fly off to honor and glory, but I'm distraught over losing your company."

The Dark Man stepped up and bluntly intervened. "Well, Monsieur Sam, at least now they'll get their fill of your up-to-date stuff, off in Paris," he snapped. "Huh! Up-to-date my ass!"

Sam tried to ignore him. He capered about, made faces, warbled a refrain ("A little sentimental journey . . ."), handed out candy as well as a few violets and forget-me-nots purchased from the florist's shop next to the station. He also gave me a slim volume, naïvely illustrated: *The Little Prince*—a title that meant nothing to me.

"Here," he said. "In this book you can read all the things I was never able to explain to you about friendship. Take a good look at the part about the fox and the flower, and write to me."

We hugged each other in a flurry of tears and emotion.

The train from Toulouse came puffing into the station, a long, noisy mass of gray, green, and black metal, suddenly galvanizing our drawn-out scene of departure. I'd just felt for the first time that particularly intense form of anxiety one experiences in stations, an anguish that can affect children as well as adults, plunging them into a state of guilt and apprehension. The sounds, the smell, the inhuman symmetry of the railroad tracks, the uniform colors—did they remind me that it was from this same platform that Monsieur Germain and others like him had left, never to return? And hadn't Madame Blèze bid farewell to the province from this same horizontal setting of impersonal cement, leaving without having betrayed the secret that bound her to the precociously salacious youngster, the vase-breaking little monster I'd always remain in her eyes?

"Write to me, my carissime," repeated Sam. "And you'll write to me, won't you?" he asked my brothers and sisters. "You'll write to me?"

"You'll come and see us in Paris," we said, to console him.

"No, no," he replied. "You'll be visiting me in Toulouse, at my grandmother's."

And in a last burst of comic energy he cried, "Be careful, children! Don't lean out the windows! *'E pericoloso sporghersi!'* "

We'd known him only a short while—barely more than a year—and yet we'd grown fond of him, while with us he had found something he'd sorely missed until then. And so, after we'd boarded the train, piled our bundles and berets on the wooden seats of the compartment, and craned our heads out the windows, we felt sad to see him down there on the platform waving goodbye, and to know that from now on our Saturdays and Sundays would be spent without him, without his jokes and disguises, without the subtle and captivating ways he had of teaching us things that were a valuable addition to the example and education provided by our parents.

Standing a little apart, leaning against the wall of rust-colored bricks, the Dark Man was also waving goodbye, without Sam's melodramatic flourishes, but his farewell affected me just as much. Perhaps it upset me even more: his imposing figure had been imprinted on my memory from earliest childhood.

He had symbolized the mysteries that govern the existence of grownups; he had sensed my curiosity, my awakening sensuality, and had gently steered me in certain directions. I had worshipped and admired him as though he were a second father. Together we had hunted hares and truffles, tramped beneath the chestnut trees and across the fragrant chalky terrain of Les Causses. To me the Dark Man meant grapevines, gorse, ducks, carp and crows, reeds and the scent of Caporal tobacco. In some indefinable way he had initiated me into the world of fleshly pleasures, and the secrets of sex. We had selected flat white stones together from the debris at the foot of the steep cliffs overhanging these lonely but happy valleys, and he had taught me how to skip them across the milky currents of the Aveyron, leaning back with arms and legs bent to send the stone skimming away at just the right angle. Although my parents had told me over and over that we'd all see each other again the following summer (and in fact I did see the Dark Man and his friends often in the future), my sensitive nature was going through tumultuous and irreversible changes, and for the first time I feared that, when we met again, the Dark Man would no longer be the same man, for I dimly sensed that I would no longer be the same little boy.

The train lurched, and a whole world of habits, rites, and myths was left behind on the platform of that ordinary railroad station, along with those who had helped me create this world and its protective walls, which had just crumbled at a simple blast from a locomotive whistle.

39

Caussade, Cahors, Brive, Uzerche, and soon Limoges.

The musky perfume of Gascogne, the amber light of Guyenne, the bluish mist of Quercy, the dark red soil of Périgord.

It was only after the train had passed through these cities and regions, as it prepared to leave what a British writer once graciously called "the enchanted circle of southwestern France," that I felt a strong pang of melancholy. I was powerless to master this pain, because I was unable to understand it.

I was very young, at an age when one isn't used to saying goodbye to things, and I hadn't realized that "going up to Paris" might open that first wound of nostalgia, the implacable moment when events tear you away from something you love and were foolish enough to believe would last forever. In that minute, that hour, forms the sediment of "things past." That was truly what happened in that fateful moment, although I didn't know it at the time, and since I couldn't put this parting into words, still less make any sense of it, the train did so in my place, and said farewell simply by rushing headlong across the landscapes of my childhood.

Farewell to the song of the seven poplars in the evening breeze; the shouts of the kids horsing around on the white benches of

Les Mouettes, our muddy municipal pool; our blackberry feasts; the quiet efficiency of the peasants setting out their strings of sausages, jars of cracklings, black puddings, and potted meats upon the oilcloth-draped trestles of the covered market on Place de Cazes-Mondenard; the dogs barking as they race along, down in the valley of the Tescou River; stolen kisses planted on the cheeks of the little girls at Le Jougla; the plane trees and cedars; the muffled, reassuring sound of Father's espadrilles as he made his last round along the tile floor of the halls, checking to see that his brood were all asleep; the phonograph scratchily playing "Maria de Bahia" and "Qui Sas," and the mellifluous voice of André Claveau singing *"Il pleut sur la route"*; Christmas morning, when my mother would sing *"Il est né le divin enfant"* in her pure, youthful soprano, as we rushed in our bathrobes to feign surprise at discovering the Pathé-Baby movie projector that would allow us to enjoy the exploits of Harold Lloyd or Laurel and Hardy, but which we'd already reconnoitered during the night, insomnious rascals who no longer cared to believe in Santa Claus; the taste of blood in my mouth and the sandy grass jammed up my nostrils when I was tackled too hard, and had trouble getting back on my feet to face the heartless laughter of the male spectators; the orgies of red and black cherries eaten straight from the tree as we straddled the main branch, without bothering to spit out the pits, and the delectable stomachaches that followed, requiring lots of pampering from the women of the house.

The spoonfuls of cod-liver oil fed to the students lined up on the playground of our small lycée; the jaundice of our teacher Monsieur Furbaire, caused by a snake that had wrapped itself around his belly while he was out hunting, for the reptile had slid over his boots and up his pants leg, encircling his waist like a belt, and the unfortunate man hadn't noticed until he'd gotten undressed for bed later that evening; the confident step of the German officer going upstairs, carrying a cup of coffee to the Brigadeführer as calmly as if he were in his own home, when the two of them were unforgivably defiling our sacred world; the distress in the eyes of the little Jewish girls who spent the night in the laundry room before vanishing in the morning; the singer Cajabou, a poor deluded man aspiring to a career as a lyric tenor, who came to massacre Verdi one evening after dinner in our front parlor, before the astounded eyes of our neighbors, whom our parents had invited to share this special occasion; the cackling of geese; a flight of partridges above the limestone plateau of Le Margoulliat; the savor of white peaches and green figs, of quinces with tough skins, whose fibers got between our teeth, already set on edge by the fruit's tart flesh; our locally made cookies, tasting of almonds and wheat, a flavor now lost and gone forever! The scent of Naja cigarettes, of Baltos, Salâmmbos, smelling of honey and pepper, those first illicit smokes, and the odors of Virginia or Maryland tobacco; the games of mumblety-peg on the softest part of the lawn; fishing for young lampreys in the rivers; the hanged men, the deported prisoners, the bastards and their victims, and the people who simply did nothing; the Punchinellos and their masks; the puppets and the heroes. And the earth—the smell, the feel, the color of the earth!

Who could ever tell this little boy with his face pressed against the window, waiting to be astonished by his first glimpse of the big city, that, despite everything he would discover or take pride in knowing later on, he had already learned the most important things, before he was even twelve years old, back home in the Villa?

40

"To the blackboard!"

These dreaded words seem to ring in my ears with unusual
frequency. Each time, the unlucky student must leave his seat,
walk up to the rostrum, follow the teacher's orders to face the
class ("Look at your classmates, not at me!"), and answer
questions—or stand there silently, if he doesn't know the
answer.

"To the blackboard!"

It seems to me my name is called more often than anyone
else's and that the entire class has been waiting for precisely
that moment, to see me silent, hesitant, ignorant—or, better yet,
to hear me babble my meager store of knowledge, with that
awful "Midi accent" that sets off sneering smiles, smothered
giggles, and squirms of commiseration. I hardly open my mouth
when a murmur runs through my audience, which seems to
quiver in anticipation, like an oncoming wave. And I panic.

"Silence! Let the poor wretch answer the question!"

Everything has changed, and what once appeared simple and
easy now shapes up as an impossible contest for which I am
utterly unprepared. As though, each day, I have to pass another
exam.

Back in our little provincial lycée, I used to feel as though I were head and shoulders above the other pupils my age, and I poked good-natured fun at their thick accents as fat as a rasher of bacon, as heavy as their fathers' wooden shoes. My brothers and sisters and I all shared an unavowed sense of superiority, the awareness of a difference between our classmates and ourselves. And now the very thing that used to inspire our games and mimicry is turning against me. I've become the star of that cruel comedy instead of the cool, detached observer I once was. What's going on? I talk like a nitwit, like a "country bumpkin," a complete jerk.

Everything has changed. Our teachers don't call me by my first name. I have no idea where they live. They vanish into the Métro, or the bus, and I can barely recognize them when I see them again a few days later. I don't meet them in the bakery or on the road to our house. But this distance, this impersonal aspect of my relationship with them, wouldn't be so wounding if I could find some comfort, warmth, and companionship among those the teachers erroneously refer to as my "comrades." At first they seem to me more like strangers, even adversaries.

They don't dress the way I do. They're in long trousers, and some of them wear ties, scarves, and double-breasted coats. They speak more quickly, they pack in more words; I have the feeling they do it on purpose to keep me from figuring out what they're saying. Their knowing voices follow me mockingly as I trudge up the street to our apartment, which isn't far from the lycée. I come home alone, because my schedule doesn't correspond to those of my siblings, just as we no longer set off as a group in the morning, in our proud armada of bicycles. We don't even ride our bikes anymore. Antoine is in his first-year class in preparation for the École Normale Supérieure entrance examination; Juliette and my other two sisters take the Métro to the Lycée Molière; the twins aren't in the same playground as I am. We all go our separate ways. And although we eat our meals together, I no longer feel that stirring camaraderie of a little community marching off to the same destination, the same experiences.

It's only a few yards to the big traffic circle where the twins go down Rue de Longchamp, since they're allowed to use the lycée's upper-school entrance, whereas I have to take Rue Decamps and go around to the lower-school doors off Avenue Georges-Mandel. I've already gotten lost several times in this vast gray and black edifice of metal and stone with cement-paved courtyards. The building isn't really modern; it is, however, huge, urban, without warmth, and often empty.

It resembles the streets of the neighborhood and what I've seen so far of the big city: the same colors, the same lack of green, of blue, of earth. What has happened to my native clay? Has it been covered with an endless coating of asphalt? Will it ever manage to break through somewhere?

When I arrive at the entrance, my "comrades" are already there. They're looking at me the same way they do when I'm suffering up at the front of the class, a look I can only describe as that of a judge, a sentinel, a customs inspector. The crafty look of someone who knows more than you do, an initiate who belongs to the inner circle, who knows the codes, and has the keys, and the right to evaluate you, to pass or fail you. They cast an appraising eye on the little country boy, waiting for him to make his first silly remark of the day, with his ridiculous accent and his slow way of doing everything, and their expectant attitude makes me even more nervous.

In time I will amend myself, and defend myself; I will gather up my strength, gather into myself what remains of my childhood so that I may catch up with them, with their liveliness, their lewdness, their propensities for disloyalty and casual forgetfulness, their eagerness to strike out in all directions in matters of the heart and mind. One day I will be as "Parisian" as they are, and they won't make fun of me anymore, nor will café waiters or bartenders be tempted to imitate my accent and manners.

239

Eventually, I'll be allowed to join in my classmates' games of marbles, then in their roughhousing, their sports, and finally I'll get to match wits with them as an equal, but when they invite me home with them, to those big apartments on the solemn, sad, deserted, cold, dark streets of the sixteenth arrondissement in those years of 1947, '48, '49, I'll still feel as though I don't quite belong. I'll still be too innocent to see that most of my classmates—like me, and before me—came to Paris from other cities and provinces, seeking the same acceptance as I do from this new city, and I'll still feel the weight of their eyes upon me, still behave as though I have to prove myself, give some account of myself. They'll introduce me to their mothers apologetically, as though ashamed of having brought such an oaf into their homes, which seem to me more organized, well appointed, and stylish than our own apartment. Their mothers will look at me with a twinkle of amusement, while their fathers will size me up impassively. I'll do my best to charm their sisters.

I'll wonder, beneath the chandeliers of Rue de Passy, on the carpets of Impasse du Ranelagh, in the parlors of Rue de la Faisanderie, in the halls of Square de l'Alboni, or in the elevators of Rue Vineuse, just how long life in Paris will go on seeming like some perpetual rite of passage, and how old I'll be before I stop hearing that threatening summons, "To the blackboard!"

And I'll wonder how many times I'll have to triumph over the others, but most of all over myself, before I no longer have to stand up from my seat and be judged by a jury of my peers.

41

At first my days at school seemed unhappy and constrained, but I discovered places in Paris that filled my spare time with pleasure and finally overcame the last of my provincial shyness.

Like a cat transplanted to a strange house, who identifies its territory by prowling in ever larger circles around its new home, venturing at last beyond the garden walls, I set out—alone or with my brothers—to explore my neighborhood, and then its outlying zones. The more I saw, the more fascinated I was by this city of endless mysteries, a city with underground trains and artificial lights illuminating what were known as the Grands Boulevards.

And so, beginning with Le Trocadéro and Avenue Raymond-Poincaré, we systematically reconnoitered that sweeping, magical avenue with its stone borders of architectural elegance, the Champs-Elysées!

We loved to puff on Gauloises, hiding in the subterranean darkness of the aquarium at the Palais de Chaillot; we lounged on the gold-and-white wicker chairs of the terrace at the Café Scossa, on Place Victor-Hugo; we listened to a man dressed entirely in brown sing at the Théâtre de l'Etoile, on the steeply sloping Avenue de Wagram, and after the show we had a *café liégeois* at the stand-up tables of La Maison du Brésil; we checked out the prostitutes showing their ankles at the top of Avenue Carnot; we smelled the fragrant smoke of roasted chestnuts, mingling with billows of that "Métro smell" that intrigued us all one winter because it was an indescribable, entirely artificial odor, unrelated to any of the smells we'd grown up with. We loved all those things and many more, but nothing rivaled our interest in the majestic perspective of the Champs-Elysées.

What a handsome avenue it was then! How we loved to walk up and down its broad sidewalks unsullied by a single car. We were filled with pride at having come from our small town's Rue Delarep to this spacious parade of marvels. On a foggy day, we sometimes wondered if the avenue didn't lead straight to the sea.

We'd leave the sixteenth arrondissement via Avenue Kléber, going up to the Arc de Triomphe and swinging right to begin our descent of the Champs-Elysées. There was an obligatory pause to admire the beautiful customers at Le Pam-Pam, a café made famous by three little music-hall songs and a few racy write-ups in the newspapers. The name had an insolent ring to it, like a challenge issued by the young lounge lizards who'd made the café their home-away-from-home during the Occupation. Almost exactly across from it, on the left, a few yards down a street perpendicular to the Champs, there was a small bar that attracted our attention, provoking envy and speculation: Le Val d'Isère. We were still woefully unsophisticated kids, and we took these two establishments for the heights of elegance, showcases of true Parisian behavior. There we saw tanned faces, men wearing silk scarves, pencil mustaches, women in flowered frocks, their busts overflowing their strapless bras. But I was even more entranced by Le Passage du Lido.

This vast gallery of stores blooming in the middle of a block of houses and filled with a noisy, cosmopolitan crowd I imagined shopping, trading, coming and going about its business, all regulated by some invisible clock, this bustling flood of human activity symbolized more than any other place the complex, dangerous, but enthralling nature of life in Paris.

I was so astonished by the Passage that it took me a while to muster the courage to go inside. I stood mutely before the entrance, unable to plunge into this universe that never saw the light of day, where crooks might lie in wait, as well as pickpockets, fast women, and maybe even kidnappers! Then I grew bolder. And what impressed me the most inside was not so much the profusion of stores, the places where you could stand at the counter and consume concoctions with exotic names, the shop windows full of women's underwear or records imported from distant continents, but rather this movement itself: the constant procession of men and women whose faces, clothes, shapes, voices belonged to so many social and ethnic groups that I concluded I'd chanced upon the heart of Paris. And for a long time I believed that the eye of the cyclone, the very center of the Capital, was here in this Passage, where you could—it was just fantastic!—have your shoes shined, drink a glass of milk flavored with strawberry syrup, ogle the legs and hips of flashy dames, hang out by the music stores to hear the sounds of Duke Ellington and Jacques Hélian, and if you were really lucky or really patient, you might catch an admiring glimpse of the legendary Jimmy Gaillard.

Everyone knew that he stopped by regularly, late in the afternoon, to sip an aperitif and shake a few hands at the Bar du Lido, a narrow hole-in-the-wall with a single counter and eight barstools, right at the entrance to the Passage, just inside the swinging glass doors that led to this troglodytic universe.

"Come on, it's time," my brother would tell me. "Let's go see Jimmy Gaillard."

Just as some people go on journeys to gape at the sunset on a beach or a herd of elephants crossing the savannas, we used to go observe that singular animal, endowed—in our opinion—with all the graces of Parisian chic, who allowed us to continue filling the pages of our Album for a while longer.

Jimmy Gaillard! Was it the name, that audacious conjunction with its Anglo-Saxon beginning and earthy, down-home finish that had made him a hero in our star-struck eyes, or was it his style, or his regular appearance at the appointed hour in this Parisian wonderland?

He'd been a singer and tap dancer with Ray Ventura's orchestra. He was a man of average height, with a handsome, fleshy face and brown hair shiny with brilliantine. He wore a bright red blazer with gold buttons, shirts with English collars, and shoestring ties. Some days he varied his wardrobe, opting for a navy-blue blazer, but the rest was always the same. When recognized by passersby, he'd smile and hold out his square hand with its stubby fingers to anyone who seemed eager to shake it. He'd have long conversations with the white-outfitted barman, who resembled him like a brother, with the same insipid smile, the same mannerisms, and he often chatted at length with the doorman at the nightclub next door to the Lido. Then he'd take off again for parts unknown; we imagined him busy with intricate schemes or the negotiation of complicated contracts. He wore glossy shoes with gold buckles, probably to complete the effect produced by the blazer buttons.

One day, we suddenly lost interest in this guy and his whole little world, so we crossed the Seine to take a look at the Left Bank, which our oldest brother had already begun to explore. I don't know exactly how many sessions we spent closely scrutinizing Jimmy Gaillard and his atrocious blazers before deciding he was a comical, even vulgar nobody, but I suppose it was at about the same time that we realized we were losing the last traces of our Midi accent.

42

At the lower end of the Champs, on the right side, was a single big movie theater: Le Marignan. A long, straight, and orderly line stretched from the box office all the way to the curb at the edge of the traffic circle. I'd never seen so many people standing motionless, two by two, waiting to buy tickets for a show.

Since I was slender and agile and had learned how to sneak in for free, thanks to my classmates (who were no longer the sly "comrades" of my first weeks in school, but real pals), I slipped between the first two couples at the head of the line and went straight inside.

The black-and-white film was called *Quai des Orfèvres*. I watched it openmouthed with astonishment. It showed greedy, violent beings driven by jealousy and sexual impulse, loners drifting through a dead-end world of smoky bistros, murky nights, and rain-slicked cobblestone alleys, seeking a substitute for the love and friendship they lacked. In these low-life surroundings, laughter curdled into derision, and there was flesh-and-blood realism in the odd or outrageous types served up: cops, tarts, a murderer, some pathetic minor characters, people depicted without hope, without charity, their souls laid bare with a scalpel by an expert in depravity.

The theater was full, and the audience thrilled to the spectacle of this talented but pitiless dissection. It was the very first showing of the film's commercial run, which I hadn't realized. The spectators experienced successive waves of pleasure and terror, interspersed with the profound silence that only a master can evoke, one who knows how to tell his story with a sure hand. Jouvet gave an imposing performance, playing the cynic to disguise his need for tenderness, hiding his sadness and disillusionment behind an abrupt manner; Blier displayed the fear and weakness of a cowardly, rejected husband; Suzy Delair flaunted her curves, her stockinged thighs, and the hip-swinging walk of a woman who'll give you a good time, but one that will cost you dearly, and for the rest of your life. The harsh lighting and obsessive music put the finishing touches on a striking, almost poetic depiction of this tawdry milieu. The film gave off an aura of sexuality, of gluttony, of despair, and of callous resignation as well, as though the director and screenwriter had wanted to say (as much through the title, which refers to the French equivalent of Scotland Yard, as by the dramatic, and then poignant ending of their story): That's life in the big city. That's Paris.

When I left the theater, I was moved as I had rarely been before, because all the other movies I'd seen had seemed hard to believe, detached from reality, and they certainly hadn't seemed like anything that might change my life. They'd been make-believe, "the movies." But this film, seen in the city that was now my home, in this Paris where I was to grow up and go to school, seemed ominous and brutally truthful. It reinforced my instinctive conviction that I'd have to keep my eyes wide open and my wits about me if I hoped to survive such dangers, avoid such unhappiness, and resist such a wealth of temptations.

43

I recognized him immediately, and was left speechless.

It happened at the Palais de Chaillot, on the esplanade facing the Tour Eiffel. I was there with a friend, learning the simple and exhilarating art of roller-skating. We heard a few drumrolls, some meager applause, and a distant murmur that drew us toward one wing of the building, along the top of which are inscribed, in block letters of gold, some long sentences by Paul Valéry, which Father had patiently explained to us one day.

A few gentlemen in dark suits, surrounded by officers and ladies wearing hats, had just unveiled a plaque of blue-and-green metal, with the assistance of a two-man band composed of a trumpet player and a drum major in police uniforms. It was one of those ordinary ceremonies one could still see, at that time, on squares or street corners, because many of them were getting new names, usually in honor of Resistance heroes, solitary marksmen shot down on the sidewalks during the Liberation of Paris, or deportees who never returned from camps whose names had now taken on their full meaning for us. I wouldn't have lingered there any longer with my friend and would have eagerly rejoined the bands of roller skaters my age, happily zigzagging over the vast expanse of flagstones that had become one of my favorite playgrounds—if I hadn't noticed one of the men who seemed to belong to the small group of officials.

His hair was now neatly trimmed, less bushy and untidy, but still as greasy and black, carefully combed along his bovine nape. His gestures were just as unctuous, his step as mincing and formal as before, and he still used his hands in the same way. From where I was, I couldn't hear what he was saying, but I could tell from the way he moved his eyes and lips that he was cranking out the usual innocuous phrases in his prudent, self-satisfied style.

It was that miserable Floqueboque, the "stuffed shirt" Father had defined for my edification a few long years before, who had dared turn up at the Villa one day demanding his pound of Jewish flesh. We hadn't heard much of him after that morning when he came for Dora, repeating a phrase we'd turned into one of our hated antiphons ("a small overnight bag"), then retreating before the adamant opposition of our father. We'd been given to understand that he'd vanished from the purlieus of City Hall, where he'd "placed his experience at the service of the nation," some six months before the Occupation forces were routed. Since then, not a word. And no one, frankly, had cared what had happened to him. Now I'd found him taking his place among officials of his generation, backed up by military authorities and the French flag. He certainly wasn't the chief participant in this ceremony, but he appeared to be closely involved in it and to have easily wormed his way into the new order of things.

"Oh, no," I shouted, "that's just too much!"

A passerby who had watched the unveiling of the plaque with a few other gawkers took me by the shoulder. "What's the matter, sonny?"

I was furious, choking with indignation.

"That guy, over there . . . That guy," I finally stammered, "he's a bastard!"

The man laughed carelessly and turned away, as the spectators and actors in the brief ceremony began to walk down toward

Avenue Albert-de-Mun. Feverishly, I tackled the laces of my
roller skates; I hadn't much time. Carrying my skates, I stepped
over a low hedge between the flagstones and the place where
Floqueboque had been. The officials were getting into two cars.
I saw Floqueboque put on a hat that was smaller and less flamboyant than the insolent felt number that had once so intrigued
me. He got into the front passenger seat of a Prima Quatre, and
I realized I'd never be able to catch up with him. So, before he
slammed the door shut, I put my hands up like a megaphone
around my mouth and shouted as loud as I could. "Floqueboque, bastard! Floqueboque, bastard!"

A few pedestrians turned and stared at me in astonishment,
but Floqueboque didn't seem to hear me. I was certain, however,
that it was the same man. Had he changed his name? Or had
he simply made one up for himself when he arrived in our area,
then taken back his original name once he'd deserted the losing
side to weasel his way cleverly in among the winners? I didn't
stop to wonder about this, however; filled with bitterness, seized
with a feeling of disgust, as though I'd been doused with something as revolting as a batch of spittle from a swarm of sick
toads, I sped back to our apartment.

With my skates tied at the laces and slung over my shoulders
the way I'd seen my most savvy friends do, the heavy wheels
and metal frames raking my skin through my shirt, I ran like a
madman, bumping into people right and left, across Place du
Trocadéro, down Avenue d'Eylau, reaching the traffic circle and
swinging to the right on the sidewalk for the last thirty yards
along Rue de Longchamp, where I pulled up completely winded
in front of the building where we lived, and beat on the door
with my fist.

"What is it?" asked my mother as she let me in. "You're all
out of breath. Did you hurt yourself?"

"No," I managed to gasp. "I have to speak to Papa."

I entered his office without fear of disturbing him, because in
those days his visitors were few and far between. We knew that

Father spent hours alone, doing his accounts and tightening his budget, telephoning former clients and friends in an effort to get his business back on its feet, occasionally deciding to forget his troubles by burying himself in one of his favorite books. In those difficult times, he seemed to prefer Chamfort, Sainte-Beuve, and turned invariably to Pascal. He had re-created the legendary interior of his office in the Villa: a room as big as the other one had been, with paneling and woodwork in the same colors, the same walls of books, the same niche for the bust of Voltaire, the same furniture. The only difference was that it was quite chilly—full northern exposure—and that the French windows no longer looked out over poplars, orchards, and the pleasant, hazy valley of the Tescou, but on the edge of a building on the corner of Rue Saint-Didier, with a horizon graced solely by the red sign of a local garage and the silhouette of a streetlight the color of boredom.

"Tell me everything, my boy," said Father. "Take your time."

After I'd caught my breath, I gave him a detailed account of my sighting of Floqueboque. He listened without comment. When I'd finished, I waited for him to ask me questions. The thing that amazed me was that he never seemed surprised by what I was telling him. It was as though this apparition that had so shocked me were for him simply a case of déjà vu.

"Is this right?" I asked him. "Is it fair? What are you going to do? We have to do something about it!"

He smiled at me kindly, and murmured, very gently, "Inform on him? Denounce him? That's not my way, you know."

He took a deep, slow, tired breath, then rose and began to pace back and forth, as I would often see him do in the future. Since he no longer had a large terrace at his disposal, or a spacious garden, he'd fallen into the habit of opening the doors of the office and the dining room so that he could stride up and down the apartment with his hands jammed into the pockets of his jacket. He now wore respectable ties and well-polished shoes, no matter what his daily agenda was to be; gone were the days of woolen pullovers and English canvas slippers. Back and forth he'd go, in a rhythm that finally wore on those who watched and saw him withdrawing ever deeper into his thoughts and silences, in this tour of his room, this voyage around himself.

"But, Papa," I objected, "we can't just ignore this Floque-boque like that."

He stopped and replied, "But you see, my boy, we could. We could ignore him, because going after him won't bring back Monsieur Germain."

Heartsick, incapable of understanding how his clearheaded skepticism reflected the weight of his own experience, I tried to protest, tried to put my feelings into words, but could only exclaim, "Even so! Perhaps it wouldn't bring back Monsieur Germain, but, Papa, even so!"

Again and again I said this: "Even so!"

With those words I'd reached the limit of what my outraged sense of justice could express. Father smiled at me warmly, tenderly, and took my hand. He gave me a long hug, a rare gesture from this modest man.

"Even so," he said. "That's the truth of it: Even so!"

After holding me in his arms for a while, he sent me kindly away to the room I shared with my brothers, and I couldn't tell whether he was going to remain in this attitude of blasé tolerance, of stubborn fatalism, or whether one day he would "do something," because one of his children had exclaimed "Even so!", which had made him smile and had roused him—momentarily, perhaps—from the philosophical resignation toward which the contemplative side of his nature was increasingly inclined.

He was alone, pacing in his large office. Outside, the city street lamps had blinked on, shedding a stale, glaucous light. A taxi waited for a client, its idling motor clicking away monotonously. Finally, he sat down.

Like Jérôme Coignard—whom he liked to quote, even though he claimed there was no one else around who read his cherished Anatole France anymore!—he felt that life was an absurdity, that society was a magma of ludicrous rules, and that only by holding firmly to principles that are unprovable, and thus impervious to reason, can one avoid sinking into chaos. He was careful not to express such ideas in front of his children, and tried to keep his doubts and misanthropic tendencies from distressing his wife. He bared his soul, however, to Paul, the friend he'd left behind, and he had returned to his former habit of writing once a week to the Dark Man. He hadn't realized how much he would miss his friend's presence, their affectionate arguments and shared intellectual games. And so he sent him frank, detailed reports of his daily activities and observations.

He worried about how his wife would manage after he was gone. He expressed the wish that by then his children would be sufficiently independent and settled in their lives to be able to help their mother bear up under the blow, because he feared she would suffer for a long time after their parting. He spoke of each of his children, giving them good marks and bad. He mentioned the unwonted visit, which was never repeated, of young Diego, who had turned up disguised in the cheap finery of a postwar dandy to borrow some money. When last heard of, Diego had returned to the Côte d'Azur.

Father wrote: "The break caused by the war and the Occupation has produced an unimaginable number of worthless, amoral leeches. The ends justify the means, and no one cares what falls by the wayside: a love of truth, a sense of honor, a feeling of compassion." His pessimism was unchanged, and he saw no reason why the behavior of men or their governments might be expected to improve. He feared, rather, that the situation would grow worse. This "old liberal" admitted to the "old leftist" that he was deeply demoralized by the way things were going in the world.

It had been a hard winter. He confided to his friend that his business had picked up slowly, and that some days he had felt so discouraged as almost to lose hope. For a while now, however, he had been increasingly busy, as his clients spread the word about the eminent and experienced legal adviser they'd rediscovered after such a long absence. He was regaining his strength and his clientele.

"You'll laugh," he wrote, "but strangely enough, now that things are going better, I notice a feeling of disappointment when the telephone rings to bring me a new case. Would you explain to me why I would rather my office and appointment book remain empty? But there are the children! After leaving behind our home in the country, it would be unthinkable for me not to struggle here for them, and for their future. Even so!"

Not without humor, he compared himself to Sisyphus. He had his rock to push laboriously up his hill, like everyone else. And that was why he felt it would be useless, and too petty an action for the man he thought he was, to pursue the traitor with the greasy hair whom fate had placed ironically in the path of his little boy.

But the reminder of that "Even so!" had led him to recount in detail, and as though through the eyes of a child, what had happened at the Palais de Chaillot. As he described the incident for his dear "country correspondent," his one true friend, he thought more deeply about its implications. He ardently hoped that his child—like all his other beloved sons and daughters, who with their mother were his sole reason for being and for having started his life all over again—would always react with indignation to the Floqueboques of this world. In the end he congratulated himself for having immersed them in the stark reality of the big city, in the dawn of a new era whose end he would never see but which he prophesied would be an age as barbarous as it was modern.

He felt that he had given his children enough strength, enough heart and soul, to face whatever lay ahead. He had brought them "up to Paris" to complete their educations; perhaps they'd been too protected in that small provincial town, a paradise now lost. He realized that, from now on, they'd find more than enough here to put to the test what mattered most, in the end: character.

He closed his letter as he always did: "Farewell, old friend, I embrace you fondly."

Outside, the taxi was gone, and the street had nothing to say, nothing but its own noise, neutral and artificial, like the gaslight from the city street lamps.

EPILOGUE

One September about forty years later, I was attending a ceremony hosted by an organization located on the Right Bank, in
rooms with a view of the great glass canopy of the Grand Palais.

The autumn sky had a radiance one sees only in Paris, and
as the setting sun, with its mauve palette, gave a brief wash of
cerulean blue to friezes, bridges, and the tops of monuments,
the delicate alchemy of colors and ancient stones reassured you
once again that you could never, ever, live anywhere else.

An "important personage" was being honored. This gentleman was all the more important in that he wasn't famous, but
played a role of some prominence within this society, so there
was a large crowd of well-dressed people milling elegantly
about.

Ministers and bankers emerged from their black automobiles
to climb the entrance steps alongside artists and smiling celebrities, since in the realm of appearances the first commandment
is that celebrities must smile. Business, finance, and the market
had come to rub shoulders with beauty, glamour, and literary
lions. Everyone was glad to be there, even though the evening
promised no surprises, since the guests all knew one another
already, had seen one another the day before, and would meet
again on the morrow. The exceptionally mild weather, as well

as the extraordinary profusion of powerful names and famous faces, made this gathering an unusually distinguished one, of the kind that makes people feel they really should "be there," thus dispelling any distressing suspicion that it wouldn't actually have made any difference if they'd simply stayed home.

The man who was being honored that evening had never done anyone any harm. As far as everyone knew, he had no enemies, which might mean that he possessed not a single outstanding quality, or else that he'd managed to efface them all, so as to show those whom he'd wished to court the reassuring guise of mediocrity that is one of ambition's most subtle weapons.

He had managed to last. He had become an influential man within his sphere, a man toward whom flowed a constant stream of offers, advice, requests. Over the decades, he'd acquired a reputation as someone impossible to dislodge from his high position, for he'd survived several crises, shareholder turnovers, and shifts in the reigning alliances. A flexible man, careful to flatter discreetly both those who were in power and those who'd just lost it, he garnered the favors of the masters of the moment as well as the appreciation of those who would one day return to authority, and spiderlike, he had politely, patiently, woven his network, putting his experience and ability to work finding and developing the talents of others—which is an authentic talent in itself, but a frustrating one.

He had kept his anger, spleen, and resentment to himself, which should have cost him a few ugly wrinkles, but through self-discipline, or one of those little miracles of nature that also bless the homely, he'd managed to keep a cheerful face, and pink, healthy skin that showed no signs of wear, so that he resembled a baby the whole world couldn't help patting on the cheek.

This, then, was the person who stood in the middle of the buzzing and humming room, stood as straight as a wooden soldier, serious, but not solemn, his frank countenance illuminated by the last rays of sunlight beaming through the double windows.

An unforeseen problem was threatening to ruin the occasion. The room was growing hotter and hotter. The windows ought to have been opened, but the clatter of rush-hour traffic on the Avenue Franklin Roosevelt would have drowned out the speeches. The temperature was soaring. The many guests were packed uncomfortably close together, and perspiration stood out on their powdered noses, at the roots of their dyed hair, and on cleavages daubed with foundation makeup. The atmosphere quickly grew stifling. Men mopped their brows with handkerchiefs. Soon people were going to start fainting. The euphoria of self-congratulation in which the evening had begun was about to turn to irritation, exasperation, and disgust.

The speaker, an old hand at this sort of affair, had realized early on that he should cut it short, and so had turned the podium over to the evening's guest of honor in record time. This gentleman's adaptability was indisputable (which was actually one of the reasons he was being feted that evening: he had known how to get by, whatever the circumstances), and he had also understood that it was useless to prolong what had started out as a pleasant occasion but now threatened to become an endurance test, even a fiasco.

And then he did something that earned him the gratitude of his audience, particularly the women. He drew from the pocket of his jacket a thick sheaf of papers on which he had labored for several evenings, composing his speech of thanks, carefully mentioning every single person to whom he owed so much, without whom he would not be there, without whom he would be nothing. With a comical gesture, he rolled his speech up and shook it at the guests as though menacing them with a weapon, then stuck the thick roll back into his pocket and said modestly, "I'll say just a few words: My thanks to all of you. And now get those blasted windows open, and let's move on to the buffet!"

There was a burst of applause, mixed with laughter and approving comments. The huge windows were opened, letting in a gust of fresh air that ruffled hairdos, fluttered veils, soothed damp and sticky skin. The guests, satisfied with themselves and with life once again, moved gaily off toward the buffet tables set up in the main salon and surrounding rooms.

A party atmosphere sprang up, as at a reunion, with each profession gathering naturally into its own group, and everywhere reigned a good humor that was not necessarily compatible with the sanctimonious reserve of the hero of the hour. A man I couldn't recall ever seeing before came over to me, pointed at the bemedaled honoree, that little VIP of no importance whatsoever, and spoke to me, using the familiar *tu*.

"When I caught sight of you tonight, I was reminded that it isn't this kind of man we should be honoring, but another."

I didn't say a word. I stared at this stranger. He was my age, or thereabouts. He had a thin mustache, curly gray hair, and a kindly air.

"You don't recognize me," he said softly, with a strange smile.

"I'm sorry, but no, I don't recognize you," I replied. I thought I glimpsed something in his eyes, something that had come from far away, over such a distance that I was immediately shaken to the core.

"It's thanks to the man I'm speaking of," he continued, "that I am alive today."

He was still smiling, but I saw his face, his entire body, gripped by an emotion he struggled vainly to control. As though his trembling were contagious, I began to shiver as well, and to hear voices that belonged to another time and place.

"I'm thinking of your father," he said.

"Maurice . . ."

In those brown eyes dimmed with tears, I'd just recognized the frightened little boy desperately warding off sleep on the camp bed in the laundry room one night in June of 1944, while overhead, as he and his parents listened, German officers caroused in our dining room at the Villa. It was such a shock that all I could do was repeat his name, over and over.

"Maurice, Maurice, Maurice . . ."

His name opened the floodgates of my past, which swept over

me in an endless wave. Finally, I was able to say, "Now I recognize you."

He drew me close and embraced me tenderly. I stayed pressed against him, overwhelmed by my inner turmoil, the chaotic rush of images. A few friends standing next to us had no idea what was happening, no way of knowing how heavily the past had come crashing down on us, and how helplessly we clung to one another. As I held Maurice in my arms, I whispered, "He's gone, you know. He left us a while ago."

I felt him give a start. "Ah," he said sadly.

Then we let go of each other and stepped apart, for we had to regain our composure amid this festive crowd swirling around us. In answer to Maurice's first words to me, I tried to tell him how my father had been offered everything after the Liberation: honors, rewards, even power.

One morning, a delegation of distinguished citizens, men wearing tricolor armbands and berets hastily embellished with gold braid, had arrived at the Villa to ask him to accept the office of mayor. He had politely refused. Later, numerous "visitors" had gotten in touch with him to let him know how they were doing. Some of them had sent him letters "To whom it may concern," attesting to their gratitude for his selfless actions. These letters had remained in a drawer in my father's office. He had not disdained these tributes from his "visitors," but what had been most important to him was learning that the refugees had managed to survive. As for the rest, the ribbons, speeches, official ceremonies, and *vanitas vanitatum*: no thanks, that wasn't his style, that had never been his way, as he'd once told me apropos of something else.

It was hard for me to say goodbye to Maurice that night. Together we traveled several times back down that lane of bittersweet memories, and all the tears we wept, and all the tears I shed after he left, tears that racked me all night long, could not console the little boy I had become once more—the child I've never ceased to be.